Lemhi Overhang

ADVENTURES OF AN IDAHO PRIVATE EYE

STEPHEN T. WATTS

Bo-Tree House

Published by
Bo-Tree House, LLC
1749 Del Mar Drive, Idaho Falls, ID 83404 USA
For more information about Bo-Tree House, please visit the website www.Botreehouse.com.

First U.S. edition 2015

Lemhi Overhang is a collection of fictionalized stories based on some adventures of a retired policeman who owned a detective agency in Idaho. The author has recreated events, locales and conversations from his imagination of them. Names, characters, places, and incidents are either the product of the author's imagination based on his detective work or are used fictitiously. Any resemblance to actual events or locales or persons, living or dead, is coincidental.

Publisher's Cataloging-In-Publication Data
Watts, Stephen T., 1932 – 2015
Lemhi Overhang – a collection of fictional stories based on the experiences of a private detective, Steve T. Watts, in Idaho.

Summary: Lemhi Overhang describes some fictionalized adventures of a retired cop as owner of a detective agency in Idaho: on the road to Arizona to investigate a murder-suicide; combating government bureaucracy run amok; and interacting with a fascinating cast of characters in the tiny cowboy town, Leadore.

ISBN 978-0-9968516-1-9
1. Detective Agency – fiction. 2. Idaho – fiction. 3. Leadore, Idaho. 4. Horse. 5. Idaho – Culture and customs. I. Title

Library of Congress Control Number: 2015956921

Cover Painting By Alexandra Vivian, Idaho High School Student.

Stephen Thomas Watts
(December 12,1932 – May 9, 2015)
On his horse, Ranger

Steve Watts on Whiskey, his early love.
They spent many hours together in the Lemhi Overhang
area.

Dedicated to Bill Maeck without whose support this book would not have been possible

Table of Contents

Foreword

There was a great deal to admire about my friend, Steve Watts. The man had guts. The list of ex-cops willing to publicly question the actions of police on the job today is short indeed. But Steve knew from long experience that those who carry guns and badges must be held to the highest standard, and that it takes a special person to do the job and do it right.

His columns for the Post Register, which he wrote nearly until the day he died, were valuable tools that educated readers and, if they were willing to look at what he was saying, served as a guide for those who enforce the law today.

Steve was a man of great empathy who was compelled to fight for the underdog. Perhaps that's because he came up the hard way and earned everything he had in life. These traits are evident in every page of "Lemhi Overhang," which Steve completed just before his death at the age of 82 and I had the honor of editing. You feel it as Steve investigates the death of a friend's daughter and her baby; in his befriending and helping an aged logger who spent much of his life on the wrong side of the law and an ex-cop permanently damaged by the Vietnam War; in his effort to reunite a father and son and through his fight to see that a small child endangered by the "System" ended up with those who could best care for her.

Steve liked and cared about people. He had an insatiable curiosity and did not jump to conclusions. A man was to be judged on the content of his character and by his actions, not the numbers in his bank account or the title in front of his name.

But what I admired most about Steve was his commitment to justice. Not just enforcing the law, doing his job or being part of a team. Steve was a man who I imagine could look in the mirror and feel good about what he saw because his life was spent in the pursuit of justice, that elusive outcome which occurs only when the right thing is done for the right reasons. If that meant taking on government paper-pushers, fellow cops or a bar filled with construction workers looking for a fight … well, so be it. Right is right. Wrong is wrong. And a man damn well better be willing to stand for what he believes.

Steve would drop by my office in the Post Register newsroom from time to time and I always enjoyed those visits. Here was a man whose mind belonged to him. Nobody told Steve Watts how or what to think. Anyone foolish enough to try would have had a fight on their hands. Steve's death was a huge loss for his family and many friends, and also the community he served for so long in so many ways.

But my old comrade performed one last service by writing the stories you will soon be reading and sharing his insights on that one subject we must all someday confront. I hope you enjoy and profit from them as much as I did.

Corey Taule
Idaho Falls

Introduction

The crack of the lightning bolt was deafening. The hair on the back of my neck seemed to be sticking straight out. With my free hand I reached up to see if I could feel anything different. I seemed to be okay. The acrid smell of singed, wet wood permeated the air. "Hot damn, that was close," I thought.

Whiskey reared up under me. He was getting older and had survived his share of high mountain summer storms, the kind that come up on you quickly in the afternoon of what had been a really nice day. Some instinct in his genetic makeup told him that lightning can kill and compelled him to race away from it.

I had the same instinct. I saw the black clouds boiling over the peaks and urged Whiskey down the trail, hoping to reach my pickup and horse trailer. But the storm was almost upon us and safety was still four or five miles away: land covered by large and rugged pine trees that were squeezed between massive cliffs and containing a stream flooded by spring run-off – all seemingly designed to slow our progress.

I couldn't allow Whiskey to run the way he wanted. When I was younger, I might have, but it seemed as though all these years of living had, in the words of the old cowboys, "smartened me up somehow." A racing horse can slip on wet rocks, drag his rider through low-hanging branches and stumble on roots protruding above the ground.

Whiskey had been my horse for a lot of years. We formed a bond that men and horses, if they're lucky, get to experience. This bond is difficult to explain to non-horse people, but it's a feeling that goes beyond friendship. Whiskey takes care of me on these rides and I take care of him at the corral. I spoke softly to him and pulled back on the reins. He mastered his fear and slowed to a comfortable trot. I was alone and walking out of the mountains in my riding boots didn't appeal to me. Besides I had been noticing, now that I was in my 70's, that it took longer to lose the soreness and heal bruises that result from being dumped on a bunch of rocks.

Earlier that morning, as I rode up to the mountain lake, I marveled at the beauty of the canyon. But then we were picking our way slowly. Now we would be confronted with another, less tranquil kind of beauty: the raw power and majesty of a storm pummeling the high mountains with its might and force. Thunder would come first, accompanied by lightning, to be followed by sheets of rain driven by high winds. It would soon become most uncomfortable.

Whiskey tossed his head, rolled his eyes back and grumbled the way horses do when they don't get their way. We moved at a slow trot and I recalled a cliff that leaned out over the trail, an overhang that should be just ahead and would provide some shelter.

I often ride into the Lemhi Mountains of Idaho, where I live, and have developed a habit of watching for and making mental notes of sheltered places. Whiskey and I swung in under the cliff just as the storm broke around us. I carry a large rain poncho behind my saddle. Thankfully, this time, I would not need it.

I stripped the saddle and blanket from Whiskey's back and tied him to a small sapling just out from the overhang. He turned his tail to the wind and the rain pelted his rump.

Whiskey is a Leopard Appaloosa, a breed developed by the Nez Perce Indians of northern Idaho. When he's clean, his color is a brilliant white. His rump and most of his body is covered with two-inch black spots that look like rosettes as the outer rim have a brown tinge. He is a beautiful animal at any time, but as the rain struck and his coat began to glisten, I marveled at what a fortunate man I am to own such a horse and share with him these rides into the wilderness.

At times like this, I think about how good life has been to me since I was 12-years-old and had just walked out the gates of the reform school. Life, up to that time, had not been very good. My family life could be described as dysfunctional and I was in and out of trouble, leading to my sentence to the school, a place filled with young and angry males who were ready to strike at whatever agitated them in the moment.

Fights were easy to start and there were lots of them. The youngest kids at the school got picked on a lot and I was the youngest there. I survived by proving a willingness to fight. By the time I left, I could best be

13

described as an angry young man with my fists clenched and a chip on my shoulder. All these years later, I've added love and laughter to my life and my fists are no longer clenched. The chip on my shoulder, while still there, is usually kept out of sight. I feel its weight from time to time, especially when I encounter injustice.

I have divided my life into phases. When that first one, involving my early life and time at the reform school, passed, I moved into my "cowboy phase." These encompassed my teen years after I moved to a small Texas town to be near my great uncle, who had a ranch and I assume had volunteered to offer me a place to stay and some badly needed guidance.

I worked with and learned to be a cowboy. As the years passed, I went to school and worked part-time jobs of all kinds. The best was working with an old-time Texas cowman who had sold his outfit and retired to be a cattle buyer. I rented a sleeping room from him and helped move cattle and did odd jobs associated with the business. When I look back to those years, I recognize that he had chosen to mentor me. The old cowman shared his knowledge freely, teaching me how a man should live and conduct himself.

I remember him telling me that for a man to be whole, he needed a piece of land, a good horse and a good gun. Today, I can argue – from an intellectual standpoint – that premise. Those things may not really be necessary. However, as the years have gone by, I have acquired several pieces of land, many good guns and have owned good horses throughout my life. I recognize now how much they have contributed to my happiness, even as I pursued other ways to make my living.

Next was my "soldier phase," which began with me volunteering for a 3-year enlistment in the Army at the start of the Korean War. Those years were good for me and broadened my outlook on life. Looking back, I can say I grew up and learned a lot during that phase. Every young man who experienced those years could write a complete book about his experiences. Each came out far different than when he entered. In my case, that chip on my shoulder seemed to get in my way a lot; there seemed to be so many incompetents in the wrong jobs and though I was given the opportunity to see the world, I was happy when my discharge came through.

The next phase was the life of a commercial fisherman in Alaska, a time I truly loved. Each day was a new adventure. I spent a year living with an Indian tribe, learning to fish. Then I joined some of Alaska's best fishing crews and learned to survive an ocean that didn't seem as though it wanted you there. Many times I have been tempted to write a book about those experiences, but it's hard to slow down long enough to gather my thoughts. That is where I met and courted my wife, which led me to my next phase.

I needed to settle down. For a lot of reasons, mostly involving my hatred of injustice, I wanted to become a police detective. Knowing I would have to start at the bottom and realizing I would need more education, I left Alaska and started my first semester at Oakland Junior College in California. My love and I were married and started our life there. As time went by, we relocated to Idaho, where I found employment as a policeman in Idaho Falls. At the end of the first year, I became a detective and attended school part time to earn my degree.

I spent 12 years as a detective and was recruited as a criminal investigator with the Idaho Bureau of Investigation, where I stayed until I took early retirement to accept an appointment as a contract federal investigator with the U.S. Government. This phase was can best be described as extensive, interesting and full of adventure. At its completion, I did actually write a book about it, "Better an Honest Scoundrel." I've yet to hear from anyone who has not raved about it. And it seems to have left me with the bug to write once again.

On to the next phase – going into business for myself.

With the raging mountain storm allowing me a couple idle hours sitting comfortably with my back to the cliff, I found myself musing about the years that passed so swiftly. In 1985, I created my own private detective agency. I named it "Idaho Protective Specialist, Inc.," to inspire confidence. My purpose in starting this business was to right wrongs and the scope of operation was to be wherever our services might be required.

That purpose was ambitious, but with one exception I have stayed with it. The exception was the scope. I ended up limiting myself to the west, from Arizona to Alaska. My one early foray into extending the company involved a security contract with a small company of entrepreneurs in Colombia. My wife, Marilyn, was so opposed to me running that kind of risk in an unstable and violent area that she used the ultimate threat: splitting our property if I went through with it. Marilyn feared I might not have made it out of there.

So there I was, many years later, dry and snug, protected from the elements, much as an Indian hunter might have in decades past taken shelter under this same overhang. And while I can muse over the interesting and exciting years since that beginning, I could not help but ponder: What thoughts may have preoccupied that Indian's mind as he patiently waited out a similar storm? Could his life have been filled with mystery, intrigue, dangers, satisfactions and occasional disappointments? Did he use his time, in this place, to review his life, as I did? Or did he just take his life for granted, not knowing there were other choices? I hope he used that time to review his life, as I did. If he didn't, our Indian hunter wasted a good opportunity in a wonderful setting.

So, as many have asked at various social gatherings, what is it like to be a private detective? And what is it that a private detective actually does? Everything that follows is true. I have changed a few names to protect the innocent, but as I sit, watch the storm and reflect, I cannot imagine anyone writing fiction when the real stuff is so interesting. Enjoy.

One

INVESTIGATING MURDER IN ARIZONA

I t was winter in the late 1980's, a typical cold Idaho day: the kind I had become accustomed to and even looked forward to - that special time of year when you pull in your horns, hole up and tackle those indoors activities so easy to put off when the weather is warm.

Even so, those activities don't always hold our attention. On this day, I was in my office, surrounded by books, reports and paperwork. An occasional glance out the big window behind me offered a second-story view of the intersection below and a park across the street. Watching gusts of snow swirl against buildings entertained me for a while. Inside, however, was a nagging knowledge that I would be more comfortable wheeling down some highway in the snow and working a challenging case.

My Secretary, Geri, understood my struggle, but worked to keep me on task. We had been acquainted for many years and she knew I was an active man who liked moving around ... outdoors. As secretaries have done since the beginning of office work, she attempted to isolate me from distractions, restricting access to my inner office retreat. Anyone coming into the office was asked about their business and told to take a seat while she evaluated who they were allowed to see.

Geri and I were friends who had come to know each other years before in troubled times. I asked her to join my company because I knew her to be talented and competent, but mostly because she was the kind of person who could be trusted to keep everything she saw or heard confidential. Besides being an intelligent woman, she was also striking in appearance, with long flowing black hair. Geri gave class to a place that may have looked ordinary without her.

As the years went by, Geri's role in the company expanded and she took on assignments in the field when I needed someone to work undercover on special projects. We discussed every case in detail, sharing thoughts about people and clients. She collected fees, paid bills and kept me alerted to any problems that came up. I don't know how someone could manage a company without an employee like Geri.

On that winter day, I heard voices in the waiting room: Geri's low and pleasant voice that puts visitors at ease and a man's deep voice filled with urgency. It was just the excuse I needed to drop the bid proposal I was putting together and head out to the waiting room.

I knew the voice of the man talking to Geri, but couldn't place it. His back looked familiar, but the cowboy hat was the trigger I needed to make the connection. It was a friend from way back in time, a former county sheriff, Manfred Peterson.

As I walked in, he turned, grinned and stuck his hand out. I could tell this was not a social visit. Normally, Manfred's whole face lit up when I saw him. This time, I observed something heavy in his eyes. I invited him into my hideaway, waving at Geri and receiving her nod.

Manfred was a cattle rancher on the Big Lost River Basin above Mackay, in the very heart of central Idaho's mountains. From his ranch, he had access to the Boulder-White Cloud, Pioneer and Big Lost mountain ranges. In a moment of weakness, he had gotten bored with the cold Idaho winters and joined the sheriff's department for something to do. Like me, Manfred got impatient sitting around and waiting for the weather to break.

I got to know Manfred a year or two later when, after deciding the sheriff was not doing a very good job, he ran for the office. He surprised himself by winning. When he told me that, I thought it should not have been a surprise because Manfred was a quintessential straight shooter right out of a western novel. He was honest almost to a fault and had an easy-going and affable air that put everyone at ease. At the same time, he had no fear and did not hesitate to exercise the power of his office in going after those who broke the law.

As a state criminal investigator, I worked with Manfred on a complex cattle-rustling case and in pursuit of a psychopath who made the mistake of hiding in Idaho's mountains after killing a child in the Seattle area. We had shared experiences that draw men together. In the military, they call it "comrades in arms."

I retired and Manfred went back to ranching. I had not seen him for several years, but as is often the case with good friends, time is of no consequence. We didn't need to get re-acquainted or waste time with small talk.

"What's happening," I asked. It was as though I had turned on a tap. He began his story:

"You know I'm LDS," Manfred said. I nodded and he continued: "My whole family is active in the church. My daughter, Nancy, was chosen to go on a church Mission to Australia about five or six years ago." I nodded again, knowing the Mormon practice of having young people serve missions promoting their church throughout the world. He went on: "While she was on her mission in Australia she met another missionary, a young man named Jeff Banks. They hit it off and made a decision to return to Idaho and attend Ricks College together."

Ricks was a two-year Mormon college in Rexburg that has expanded into a four-year school known as Brigham Young University-Idaho. I knew it well because I had received my own degree from there. Manfred said that after completing their schooling, Nancy and Jeff decided to get married.

They lived on Manfred's ranch for a while, before deciding to begin their lives in California. Manfred said his daughter and new husband ended up in a second rate trailer camp near San Diego. Nancy wrote about the neighbors, who had lots of problems with drugs, alcohol and poverty, and how she would have liked to help them but there was not much she could do. Jeff was unable to find a good job. After struggling for about a year, Nancy and Jeff moved to Phoenix, where his parents lived.

Jeff's brother helped him get a job with an armored car company. Their policy was to hire only returned Mormon missionaries, who were considered more honest and reliable than the general population. They rented an apartment, bought a better car and had a baby.

About a year and a half went by. Nancy called often, keeping Manfred updated about their lives. On one of the last calls, she talked about spending time talking with their Mormon bishop. Jeff had been acting strange. He seemed to be in danger of "losing his testimony," as Manfred put. Looking at me, he said: "You understand that, don't you?" I nodded.

I assumed Manfred knew I was not Mormon, though it was something we had never discussed. Mormonism is the dominant religion in this part of the country and you cannot live here long without learning something about their belief system and practices, even if you have no interest. When one loses his testimony, it means they no longer believe in or adhere to Mormon doctrine. To lose it is considered a very bad thing. I knew this would have been unsettling news to Manfred and his family.

About two weeks later, Nancy called home again and spoke to Manfred's youngest daughter. Nancy told her sister she would call back, but never did. That wasn't like her at all, but Manfred and his wife, Mary Jane, saw no reason to panic. That came when they received a phone call from a detective with the Phoenix Police Department, asking to talk with Nancy.

Manfred told him she was not in Idaho and demanded to know why he was calling. The detective's voice softened as he told Manfred his daughter and grandson were missing. "We were told she went home to Idaho to visit her family," the detective said.

The detective told Manfred that Jeff had been killed in a car wreck. Jeff had provoked a chase by peeling out next to a state trooper on a freeway entrance in Phoenix. After getting up to more than 90 miles an hour, he deliberately left the roadway and crashed head on into a massive steel power pole. Police found no one at home. Neighbors hadn't seen Nancy or her child for a couple weeks. One had seen Jeff about a week prior to the accident as she was returning a borrowed cookie sheet to Nancy. Jeff told her Nancy was on a trip to either Utah or Idaho to see family. Neighbors reported a strong smell of Lysol and assumed it had come from Jeff's apartment.

Police discovered honey and feces spread around and rubbed on the walls of the apartment. A note from Jeff said he was having marital problems. Based on the note and the accident, police assumed Jeff committed suicide.

When Manfred and Mary Jane got off the plane in Phoenix, there were television cameras and newspaper reporters waiting to meet them. He showed me a front-page newspaper clipping with a picture of him and Mary Jane coming off the ramp. The caption read: "Idaho sheriff arrives to search for daughter and baby."

I could see why the press picked up the story and ran with it. Manfred looks exactly like anyone would imagine an Idaho sheriff should look: broad shouldered, cowboy hat, jeans with large buckle, boots, a western cut jacket and a good-looking wife next to him. Manfred thought it might help if he talked to the press and made a public plea asking for anyone with any information about where she and the baby were, to please come forward.

"We provided them with pictures and descriptions," he said. "I know now that it may have been a mistake, but there was no way for us to know that then."

I asked Manfred why he thought that was a mistake. He replied: "I'm getting a little ahead of my story, let me go back."

After Jeff's crash, which had been big news in the Phoenix area, a young man told police that he and Jeff had been working together for the armored car company. They were teamed together on a truck and followed a specific route each day. The week before the wreck, they pulled into a mall parking lot in Phoenix to make a pickup. They were carrying about $2 million in various denominations that would have been untraceable.

Jeff's partner said he pulled a pistol on him, handcuffed his wrists from behind, commanded him to sit down on the truck floor, where he put a second pair of handcuffs on his ankles, shackling them together so he could not move. Jeff put his pistol back in the holster and started stuffing money into a duffle bag.

The young man told police he was able to slip one of his hands out of the cuffs and, being larger and stronger that Jeff, pulled him down, overpowered and subdued him and took his pistol. He forced Jeff to free his legs and remove the dangling cuff from his other wrist.

His next move was probably not a good idea, but may have been consistent with the inexperience of youth and strong hold of Mormonism on its members. His companion, also a returned Mormon missionary, lectured Jeff on the responsibilities of his faith.

Believing Jeff was contrite, he offered a proposition. "I'm going to give you another chance and not turn you in," the young man told Jeff. "However, I want you to quit; you should not be working in a job like this, the temptation is too much for you."

A polygraph test determined he was telling the truth. The robbery story gave police a motive for Jeff taking his own life. The only loose end was the missing wife and baby.

Manfred described the events that transpired after he asked people with knowledge to contact the Phoenix

Police Department. Calls started coming in. Detectives kept him informed and he worked with them as much as he was able from his ranch in Idaho.

An attorney in California said he had a client who knew where Nancy and her baby were. His client wanted an up-front payment of $10,000. Manfred said he would try to raise the money, but police discouraged him, believing it to be a scam.

A man called to say he had recently been sentenced to a term in the Nevada State Prison, but had lived with Nancy before he was caught and could provide information on where she might now be, implying she had been moved to California. He said he would be glad to help but needed money for an appeal and suggested Manfred help him first. Phoenix police went to Nevada and interviewed him and told Manfred their best guess was that he had no knowledge and was trying to use Manfred's loss to raise money.

As Manfred related these events to me, his pain was evident. He couldn't bring himself to discount any possibility, however remote. I knew Manfred also would not have believed anyone debased and evil enough to take advantage of grieving family members. In the remote Idaho Mountains, you don't run into many people like that. I knew of Manfred's high personal and moral standards. His clenched jaw, furrowed brow and hands constantly opening and closing as he talked showed how difficult it was for him to relive the experience. But the worst was yet to come.

More information was coming in. Jeff had rented three cars prior to his botched robbery, but police were able to locate only two, including the one destroyed in the crash. Several people had called the police to report seeing the third car being driven by a woman at various times and places, as far away as California.

My police experience taught me that a lot of people want to be involved and in their desire to help will provide leads that many times have no basis in fact. Often these are hunches or wishful thinking. Police learn after a while to sort them out and if busy on other things it becomes easy to discount all calls coming in.

One call involved a young pregnant woman who had shown up at a truck stop in a small town in eastern Wyoming. The woman had no identification and seemed unable to remember who she was. Wyoming deputies came across the APB on Nancy. During the exchanges of information, first to Phoenix, then to Idaho and then back to Wyoming, the information coming to Manfred indicated that this woman could be Nancy.

But this lead proved false. The woman was not Nancy. Another disappointment added to the growing anxiety being felt by Manfred and his family.

Thirteen long months passed with no word from Nancy, time spent wondering if she needed help and trying to answer questions from the younger children, wondering where she was. Finally, Manfred received the call he had feared. Dove hunters found a gravesite in the desert several miles out of Phoenix. The coroner unearthed the dismembered bodies of a woman and baby buried in black plastic trash bags. At that point, they had not made a final identification, but were alerting Manfred to the possibility that it might be Nancy and her child.

Manfred said the next few weeks were a blur. The identification came back positive and he and Mary Jane flew down and arranged to accept the remains and to set up funerals in Idaho. Manfred contacted Jeff's parents to try and get information about Nancy and Jeff's last days leading up to Nancy's death. He said they seemed to be in shock and were reluctant to talk to him, other than to tell him that there was no way Jeff would have killed his wife and baby.

He contacted the local bishop of the Mormon Church Jeff and Nancy had attended, and the bishops in charge of the mission field in Australia. He learned that Nancy was highly thought of and Jeff had been a disappointment, although no one would have considered him capable of murder or robbery.

Arizona police were convinced Jeff was the murderer and closed the case. Manfred was angry about the case being dismissed summarily by the police. He wanted to know why they thought the way they did. I had worked with detectives who were totally insensitive to families of victims or survivors of crimes. Getting rid of the cases became their only goal. I could not completely fault them as new cases are constantly rolling in, and you need to move on quickly, particularly in large cities where murders can be commonplace. At the same time, from my own experience, I knew that it only takes a few minutes to sit down with someone and share your thoughts. Most of the time, just showing your concern helps people come to grips with what happened to them. I could see where Manfred was going with our meeting.

He wanted me to go to Arizona and find out what really happened. "There are too many unanswered questions," Manfred said. "Did Jeff's family play any part in this? Is there a chance someone else, a gang or something, is involved? I don't think we know enough to be satisfied with just closing the case." Manfred looked me in the eye: "I know you know what you are doing and

I trust your opinion. I need to know for sure. Will you help me?"

How could I have said no?

A few weeks later I found myself in Arizona. Friends in Tempe invited me to stay the duration of the investigation, which gave me more time to work the case and not run up expenses for my client.

I contacted the bishops who supervised Jeff in Australia and Phoenix. Both were open and related the same information they had given to Manfred. They said Jeff caused them considerable concern, both as a missionary and a church member. His home bishop said that some of the problems between Jeff and Nancy involved him developing a sudden interest in bizarre sexual acts. While it saddened them that Jeff committed at least one crime, it did not come as a total surprise or shock.

I talked to the armored car employee that had foiled Jeff's robbery attempt. He came across as a credible young man and, unless something new revealed itself, I was inclined to believe his story. It was time to find out why the police had arrived at the conclusion this was a murder-suicide.

My first stop was the police department, where I contacted the lead detective in charge of the case. Detective Bob Mills reviewed what facts he had unearthed about Jeff and his activities. He was unable to add anything new and told me the county sheriff's department had taken over the case. My impression was that he was a good man who knew what he was doing.

I had the same experience at the sheriff's office. I met detective Russ Kimball, who also impressed me as being competent. I spent considerable time with him reviewing his information about the follow-up to the original crash. Russ said Jeff's family had not been very cooperative. They had taken the position from the beginning that Jeff was innocent and didn't want to hear anything else. Every lead he followed came back to the premise – that it was a murder/suicide with no one but Jeff involved.

As I left, my thoughts were that they would, under normal police standards, be justified in closing the case. While there were gaps in the story, it was still just speculation that anyone else was involved. I wanted to clean up that speculation.

I had called Manfred and asked that he and Mary Jane meet me in Phoenix the next day. They needed to be involved as a way of mentally coming to grips with what had happened. I systematically retraced Jeff's path, beginning at the lot where Jeff had rented the three cars.

Keeping track of distances between places, we went to the mall parking lot and concluded it made sense as a place for a robbery attempt.

We drove to Jeff and Nancy's apartment complex. It was a typical large city complex that was crowded but reasonably nice. Manfred and Mary Jane seemed to feel better when we left there. I speculated they were able to see that Nancy and her baby had a more comfortable life than she had described living in the camper in California.

I took them to the crash scene. The evidence was gone, but the physical characteristics of the freeway and pole were just as described in the accident report. It did not take much imagination to visualize what had occurred that bleak night. The powerful steel and concrete pole dominated the roadside. Retracing the events made the whole sequence come alive. It was not just a story someone was telling, but rather tangible places with reasonable connections that fit together

It was time to contact Jeff's family. We drove to their address north of Phoenix. They lived in a small, older trailer home on an unimproved lot. There was no grass or shrubbery. They drove a beat-up sedan and owned an old van with a homemade camper built on it. It appeared that they did not have a lot of money.

Terry and Lottie Banks greeted us in a friendly fashion and invited us inside. My initial reaction was that they were frightened, which stirred my curiosity, but I was not there at this time to push for information, so I tried to put them at ease with small talk. I observed Jeff's framed picture in several prominent places in the living room.

Lottie went into a back room and woke up her daughter. She was severely handicapped, appearing to be about 12 or 13-years-old with an IQ of a baby. Lottie held the girl on her lap for the duration of our visit. My feeling was that it was done to elicit sympathy from us and I felt a tinge of irritation. I quickly suppressed it as I had not experienced her obvious travails in life and I knew I had no business making judgments. But I did have sympathy. I thought of how it must be to lose a son and a grandson and to have an imperfect child that needed constant attention. On top of that, these folks had to face the reality that their son had done horrible things.

I could tell Manfred and Mary Jane had the same thoughts as they kept the conversation light, avoiding the questions we wanted answers to. We were joined by a teenage boy, their youngest son. He seemed to be a pretty nice kid. It was not a situation that I wanted to "pull anybody's chains." The visit was short. Manfred arranged a time when he could pick up Nancy's things to take back to Idaho and we said our goodbyes.

Our next stop was the place where the bodies had been found. Manfred said he wanted to go. I felt it had something to do with the healing process and did not try to discourage it. I had been there the previous day. It was about 10 miles out of Phoenix and we did not talk much as I drove. When we arrived, Manfred and I got out, but Mary Jane said she wanted to stay in the car.

Manfred approached the site, leaned forward to look, gazed at the sky, then walked around the area, occasionally kicking at a rock, taking his time, moving slowly. I could imagine memories of a little girl, loving her and watching her grow into a delightful young lady. I remembered his emotion as he told me of his new grandson. That it all came to an end in this ugly place in the desert. I looked away, trying to think of other things as I waited for Manfred.

Things were quiet as we drove back to the city. I dropped Manfred and Mary Jane at their motel and met with another sheriff's detective, who told me both skulls showed an indentation on the foreheads that matched the characteristics of a standard carpenter's claw hammer. He said they were sure the blows were sufficient to cause death. A canvas of Jeff's neighbors revealed he had a toolbox with a hammer and handsaws in it. Police speculated that a hand saw may have been used for the dismemberment. When they attempted to retrieve his tool box from Terry and Lottie, they denied having it, although police knew Jeff's parents had cleaned the apartment. The detective said he saw no need to pursue the issue as they felt justified in closing the case with what they had.

He also said they had observed that most of the tenants of the apartment complex were young people, such as Jeff and Nancy, and that it would have been unlikely that any organized criminals could have kidnapped anyone without neighbors hearing or noticing it. Without any direct evidence to prove otherwise, detectives ruled out the possibility that anyone else but Jeff was involved. We speculated together that after Jeff had conceived his plan to commit the robbery, he told Nancy of his intent. Being the kind of person she was, Nancy would have attempted to dissuade him, which could have provoked him into hitting her with his hammer. Having killed her, he might have thought he had no choice but to kill the baby.

Later that evening, Manfred, Mary Jane and I went out to dinner. I shared with them that Nancy and the baby's death would have been quick with no suffering. I also gave them my opinion that the killer was someone who was known to them, not a total stranger. I based my opinion, influenced by past experiences, on the careful way they were dismembered and wrapped prior to burial.

Manfred and Mary Jane were heading back to Idaho. I took a needed day off and with friends visited some of the sights around the area, ending the day with a chuck wagon dinner and western entertainment at the Rocking R Ranch. I have found that a little fun helps to reorient my thinking. I was ready to continue.

The only place left to pick up any useful information was from the Banks family. They had refused to talk about Jeff to everyone else. I felt the need to get through their barrier and discover if they knew anything beyond the speculation we were dealing in to this point.

I arrived unannounced at the trailer home about 10 the next morning. I did not want anyone to prepare for my visit. I knocked on the door and heard movement inside. No one came to respond to the knock. I knocked again, firmly. I hoped to let them know I would not allow myself to be waited out. The third knock worked. Lottie came to the door, opening it just enough that she could keep it as a barrier between us, leaving a narrow gap we could talk through. I again sensed fear: an extra challenge to overcome. I used my best weapon. I smiled. In spite of herself, Lottie smiled back. It wasn't a large smile, but it was there.

On our first visit, I had been introduced as an Idaho detective working with Manfred. It was obvious she had developed a fear or distrust of law. I quickly assured her that I was a private detective trying to learn what had happened to her son and his family. "Over the years, I've learned that the best way to find anything out is to go directly to the people most involved and listen to what they have to say," I told Lottie. "I would sure like to know what you know. Will you talk to me, and tell me?"

I had hit upon the exact right thing to say. Her tiny smile grew slightly, the door came open and she stepped back. I entered and saw Terry standing just behind her. The look on his face reassured me that he was okay with me coming in. "Honey, I've got to be on the job, you talk to him, fill him in on everything and I'll be back when I can get away," Terry said.

I had the impression there was no job and for some reason he did not want to be there. He closed the front door and disappeared. It was an odd situation and one I had not encountered in many years of interviewing people. Usually the husband wants to stay and, if not dominate the conversation, at least listen in.

We sat in the living room and talked for five hours. It was like Lottie had been waiting for someone to come and give her a chance to say what was on her mind. One thing I had learned about many detectives is that they were often in too big of a hurry, demanding quick and direct answers to only the questions they ask. It's not a good formula for people who frighten easily.

We talked about Lottie's family and her life. It was obvious that her family was her life. I knew as a Mormon she had been taught that the family must come first. In many Mormon households you will find a plaque inscribed with the words: "Family is Forever." Most believe that the complete family will rejoin together in heaven after death. But as I talked with her it was obvious to me that her attachment to family was all encompassing, more than just a religious belief; it was her purpose for existence.

Lottie said that because of her handicapped daughter and limited income, she was unable to work or have a life outside the home. That suited Lottie, who said she had no desire to seek a life beyond her family.

Because of this attachment to family, the loss of any of them would have been extremely difficult under the best circumstances. The loss of her son, daughter-in-law and grandson was anything but that.

Lottie had been very happy when Jeff and Nancy had moved to Phoenix. She developed a close relationship with Nancy, visited them weekly and talked on the phone with them every couple of days. She said Jeff and Nancy seemed to get along fine, at least they had not told her there were any problems between them. They had talked about getting a better job in Bakersfield, but she didn't know the details. Lottie said Jeff had not planned to take the job with the armored car company, but his older brother had been working there and had quit to become a policeman in a neighboring town and recommended Jeff for the job. It did not pay much money.

Lottie said Jeff and his older brother joked about having all that money they were "hauling around." She understood that all the drivers did this. Lottie said when she heard about the robbery, she didn't believe it. But, after hearing the young man tell about it, she came to believe it was true.

Lottie said that during the week the robbery occurred, she had a terrible urge to contact Jeff or Nancy – the same kind of feeling she had experienced when members of her family died. But, at the time, Lottie wasn't feeling well and Terry needed the car to go to work. On Tuesday evening Jeff called and she was extremely relieved to hear his voice.

"How are Nancy and the baby doing," Lottie asked. "Fine," Jeff answered. "I'm coming over," Lottie said, but Jeff told her not to because he was going shopping. Jeff then asked to talk to his dad. Terry took the phone and they exchanged casual greetings. Jeff asked Terry how things were and was told they were fine. After a more small talk, Terry said, "Good to talk to you son," and they hung up.

Both Lottie and Terry thought the conversation strange and they came to realize Jeff was calling them to say his last goodbye. A few days later, they were informed of Jeff's death and she had a difficult time coping with everything that was happening. She believed Nancy and the baby were alive somewhere and needed help.

Lottie continued to talk: A few days after learning of Jeff's death, she had been awakened in the night and saw her son. It was very real to her. Jeff was wearing a white robe with a cowl over his head. Nancy and the baby were at his feet and looked frightened. She said it appeared that Jeff was trying to tell her where Nancy and the baby were, but could not speak. He would look down at them and then look at her and try to speak, but no words came out. Lottie did not recognize where they were, but it looked like desert and there was a raised area behind him and a telephone pole and a saguaro cactus nearby.

As she spoke I thought back to the two trips I had made to the gravesite. I had used a telephone pole as a marker to turn off the highway down into the dry river bed. Once into that river bed, the area beyond was eight or ten feet higher than the gravesite. There was saguaro cactus trees scattered all over the place.

Lottie told me the same vision returned the next night and again a few days later. The last time, other figures appeared next to Jeff, also dressed in white robes. She could not make out their faces. She said she became aware, as did Jeff, that it was time. He would have to go with them. She said they left together and the vision did not come back to her again.

As Lottie spoke, she trembled with emotion and there was no doubt in my mind she believed every word she was saying. Later I thought of my long career as an interrogator and the many schools I had been to all over the country learning how to interpret body language and speech patterns for deception and how I had taught those same subjects in the Idaho Police Academy. As I watched

Lottie speak, all non-verbal communicators indicated she was telling the truth.

Lottie saw in her visions proof that Nancy and the baby were alive and afraid. "I felt that they would be found and I delayed Jeff's funeral for nine days, believing that they would turn up," she said. Lottie said subsequent events reinforced that belief. She became convinced that the inmate from Nevada who called police had knowledge of Nancy and the baby. Lottie and Terry attempted to verify his information, that Nancy had been seen in California and that others may be involved, but that the inmate couldn't tell her everything because he and his family might be in danger. Lottie said he referred to an organization in California he had been connected with and implied it was involved in the death of Nancy and the baby.

Denial has always baffled me. I know it exists. In fact, it is one of nature's most powerful forces. I use it once in a while, when I look at my waistline, for example. But the kind of denial I was seeing in Lottie was jarring. I kept my opinions to myself and continued asking questions.

"What is your opinion of what has occurred," I asked her. Lottie said she is "98 percent sure" Jeff tried to rob the armored car. She also is absolutely certain Jeff would have been incapable of killing Nancy and their baby. She never saw any violence or loss of self-control in Jeff that would lead him to commit murder. Lottie was aware police investigators viewed Jeff as a suspect and didn't think their suspicions were justified.

Lottie remained convinced that someone, maybe in the same apartment complex, learned Jeff worked for the armored car company and kidnapped Nancy and her son to force Jeff to commit the robbery in return for their lives. When the robbery failed, Jeff took his own life in his grief. If it was not someone in the apartment complex, Lottie believed it might have been the organization the Nevada convict talked about.

Terry had returned home, but did not join in our conversation. From the look on his face, it was apparent he had heard this version of the story many times. I guessed that if he had other ideas, he was unable to dissuade Lottie. Or he may have been inclined, as was I, to allow Lottie to believe what she could emotionally deal with rather than what logic dictated. I didn't need to cause this woman any more grief. Truth can be a terrible thing, particularly to a mother.

It was time for me to leave. Oddly, Lottie's whole demeanor had changed. She was smiling broadly and her face was shining. My being there and listening had made a difference to her. We said our goodbyes and I wished them well in the future.

The trouble with murder cases is that the best witnesses are no longer around to tell you what happened. In this case, both victims and the killer are dead. Any conclusions must be drawn from whatever physical evidence is available.

Years before, when I was a young police detective, I was on a witness stand testifying about gathering evidence relative to a murder in Idaho Falls. I did not have a lot of experience and the defense attorney obviously sensed that. He was a very competent attorney. He strode across the room near the jury box, turned and, in a loud and contemptuous voice, said: "Detective Watts, you're trying to tell us you have found some evidence, will you please tell us what evidence is?"

That's a tricky question if you don't know the answer. I was lucky. I had attended an investigation class a few weeks earlier and remembered the answer. I sat up straight and in a respectful tone, looked at the jury and said: "Evidence is anything – and underline the anything – that purports to show that someone did something or that an event occurred."

I heard the judge stifle a laugh and saw the jurors grin. I had scored big. The attorney moved on. I never forgot that lesson.

I've been privileged to train quite a few detectives, and some turned out pretty good. I like to think that their success had something to do with my constant admonition to them that: "Your final report is everything, You may be extremely skillful at digging out facts and information, but if you cannot organize those facts and write them out in a logical sequence in a persuasive manner, all those skills are essentially worthless."

It was time for me to live up to my own words. I returned to my office, holed up and wrote a detailed report of what I had done to reach this conclusion for Manfred and Mary Jane:

Circumstances indicate that Jeff Banks committed the attempted robbery of the armored car and killed his wife Nancy and their baby. In all probability, he acted on his own.

My opinion is based on the following facts:

(1) There appeared to be some disagreement or trouble between Jeff and Nancy, as evidenced by Nancy having contacted her bishop for help, and that she had called her parents in Idaho in an unusual manner. That

indicated she had a problem just hours before her disappearance. No one saw her alive after that call. This does not fit a kidnapping scenario.

(2) Jeff did not go to authorities for assistance, nor did he show any outward signs of having been coerced by other parties.

(3) Jeff probably killed Nancy and the baby on the Sunday prior to the visit of his neighbor returning the cookie sheets and his claw hammer was most likely the weapon used. The strong Lysol smell the neighbors complained of was a result of Jeff dismembering and preparing the bodies for burial.

(4) Jeff disposed of the bodies and carried out his robbery plans before discovery of Nancy and the baby being missing was evident to family members.

(5) Jeff, not being physically or mentally strong enough to succeed with the robbery, could find no alternative course of action open to him but suicide.

(6) Jeff deliberately provoked a chase on the freeway, left the roadway and destroyed himself.

(7) There is no known or reasonable connection of any other person having been involved with Jeff as an accomplice.

(8) The actions of the Banks family most likely were based on denial and their unwillingness to perceive Jeff as a murderer.

(9) Greed has always been a sufficient motive for robbery and murder and that $2 million may have tempted Jeff beyond his capacity to resist.

(10) There was considerable reason to believe Jeff was in mental turmoil relative to his marriage, his religion and his perceived lack of money, all leading him to step over the edge.

The case was over for me. It seemed like such a long time since I had heard Manfred in the front office talking to Geri. For most people, time is measured in days and years. For me, it has been measured in experiences. And this was a tough one. I have never found a way to avoid feeling enormous empathy for people in grief.

Two

A TOUGH OLD CODGER

Most of us live in neighborhoods filled with people just like ourselves. We work at jobs with people who share our tastes and backgrounds and we socialize with those of similar values and economic status.

We rarely see, except at a distance, those who are different from us … and then only when they do something to disrupt our routine. One benefit of having been a state criminal investigator was that I often came into contact with people different from me.

Harry Byers was certainly that.

I first met Harry in the early 1970s. My partner, Jim Mason, and I were making a routine call on Lemhi County Sheriff Bill Baker in Salmon. One of the duties of a state criminal investigator was to help local sheriffs and police chiefs with problems. Sheriff Baker would sometimes ask us to take on tasks he could have handled himself. The problem, as he often told us, was that limited time and a small budget restricted his ability to travel around the very large county for which he was responsible.

On this occasion, Sheriff Baker asked us to check out a complaint made by some folks in Leadore, a small town about 45 miles from Salmon we would be passing through on our way to Idaho Falls.

In later years, I would buy land in Leadore, build a lodge and raise horses. It is a small Western town located in a 6,000-foot-high mountain valley sandwiched between the Lemhi and Bitterroot mountains. About 85 people live in Leadore. This is cattle ranching country and the town owes its existence to the ranchers and influx of hunters and recreationists that use the surrounding mountains.

I asked the sheriff what the problem was. Surprisingly, his was a political issue. Baker told me the upcoming mayoral election featured two candidates, each of whom had exactly 36 votes locked up. One family revealed a plan to swing the election to their candidate by bringing a couple of sons home from Pocatello. Not everyone was happy. In fact, the sheriff told us, there is one tough old codger who said that if the boys show up and try to vote he will kill them.

That tough old codger was, of course, Harry Byers. Baker told us he was 75 or 80, an outlaw miner and logger who had been living in Leadore for half a century.

Nobody knew much about him, except that at one time or the other he had whipped everybody in the county who thought they were tough. More than once I had heard him described as "a tough, mean son of a bitch!"

The stories about Harry had taken on the stuff of legend in Lemhi County. Once, in the late 1930s or early

'40s, he caught a young cowboy named Purcell putting a brand on a calf that belonged to Harry's employers. Harry pulled his gun, turned Purcell's horse loose and made him take off his boots and head for town on foot, about a 10-mile walk.

A few days later, Harry was in the Railroad Bar in Leadore when Purcell walked in. The fight was on and Harry kicked the stuffing out of Purcell. Both were bloodied up some and Purcell staggered off somewhere while Harry went outside to wash the blood off in a horse trough.

Purcell showed up behind him and put six rounds into Harry's back. Harry survived the shooting. Purcell was charged with a misdemeanor and freed within a year. The following year, Purcell was found dead in his cabin, with a bullet hole in his head and his pistol on the table.

Purcell was not seen as the kind of man to take his own life. It was widely believed that Harry had killed him and made it look like a suicide. There was no real evidence against Harry, except that he could not account for his whereabouts at the time.

The sheriff told us that, over the years, FBI agents had arrived in his office, claiming Harry was a notorious bootlegger, had shot at people and blown up vehicles. He was, Bill told us, "a bad actor."

"These agents always wanted information and never gave any back so we kind of ignored them," the sheriff said, admitting "I don't know what is true and what is not."

All the sheriff wanted was for us stop by Harry's place and figure out if he had a problem.

There were no street numbers or signs in Leadore, but we found Harry's place through Bill's description. He lived in a simple, old one-room log cabin. This wasn't a modern home with machine-matching logs. These were large logs of various lengths and sizes that had never known a single coat of preservative or lacquer.

Harry's house had been built in the old style, with two very small pane glass windows designed not for beauty but to conserve heat. It had a low roof made of 1 X 12 boards laid on log rafters that protruded at various lengths from each end of the house. Heavy faded green roofing paper covered the boards. There could be no attic in this house. In the old days, there would have been dirt or sod on the roof to conserve heat.

Jim and I noted an old and faded wood outhouse at the rear of the place and an obvious path to and from the cabin. There was a large stack of firewood near the house, with a chopping block that looked well used. Smoke emerged from a stove pipe punched through the roof. If not for two skinny electric wires running from a pole to the cabin, we could have been stepping back a century.

The cabin sat a couple hundred feet back from the street. Outbuildings, logging trucks and caterpillar tractors in various states of disrepair sat on the property. It was obvious the man who lived here did so by his own rules. There were no feminine touches anywhere and no concessions to community esthetics. The world would have considered his place a cluttered mess, but to my eye it looked functional.

He had a porch, which contained more firewood and several 20-gallon milk cans, which held his water supply. An old refrigerator chugged away.

I knocked on the door, feeling vulnerable, and was happy to see that Jim had stepped to the side, where he could cover me, if necessary.

I had no idea what to expect. A fiery-eyed wild man with a shotgun pointed straight at us? Thinking back to the stories, that seemed possible. At the very least, I thought, we could expect hostility. Experience taught us that people who live by their own rules in remote places often take offence at being questioned by lawmen.

The door opened and there stood Harry. A big man with thick graying hair, he stood tall, was wide shouldered and had a large chest and torso. He had probably been handsome in his younger days. Now lines creased his face and he wore a weathered look.

He was slightly stooped and his bare arms and gnarled hands showed hard use. There was nothing soft about this man. His body was that of a man who had worked hard all his life and was prepared to continue.

He dressed in a typical logger garb: a well-worn flannel, checked shirt, sleeves rolled up, black jeans held up by wide red suspenders and scuffed logger boots that showed lots of wear.

The man before us had an awareness about him and confidence in his movements. In a second, I knew this was going to be an interesting meeting.

I introduced myself and then Jim, telling him we were state criminal investigators. We showed him our IDs and I asked if we could speak with him.

He gave a small grin and waved us in, as if ushering us into the great hall in a castle. There only two chairs in the room and he pulled them away from the table and set them out for us. He sat down on the edge of a large bed that dominated the room, facing us.

47

An old squat metal wood stove was the only appliance in the room. An array of pots and pans and a large skillet hung on nails driven into the logs behind the stove. An old wood kitchen table had been placed between his bed and the stove. On the back side of the table, a crude set of shelves held condiments, canned goods and utensils. A bucket of water with a dipper inside sat under the table. It looked as though Harry could sit at that kitchen table, prepare his meal, cook it, eat, wash the dishes and put them away without ever getting to his feet.

A single bare light bulb hung from the ceiling, with a pull string to turn it on and off. There was no TV set, phonograph or tape player. It appeared his only concession to the outside world was a small radio stuck on one of the crude boards that were nailed to the wall logs and formed short uneven shelves. Where there were no shelves, Harry had driven spikes into the logs, and they held clothing, ropes, an old saddle and set of spurs, and tools. The room also contained a rifle, some books and magazines, fishing poles, nets and traps.

If there was any question about this being the quintessential bachelor pad, it was dispelled by pictures of scantily clad women nailed to the ceiling. There were not pornographic pictures, but the kind one finds in magazines that sell tools and equipment to garages and shops throughout America.

Harry looked at us, quizzically. He was neither afraid nor in a hurry. I had the impression that he was a man who felt in control and didn't need to explain anything to anybody.

Long ago I had come to understand that a person's home is very important to him. Recognizing that gained visitors standing in that person's eyes. Partly with that in mind and partly because I found this simply constructed and efficiently laid out cabin impressive, I turned to my partner and said, "Damn Jim, I like this place!" He responded with what sounded like a heartfelt reply: "This if good living."

I think we were both sincere, but the thought flashed through my mind that neither of our wives would have allowed us near the place, for fear we might pick up some ideas.

Harry looked around his room and said: "You like a broken down old place like this? I had a pretty good house out in front there, but my last wife left me and burnt it down when she went!"

"That means you've been married more than once," Jim offered. Harry shrugged. "I've gone through six wives," he said. "I used the same divorce lawyer down in Reno. When I walked in the door he'd look up, grab his yellow pad and say, 'Hello Harry, are we ready to do it again?' That fellow got a lot of my money and the wives got the rest."

I could not resist. "If you went through six, you must have been doing something wrong," I observed. "Why did all those women not work out?"

Again Harry shrugged: "I guess I picked some bad women. Some of them were real lookers, but they weren't cut out for my kind of life. I'd bring them home and we'd be OK for awhile, until it was time to go back to work. I had a logging camp up on Grizzly Mountain. I lived up there, like what you see around here. It was hard and none of them were the kind of lady that wanted that kind of living. Some of them took off mad and some of them just took off. I had a good relationship with all of them except for my insistence that when it was time to go to the woods, it was time!"

I was getting caught up in his story: "Did you have any kids with any of those wives?"

"I have a daughter, lives in Nevada and we stay in touch," Harry replied. Our small talk had succeeded and the mood changed. Harry's hostility was gone.

"What can I do for you boys," he asked.

"We're here to check out a rumor that you plan on killing a couple of local boys who are coming back to town to vote in the local mayor's election," I said. "Do you know what we are talking about?"

Harry smiled. "There's a couple of fellows who want to vote and they are not residents of Leadore; haven't been for a couple of years." Jim said: "Well, do you plan on killing them?" Harry grinned. "I wouldn't want them thinking I wouldn't," he replied.

I had two thoughts: one that he was telling us he wasn't going to kill them; the other was that an advantage of being an old man is you can get away with saying things a younger man can't. We saw no point in taking the conversation further, so we thanked Harry, said our goodbyes and headed down the road to Idaho Falls.

Within a year I met Harry again. Two teenage boys in Idaho Falls killed their father, took his body to a ghost town near Leadore and hid it under the floor of an abandoned cabin. Harry had a gold mine up the canyon from the ghost town and passed regularly through the town on his way to the mine. He and another miner found the remains of the body and called the sheriff, who sent a deputy to gather up what was left and try to identify the victim.

It took a few months to make the connection. I was working on the case with Captain Bill English of the Bonneville County Sheriff's office in Idaho Falls. We went to Leadore after being told an old prospector had discovered the body and could show us the place.

After arriving in Leadore, Bill and I went to the local store/coffee shop where local people hang out. As we walked in, I recognized Harry sitting at the counter. I greeted him, introduced Bill and told him we were looking for the person who found that body.

"It was me," Harry replied.

He agreed to take us the ghost town. On the way, I asked him how the election went. "The candidate I was backing won," Harry replied with a laugh. "The other side didn't have as many firm votes as they thought."

I asked about the two young men who were supposed to come up from Pocatello and vote. "They evidently forgot to come," Harry said. We both laughed. Bill asked what was funny, so I filled him in on the story.

During my law enforcement career, I made a lot of good friends. Bill English was one of them. He started his career working as a sheriff's deputy in northern California and when it got too crowded for him, Bill moved to Idaho. He was an outdoors man. Through the years, he kept a couple good horses and a mule or two and spent much of his spare time riding and hunting in Idaho's mountains. Our lives paralleled each other's in a lot of ways. We were both transplants into Idaho. We both raised families and built our careers in law enforcement, albeit in different agencies, and throughout the years found ourselves working together from time to time.

Because we both kept horses, we had formed a friendship outside work. Bill possessed qualities we all admire in a man. He was smart, brave and gentle when unprovoked, but the kind of fellow you want backing you up in case of trouble.

On this day, however, trouble did not find us.

After we had secured the evidence, we thanked Harry for his help and delivered him back to his cabin in Leadore. Bill got the tour and I noticed he was as intrigued by the place as I had been. Little did I know that this meeting marked the beginning of a deep friendship between the men, once that culminated in Harry asking Bill to become the executer of his will prior to his death a few years later.

I also began to see Harry as a friend. About a year after Harry led us to that ghost town, I bought some ground on the Lemhi River, which flowed through Leadore, and began construction of barns, corrals and ultimately the lodge I intended to spend my retirement in. Harry offered to help. And so Harry was kept busy repairing my chain saws, generators and motors – equipment that seemed to be constantly breaking down. I had good stuff and perhaps things had broken down at the same rate before, but being almost 50 miles from a repair shop made me painfully aware how often it was happening on that ranch. A whole day could be wasted taking something in for repair. As it was, I was working on weekends, holidays and vacations and didn't have time to spare.

I would stop by Harry's cabin to ask him to fix something and he would open that old refrigerator, pull out a whiskey bottle and pour me a water glass full. Only then would he begin work on whatever tool I had brought. I am not much of a drinker and I protested both the drink and particularly the amount. He would reply "A man needs a good drink once in a while."

Why aren't you having one then," I asked him.

"I quit drinking about 20 years ago," Harry replied. "Booze kept getting me in trouble."

"Is this some of your stock you had left over from your drinking days or what," I asked, looking at my full glass. Harry grinned. "No, every once in a while one of my friends brings me a bottle. I guess they want to see if I really meant it when I swore off."

There was no way I was ever going to get a straight story out of him, so after a while, I gave up. I did not, however, give up listening to his stories. Harry told me about his bootlegging days, when he had a still up on Grizzly Mountain, two or three miles away.

"Having a still was the only way to make a living around here during prohibition days," Harry told me. "I'd haul my stuff over to Dillon, sell it and race the sheriff back up over the pass to the Idaho line."

Like many bootleggers, Harry was sorry when prohibition ended. He buried the still near his logging camp in case those damn fools in Washington ever brought it back.

Harry talked about his logging camp up on Grizzly … said he had a lot of trouble with the Forest Service. For some reason, the feds seemed to think Harry was cutting illegal timber; by that they meant timber the Forest Service had not marked for sale and which he hadn't paid for.

Harry said Forest Service officials were always hanging around, trying to catch him doing something illegal. One time he heard a truck driving up the mountain, then shut down when it was about a mile away.

Harry walked up the slope and sure enough saw two rangers sneaking through the trees toward his place. He went up and around them, keeping out of sight, and found their pickup parked on the road leading to his camp. Harry loosened all the lug nuts, removed the wheels and rolled them off a slope that ended in a deep canyon about a half-mile down.

He circled around, coming back into his camp just before dark and made a big deal about chopping firewood and starting his dinner, aware that he was being observed.

Harry didn't hear anything for about three days, until late one afternoon two FBI agents showed up. They were in a Forest Service pickup being driven by somebody who never got out, even after Harry invited everyone in for coffee. The agents were from Butte and wanted Harry to tell them about what had been done to the truck, demanding to know where the wheels were and threatening to send him to prison.

Harry was smart enough to play dumb, asking them what could have happened to bring two FBI agents all the way up the mountain. After hearing about the Forest Service truck, Harry had a little more fun with them.

"Why, that sounds like some local cowboy is just having a little fun," he said. "I'll bet you they rolled those tires off the hillside just to see them bounce. Those cowboys do that every once in a while around here. That's why I keep my vehicles close to camp. I'd never leave a vehicle parked off somewhere with nobody watching it. It's just not a good idea."

It's not easy to stay entertained in a logging camp, but watching those two agents back down when he wouldn't confess was a good day. But, that wasn't the last Harry saw of them.

On another occasion, Harry was dealing with someone who had been coming into his camp and stealing gas while he was cutting timber. Harry kept gas in 55-gallon drums in a shed near his cabin. He noticed strange car tracks on the road near his cabin.

Harry's solution was to stick a quarter stick of dynamite under the ground where he figured the thief would park. He wired it to his trigger in such a way that when anyone tipped the gas drum up to pour gas out of it, the circuit would be closed and set off the charge. Harry drove his truck into the woods and listened until he heard a vehicle approaching. He slipped back where he could see the shed.

Harry saw two men in a jeep with no top and the windshield folded down on the hood. They parked right where he had set the trap. One of the men got out of the jeep, took two gas cans and went up into the shed.

Harry started towards the shed, intending to warn the fellow in the jeep as he hadn't planned on killing anyone. Before he could get out of the trees, however, Harry heard an explosion. The jeep rose into the air and turned almost all the way around. The other fellow came running out of the shed, down to the jeep and jumped behind the wheel. The jeep started and he spun away, passing Harry as he came out of the woods.

Harry said it was about 10 days before the two FBI agents showed up. They had been told a couple hunters had been driving along, minding their own business, when someone threw a bomb at them. They barely escaped with their lives.

The FBI agents asked Harry if he knew anything about it. He shook his head and told them: "It's just getting too dangerous to be up in these woods. I don't know how much longer I'll be able to last it out before they get me, too."

Harry wouldn't take money for fixing my things and he wouldn't let me bring him any replacement parts. In fact, he insisted on giving me old tools he said he didn't need anymore: crosscut saws, peaveys, axes, adzes, Swede hooks and logging tongs – all antique stuff telling me Harry was through logging forever. Today, the walls of my Lodge are decorated with those old things and guests are always asking what it would take to get them away from me.

I tell them that would be impossible.

Once I asked Harry about the fight he'd had at the railroad bar and getting shot in the back. His most vivid memory was being thrown into the back of an old touring car and being driven 45 bumpy miles to the hospital in Salmon and the long time it took him to recover.

"Were you the one who killed Purcell like everyone is telling me," I asked. Harry frowned, shrugged his shoulders and looked away without answering. I changed the subject as I had the feeling it may have been true and I didn't really want to know.

Once I asked him about the traps hanging around his cabin. He got excited and opened a small wooden box he kept outside. These were his "Scents," a god-awful smelling concoction of foul-looking liquids Harry developed to lure fur bearing animals from miles around. Harry learned to trap early in life, as it was the only way he could make money as a boy. When he got old enough,

Harry travelled into the arctic to trap, and did all right at it. He said he spent months at a time in the snow and ice before giving it up to join the Merchant Marines.

This inspired more stories. Harry talked about being young and wild and willing to try anything. One of his experiences involved going ashore in San Francisco and visiting a Chinese opium den, which was legal then. They tried to get him high and rob him and he had to fight his way out. He doesn't recommend opium dens for recreation.

His best experience was a trip to Vladivostok, Russia in 1917, just before the communist revolution. Harry described it as an open beautiful city where he fell in love with several different women, which resulted in him being forced to take refuge on his ship for several days, not knowing if he would make it out of Russia. I found it fascinating to sit and exchange stories with Harry. He was taking me back to another time and he made it real.

Harry was certainly real and didn't appear to be slowing down much. When he was 83, Harry was sitting in a booth at the "Silver Dollar," one of two bars in Leadore, telling stories. A local cowboy, who was drinking heavily and may have been jealous of Harry's popularity with the crowd, looked at Harry and said: "You're lying, Harry." The cowboy, who I knew, was 29-years-old, about 6-foot-2 and probably weighed 245 pounds. Harry stood, hit him once and the cowboy sailed backwards, up and over the pool table, landing in a heap on the floor. His friends helped him up and out the door.

I think sometimes about how few of us even last to be 83, much less get in a bar fight with a sturdy young guy … and actually win it.

But even the strongest among us have limits. Harry came by my place one day to tell me he had cancer and was going to Idaho Falls for an operation. He said he'd probably be laid up for a little while. He brought me a colorful woven saddle blanket I had once admired. "Here, you can probably use this," he said, and wouldn't take it back when I refused. It seemed to me, if I accepted, that would be saying: "I don't think you're going to get over this cancer and you won't be needing it again." On the other hand, it seemed like I would have to fight Harry to get him to take it back, so I told him I would hold it for him.

Harry went into the hospital , where, among other things, they removed his testicles. After a week or so, I paid him a visit and, true to form, Harry told me: "I'm still a man, this morning it was up as good as it had ever been." He seemed quite pleased, even after I told him: "Harry, you're 85-years-old; you may not need it anymore." He replied: "I ain't planning on quitting for a few more years yet." I wondered if I would be as determined as he was at 85; that is, if I made it that far.

When Harry was released from the hospital, his doctors and nurses didn't think he should go back to a primitive log cabin until he was steadier on his feet. It was early winter and temperatures had been recorded as low as 50 below zero in Leadore. They feared he wouldn't be able to chop enough wood to keep warm. So, Harry went into an assisted living center in Idaho Falls.

By any standard, the center was a really nice place. Harry had a furnished room and private bath, good meals served three times a day in a pleasant dining room, a recreation area and a gymnasium where he could stay in shape. He scoffed at the idea of working out in a gym. Harry said he'd never been in a gymnasium in his life and thought he had plenty of muscle developed from the way he had lived. I agreed with him. In fact, I've been able to resist suggestions that I work out more often by using Harry as my standard.

About once a week I would go by to visit him. I thought he would be getting pretty lonely there by himself. I was wrong. I would stop by in the evening and find Harry sitting at a dining room table with a group of ladies. It was obvious he was the center of attention. I had no desire to interfere with his conversations, so I would signal that I was there and take a seat in one of the big stuffed sofas and wait until he joined me.

One day, I came in and started down the hall toward the dining room when a little lady with snow white hair stepped in front of me and shook her finger in my face. In a fierce, loud voice, she said: "You leave Harry alone."

It took me by surprise and I stepped back. I assured the lady that I was not going to do Harry any harm and was just there for a friendly visit and walked out around her. She repeated her warning in a loud voice. I quickened my pace, thinking: "This doesn't look good … being chased down the hall by a little old lady." I was getting a little bit riled by the time I found Harry.

"What the hell did you tell a little lady with white hair about me," I asked Harry. He had a big grin on his face as he replied: "Some of the ladies I've been visiting with have seen you come in and wait for me and they wanted to know who you were. I told them you're a FBI agent that comes to check on me from time to time."

Marilyn and I had established a tradition of having a New Year's party at our house. We would serve dinner – Marilyn is a wonderful cook – and invite as many of our friends as would fit in our house.

One day Marilyn said to me: "Why don't you invite Harry to the party?"

"I don't think Harry would really fit in with this group," I replied.

"Why not?"

"Well he's kind of a wild outlaw type with no formal education and most of our friends, while being nice folks, are still straight up and down, steady well-educated people who may not understand him."

I could see Marilyn was getting irritated. She said: "You invite Harry!" So I dropped by the center the next day and invited him, thinking he would probably decline. But, he accepted and I told him I would pick him up.

At 6 p.m. on New Years Eve, I drove up to the center and Harry was waiting. He was dressed in his best pants and shirt and had a string tie on. His hair was slicked back and combed and his shoes shined. He looked pretty good.

I was a little nervous. I had moved around in Harry's world, but he had never moved in mine. I didn't know what to expect. I was in for a pleasant surprise.

Marilyn announced dinner and we seated Harry at center table, where he would have a variety of conversation partners. I was assisting Marilyn, but kept my eye on Harry just in case. I was surprised to see him accept a glass of wine and watched how he rolled it in the glass and smelled it for aroma. The act was so casual and professional that for a second I regretted we were not serving expensive wine.

As the meal progressed, I noted that Harry had good table manners. He used the correct fork in the correct manner, ate at a slow pace, used his napkin appropriately and would have fit right in, as the saying goes, "with the Vanderbilts and Carnegies." He joined in the table conversation, speaking only when he did not have food in his mouth, and politely accepted a second glass of wine.

Our procedure was to remain at the table after the main course and allow an interval before dessert. This time is most often filled with conversation I always looked forward to, as the usual guests are interesting people with a broad interest in almost everything: politics, religion, science, philosophy and education. Harry fit right in and before long began telling stories of his life and experiences. My guests were treated to the same history that had fascinated me.

I was in the kitchen with Marilyn when one of our nuclear scientist friends came in laughing, and said: "I can't stand this anymore." I asked what he was talking about. "That fellow in there is telling those women that it got so cold up in the Arctic that the oxygen froze right out of the air," he said. "And they believe it."

"Harry has a convincing way about him," was all I could say.

We served dessert and Harry began reciting poetry. He began with Robert Service's, "The Shooting of Dan McGrew," and then offered up "The Cremation of Sam McGee." Those ballads are long and if no one else was impressed I certainly was. In past years, I had tried to learn those same verses and failed. Harry was being encouraged by the group and he started on some romantic verse, announcing: "This is some stuff I wrote myself." Harry was the life of the party all through the evening and when midnight came, we toasted in the New Year and every woman there gave Harry a big kiss, which he obviously relished.

I felt good about the evening and was glad Marilyn had insisted I invite him. I also mused about how we can think we know someone and yet not have a clue as to who they really are.

My learning was really just beginning. In spite of the soft life Harry was living, he wanted to get back to his cabin in Leadore. Bill English was also visiting him regularly, as he and his family got to know Harry well and were helping look after him. Bill arranged for him to be released early to return home. It was still cold, but hints of spring and warmer days were in the air.

I visited Harry at the cabin a few days after he returned. He was in bed and a fire was burning in the stove, so he was warm enough. I noticed a large prescription bottle of liquid morphine sitting on the table, within reach. Because of Marilyn's work with Hospice, I was aware that prescription was normally written to a dying person to make death less painful.

"Are you using that," I asked. "No," Harry replied. "I won't use it if I don't have to. I don't need to get addicted to it."

Harry was obviously hurting, but he stared at the bottle as if it was the enemy. I sensed he was having some sort of inner battle about accepting death, especially when he said: "This is the toughest thing I've ever tried to lick; I'm really having a fight." He was struggling and for once didn't seem to want to talk, so I left after telling him I would be back on the next trip through.

As I drove away, I could not help but think that Harry would end it himself, by walking out of his cabin, sitting under a tree in the cold and drinking the whole bottle of morphine. I guessed wrong.

Over the years, the subject of religion had come up more than once. Harry said he was an atheist and did not care for organized religion. The dominant religion in the Leadore area was Mormon and they became the target of his jokes. He was not mean about it. As each Mormon congregation is led by a bishop, Harry referred to himself as Bishop Byers.

Harry took baths on Sunday morning, in water heated on his stove. On a few occasions, I have been told that about the time people were traveling to church, Harry would step out of his cabin naked to get another armload of wood for the stove and to give the Mormon ladies a thrill.

Fortunately for Harry, the local Mormons didn't take offense at his sense of humor. When they learned of his illness, those folks responded by preparing food and delivering it to him each day and doing all they could to help him.

Eventually, the cancer won and Harry's long and interesting life came to an end. When someone dies, his friends sometimes gather to exchange stories and perceptions.

My partner, Jim Mason, told of having a 13-year-old nephew come out from Michigan to visit. Jim heard the boy, and his own son, who was also 13, talking about mountain men and he told them: "I'm going to show you a real mountain man."

They drove to Leadore and knocked on the cabin door. Jim said Harry could not have been more gracious. Harry spent the next couple of hours talking directly to the boys, telling them about trapping, breaking horses and logging … and showing them his things. Jim said the two boys bring up the visit to the mountain man's cabin over and over again.

That was Harry: an impressive man who made an impression, not just on those boys, but on me as well.

Three

GETTING THE FULL SWAN TREATMENT

A stocky man with a ruddy complexion, blue eyes and curly white hair walked into my office one afternoon, stuck out his hand and introduced himself as Bud Swan.

He appeared to be in his late 50s or early 60s and had a distinguished look. I'm always a little suspicious of anybody who comes into my office, but this man was so affable and talked with such an air of confidence that I couldn't help but smile and respond as he buttered me up.

Bud said he knew me from having attended a few of the chamber of commerce meetings at which I had spoken. His face did have a vague familiarity about it. He said he had been asking around about me, naming a few local business friends I knew, and that everyone had highly recommended me. I didn't know it at the time but I was getting "the full Swan treatment."

Bud had recently retired from managing an insurance company in Idaho Falls. His wife was an executive in one of the local brokerage houses and ineligible for retirement for another three years. This meant Bud faced three years of boredom unless he found something to do with his time.

Immediately after his retirement party, a local law firm asked him to investigate a couple suspected fraud cases, telling him they needed his insurance industry knowledge.

Bud discovered that he enjoyed digging into things and had some successes. The law firm did not have enough work to keep him busy and he wasn't crazy about the "ambulance chasing firm," anyway, so he sought me out to see if I might need an investigator.

I already had a few good investigators working for me, but I had learned that people do sometimes move on and to keep my eyes open for good people who pop up in unexpected places and times. So, I was intrigued.

I dug into Bud's background and found he had a career prior to his insurance agency management. He was an Air Force pilot and had lived and worked throughout the country. Bud was also an educated man who graduated from Stanford University and the Air force Academy.

My instincts told me he was an ideal applicant. But I've also learned that sometimes things are too good to be true, so I was hesitant. I asked Bud to fill out an application and told him: "I don't have anything I could give you to do right now, but stay in touch and maybe something will come up."

Field work kept me out of the office until noon the next day. Geri greeted me with a reproving look and proceeded to tell me about her morning. As soon as she arrived at the office, the door flew open and Bud walked in and began acting as though he owned the place. He told Geri he hadn't expected to see such a nice looking woman occupying her chair and what a bonus it was going to be to have someone like her to work with.

Poor Geri didn't know if he'd been hired or not and was at a loss as to know how to respond to him or how to treat him. She offered him a cup of coffee and said he should sit in the waiting room. Geri became even more flustered when he followed her with his cup in hand behind the counter, chatting all the while about himself and asking questions about the firm and what kind of things we did and who our clients were.

Geri didn't know it at the time but she too was getting the "full Swan treatment."

Bud left after asking if I would be in the next day. Geri said, as far as she knew, I would be in early. I always appreciated Geri telling everyone I was better than I really was.

Sure enough, the next morning I was late as usual and Bud was waiting in the office with a cup of coffee in his hand. He greeted me and told me that yesterday he had met this delightful young lady, waving toward Geri, his eyebrows rising up to signal approval, and I could not suppress a smile as Geri blushed, waved him away and turned back to her computer. I gave her a wink and told Bud: "Come on back to my office."

I had an inconsequential insurance fraud case in the pending case basket. It was a simple case assigned to us by a company manager who complained bitterly and often about our exorbitant rates, telling us other firms would investigate for half our cost. His boss had ordered him to give us cases because we got results and so he was stuck with us. His bitchy attitude was tiresome, so I always put his cases last on my list of things to do. If Bud Swan was assigned this case and screwed it up, I wouldn't feel bad about losing the client.

Bud agreed to work on the case and the following day provided evidence needed to substantiate fraud. He wanted another assignment. We were off and running. I passed on the few pending cases I had to him.

But Bud wanted more than just insurance fraud cases. "What do you think you want and have the qualifications to handle," I asked him. "I think I can handle anything," Bud replied, "but what I don't know maybe you can teach me." I recall thinking that if I don't take this guy on steady and give him lots of work, he may start his own business and with that enthusiasm become a real competition.

I had no reason to be concerned. Later, as I got to know him, I found Bud had no desire to take on the headaches of running a firm. He regarded the work as great fun and had a lifelong kind of Walter Mitty dream of living the life of an actual detective – digging out the truth wherever it was to be found.

We were taking in a few criminal cases from local defense attorneys. After working a good portion of my life on the prosecution side, I was having difficulty re-orienting my thinking. I knew innocent people are sometimes charged with crimes and everyone deserves a good defense. I also knew many of the clients we were being asked to defend and was aware they had long histories of being on the edge of society, by their own choice.

Getting them off the hook seemed a waste of time, as they would probably end up right back in trouble again. I genuinely hoped our competitors would occupy themselves with those cases and leave me to focus on more interesting stuff. I sometimes found myself accepting criminal cases as favors to attorneys I liked rather than on any desire to keep the criminal justice system honest.

Every once in a while, I would catch myself thinking that I got into this business to make money and here I was turning away work because I wasn't interested in it … hardly the formula for getting rich. But I had never been motivated by money and a leopard has a hard time changing his spots.

Bud took our company brochures to all the area law firms and exposed them to the full Swan treatment. The cases rolled in. He asked for advice and I told him: "There's always information out there that the police didn't want to take the time to dig out. All you have to do is convince people it's in their best interest to give you everything they didn't give to the police."

It didn't take Bud long to get in trouble. It involved a family living in Blackfoot, a community of about 15,000 people located about 25 south of Idaho Falls. The family at its best could be described as dysfunctional and a disagreement ended with one of them shooting and killing his brother. Local police conducted a cursory investigation, establishing just enough information to find out who fired the gun. The brother was arrested and charged with murder.

His defense attorney hired us. I gave Bud the case and instructed him to go out and do what he did best – get everybody talking and find out what hasn't been included in the police report.

Two days later, Bud was back in the office telling me he was convinced the shooting was self-defense and that witnesses had not cooperated with police because they didn't like their attitude.

I told Bud to get the witness statements in writing, because doing so made it less likely they would change their stories later. A few days later, Bud showed up with a large sheaf of papers, copied them and took the originals to the defense attorneys. The prosecutor could have filed a motion to obtain our reports, but he chose not to, probably having placed too much confidence in the ability of the local police investigator.

A few months later, it was time for the trial. The prosecution figured out that it had gotten sandbagged. The defense attorney presented five good witnesses police had not told him about. Those witnesses, as well as the witnesses the police had rounded up, testified that the brother who did the shooting had been physically attacked and had his life threatened by the victim. They said he fired the gun to defend his life. The jury came back with a reduced verdict, tantamount to simple assault.

The prosecutor was furious. He wrote a letter to the judge that had heard the case, claiming Bud had represented himself as a law enforcement officer and coerced witnesses into giving him information they would not have divulged if they didn't think they were talking to the law. That was a serious charge.

Bud was devastated. He had seen himself as having done a very good job. He got his client off. In reality, he had done a spectacular job — one that doesn't happen every time. Bud's problem was that he expected more from the criminal justice system than it could deliver.

He hadn't done anything wrong, and could not understand why was he being accused of breaking the law. I told him about similar experiences I had in the past and my theories about bad police, including lazy cops with attitudes that turn potential witnesses off.

I wrote a letter to the judge and prosecutor, denying the allegation and praising Bud's abilities as an investigator and man of character. I talked about how people respond to this affable man who takes the time to listen and described his ability to draw people out. The letter talked about his background, as a pilot in war fighting for his country, his education at the Air Force Academy and Stanford and accomplishments in the business world. Finally, I admonished them for presuming that such a man would deliberately violate any laws.

I signed and mailed it, though I really didn't need to. I knew the prosecutor to be a righteous man who was just venting about things he had no control over. The judge was a friend who was just passing the letter on. Neither would have taken it any further. Bud, however, appreciated the letter and my description of him.

As time went by, I found that Bud had only one character trait that didn't work well in our office. Because of Bud's military background, he felt it was necessary to keep our office, and specifically me, informed about where he was at and what he was doing.

My approach was the opposite. I found myself continually in trouble with my wife, secretary, and co-workers. All seemed constantly annoyed that I didn't bother to keep them informed. I meant well, but just did not see the need to tell people where I was.

Bud called early every morning to tell me where he would be working that day. I would tell him, "Thanks, but I trust you to be on the job and you don't need to check in with me." He would agree. A few hours later, however, Bud would call to say he was going to Pocatello or Rexburg or wherever. After a while, I reconciled myself to the fact that it was just his way. It became kind of funny.

Bud owned some time-share condos and was constantly trading for good deals, such as a week's vacation in an exotic place. He would call and say he had a week in Bermuda or some unknown island in the Caribbean and he needed time off, always asking if I wanted to go along. Somehow our schedules didn't coincide, but it was nice to be asked. Even on vacation, Bud felt the need to check in. He would call the morning he left to say he was on his way. A few hours later, I would get a call from the airport in El Paso, or some other place, telling me everything was going very well. Hours later, Bud would call from his destination to let me know he was safe and to give me a rundown.

I travelled vicariously with him and after a while began to feel I knew something about those places. My only problem was that he was calling me on the company credit card, so I would tell him he was going to have to put in extra hours to cover his bill. This would always get a laugh out of him. We both knew he was making the company good money and that he loved doing it.

Bud accepted all kinds of cases, in different places. Central Idaho is mountainous wilderness area, hundreds of miles long and wide, containing rugged trails to hike or ride horses into and cascading rapids to float. Access into this area is tough by any standard. The only exception to the wilderness access rules are a few tiny airstrips carved in strategic locations. One is located at the Flying B Ranch, which can be found at the very bottom of an immense narrow canyon of the middle fork of the Salmon River.

The Flying B consists of a collection of cabins, a large lodge, horse corrals, a pasture and the tiny airstrip. Wilderness outfitters bring tourists in for fishing, hunting and outdoor experiences.

In wilderness areas, danger is always present. A small plane leaving the Flying B had crashed on take-off, killing the pilot and passenger.

When accidents happen, the finger-pointing begins. Insurance companies don't want to pay if they can help it and need someone to determine if the accident was caused by pilot error, faulty airplane or equipment. Or, was it an act of God?

We had done considerable work for one of the insurance companies involved in this accident. They called and asked if we would be willing to take this case on. Before Bud joined us, I would have had to decline as our expertise was limited. My only experience with flying was as a white-knuckled student pilot years ago and before I realized I didn't have enough money to own airplanes and horses. I opted for horses. But now Bud was on board, a man with half a lifetime of flying all kinds of airplanes all over the world under every conceivable weather condition and circumstance. This was right up his alley and I accepted the case.

We arranged for a plane to fly him from Salmon into the Middle Fork Canyon and down to the Flying B. I noted when he loaded up that Bud included his fly rod and wading boots with his luggage. I told him I had never seen those kinds of investigative tools. Bud replied that he had developed new theories about getting the proper perspective for each case. Bud had arrived. He was now a full-fledged detective with a realistic attitude.

We were out of touch for several days because there is no phone service in remote mountain areas. Bud returned full of enthusiasm … because he caught several trout and had seen bear and elk and some goats on a cliff. I stopped him to ask about the airplane crash. He laughed: "The pilot took off, overloaded in the wrong direction, couldn't make his necessary turn to clear a ridge in time and once committed couldn't recover or back out in time to prevent what was sure to happen. It was a tragic but dumb move for an experienced pilot."

Bud had taken a day to investigate the crash and a couple days to fool around.

He spent the next couple of days diagramming the accident with maps, overlays, statistics, variants, tolerances and specific airplane characteristics, explaining to me as he went along what he was doing and why. I could not imagine that any attorney, no matter how gifted, could successfully challenge his conclusions. The insurance company felt the same way and paid us well.

One day I got a call from a law firm in New York City. The attorney said his firm represented the London Times newspaper. He said we had been referred to them as a competent firm. This always made me feel good, though I suspected it might just be a line to get us on the hook. It also meant the case was going to be difficult.

It turned out that a freelance writer had gotten on the wrong side of a movie star, who lived in Jackson Hole, Wyo., just a few hours from Idaho Falls. Jackson

Hole is a place of spectacular beauty. The Teton Mountain peaks dominate the valley, with Jackson Lake in the center and the Wind River Mountains to the east. Anyone who has seen the movie "Shane" knows Jackson Hole, as it was filmed there.

Its beauty has drawn wealthy people from all over the world to establish residences on the slopes and canyon floors, creating an enclave of magnificent homes. For years the king of Jordan parked his personal plane in Idaho Falls and motored to Jackson to ski and enjoy the ambience of gracious living. Former Vice-President Dick Cheney lives there. The Rockefeller family created and donated parks in and around Jackson for public use. Attorney Jerry Spence lives and works there. And, getting back to that phone call from the New York attorney, one of the notables who made this small western town his home was Harrison Ford, of Star Wars and Indiana Jones fame.

The freelance writer had written a story about Ford. It said that while Ford was popular with the move-going world, he was disliked by his neighbors in Jackson Hole. The story claimed Ford left several injured people at a snowmobile accident scene. It also talked about a local cowboy beating him up in a bar, which was reflective of the local antipathy against him.

The writer quoted other locals saying less than kind things about the actor and sold the story to the London Times, which printed it in their tabloid section. Ford sued the paper for slander and libel.

The attorney requested that we go check out the story and see if it could be defended in court. I always looked forward to going over to Jackson. Excellent restaurants, spectacular scenery, good shows, colorful people, art galleries and music festivals could be found scattered around in other places; but in Jackson they are in abundance in one small place. It was an extra bonus when you could visit Jackson on an expense account. Bud said this case was right down his alley, so after one unnecessary trip, which I took just for fun, he took over the investigation.

A few days, he returned. Bud thought the case was going to be a lark, but immediately he ran into a buzz saw, starting with the sheriff. Bud stopped at the sheriff's office to check their records for accidents Ford had been involved in, hoping they would give him a lead to the one the writer was referring to.

"The sheriff came unglued at the thought anyone would write an article like that," Bud told me. The sheriff told Bud people in the county loved Harrison Ford and described him as "beyond a doubt, the best citizen they ever had." He told Bud of the many times Ford had voluntarily, and at his own expense, flown his helicopter on rescue missions in the Teton Mountains to rescue injured and stranded climbers and hikers, often putting himself in danger to help others. The sheriff talked about Ford's cooperation in civic and government events and his friendliness towards everyone.

Bud said that as the sheriff talked, he got worked up and said something to the effect of: "If that writer ever shows up here again, he'll really have something to write about; the people of this town will string him up in the town square."

As Bud spoke, I thought of the square block park in the center of town where each day the stagecoach rolls up and a band of outlaws reenact a holdup and a shootout for the benefit of tourists. The large arch at the entry to the park is made up entirely of elk antlers and in my mind's eye I could visualize a hapless writer swinging by the neck from that arch and the crowd of tourists cheering.

A sheriff's deputy told Bud he had investigated an accident Harrison Ford was involved in. Ford had been snowmobiling with a group of friends and had flipped his own snowmobile over and cracked his ribs in the process. No one else was involved. They had called for assistance and a helicopter was flown to the site to pick him up. Ford was placed on a stretcher and airlifted out. "I guess he did go off and leave a bunch of people on the ground," the deputy said. "They were all waving at him and he waved back. No one else was hurt in any way."

The deputy dug out the accident report and made a copy for Bud, who then asked about the beating in a bar. Nobody in the sheriff's office knew about a fight and doubted if one had taken place. As Bud left, they asked him to, "Send that writer around."

Later, Bud and I discussed the difference between a writer who deliberately perverts the truth about someone for profit and a straight-out thief. We concluded the only difference is that the thief can go to jail. We decided we might even like the thief better.

Bud continued digging and discovered the supposed bar fight took place at Hungry Jacks, an upscale western café and bar in Wilson, a small community a few miles west of Jackson. Ford was a guest at a wedding reception. Some of the men started arm wrestling at tables in the lounge. Evidently, Ford joined in, winning several matches before taking on a cowboy that worked at his ranch. Throwing bales of hay around all day paid off for the cowboy and he beat Ford. There was laughter all around, Ford congratulated him and the party continued. Bud's witnesses indignantly said: "How anyone could have twisted what happened into a story of a cowboy beating up Harrison was beyond comprehension." This person told Bud that somebody needed to pin that writer, not just his arm and not necessarily on a table.

Bud was unable to find a single person who had anything bad to say about Harrison Ford. The local people in bars and restaurants, stores and hotels were full of praise for their neighbor and fellow citizen.

Based on Bud's investigation, our opinion was that the article could not be defended and appeared to be a total distortion of the truth. We sent it off with our bill. We received payment within a week. A few days later I got a call from our attorney client, who thanked us for the report, calling it one of the best written reports he had ever received from a detective agency. The attorney also congratulated me for having such skilled investigators.

I felt pretty good about the call, as I constantly preached to the staff that they could be the most talented investigators in the world but if they couldn't write about their findings, all that skill was wasted. The report was everything.

Once again Bud had made us look good and I could not take any of the credit, though I was the one receiving the praise. I passed it on to Bud with my thanks. Good education does pay off in the end. The attorney later called to say the case had been settled out of court for several hundred thousand dollars, which Ford donated to charity. We commiserated for a while about the fact that the tabloid paid off and still made money and how our goal of absolute justice may never be achieved.

For some reason, Bud was more pleased with the results of that case than usual. I soon learned what may have been behind his satisfaction. I came dragging into the office on Monday morning, late again and waved at Geri. As I passed, I noted her eyes were lit up with excitement:

"Guess who just called here," she asked.

"Who?"

"Steven Spielberg," she answered.

We did a lot of kidding around in this office and I had resolved not to be sucked in again. I gave a casual wave of my hand. With a straight face, I said, "That's good," and kept going down the hall toward my office. We can all play this little game. As I passed Bud's office, his door was open and he hollered at me to stop. I just knew they had cooked up some scheme to get a laugh at my expense ... just like I would do to them if an opportunity came up. I maintained my casual demeanor and said: "What's up?"

"I have to leave for a few days next week and I need you to pick up a couple of my appointments, if you will," Bud said.

"Sure, what days are you going to be gone," I replied.

"If you can pick up Thursday and Friday, I'll be OK," Bud said. "I've got nothing on tap Saturday and Sunday and I should be back on Monday." He pulled out his calendar to show me the appointment he couldn't cancel.

This didn't sound like a scam, so I asked: "Where exactly are you going?"

His face suddenly became serious, with his brow furrowed. Bud looked at the ceiling. After a few seconds he said, "I'll have to swear you to secrecy." He wasn't smiling. I raised my hand and solemnly intoned: "I swear."

He asked me to come into his office. "When I was a boy, I was in the movies," Bud said. "One of the films has been purchased by Ted Turner and he and Steven Spielberg are re-releasing it, 50 years after it was released the first time. They are throwing a big party in Hollywood to promote its 50th birthday and new release. They want to fly me and my family down to Los Angeles and put us up for a few nights to attend. I feel I need to go."

"Fine," I replied. "What movie are we talking about?"

"Citizen Kane," was his answer.

A memory flashed through my brain. Years before in college, I had taken an art appreciation class. The professor had brought up movies as an art form. I remember him saying that Citizen Kane was the greatest movie ever made and Orson Wells was a genius who pioneered all the film making methods that are used today. Routine things like flashbacks and total life spans were his invention and first used in this movie that, apparently, had featured Bud Swan. The professor had required that all class members see the movie and write a report on it. I was not likely to forget, no matter how much time had passed.

I agreed to cover for Bud, went on back to my office, picked up my brief case and excused myself as if I was going out on a job. Instead I went directly to a video store and to the classic movie section and picked up a copy of Citizen Kane. There on the cover were the names: Orson Wells, Joseph Cotton, Agnes Moorhead, Buddy Swan and others I didn't recognize. I felt badly that I had not believed him, but also relieved that I had not verbalized my doubts. There was nothing to apologize for. I even took a little pride in recalling when I first met Bud his name had triggered a memory, though I didn't make the connection at that time.

I ran the video home and quickly reviewed it and saw that Bud had played the part of Orson Wells as a young boy. It was a fairly major part and 50 years had not erased his profile or mannerisms. I could see the older Bud in young Buddy's face.

I returned to the office and found Bud working on reports. I joined him and casually asked, "Bud, why didn't you tell us about your background?"

"I didn't even tell my wife until we had been married for seven years," he replied.

"Good God, Bud, why not?"

His face contorted in a grimace and he replied: "Hollywood is full of bastards. As quick as I was old enough to get out on my own, I left and joined the Air Force." He continued: "My mother worked in the wardrobe department at MGM Studios. She was a real movie buff and pushed everyone she knew to get me involved. She got me in several films. I was a little kid in Sands of Iwo Jima. I was in an Errol Flynn movie. I was also in the Murphy Brothers, the one about the seven brothers who were killed on the same ship in World War II, causing a law in Congress to be passed that forbids brothers being posted on the same ship. And I was in two or three others that didn't do so well. I didn't like it. I didn't like the people I was thrown in with."

I mentioned that Citizen Kane was Orson Wells' crowning achievement. Bud's attitude changed.

"Orson Wells was a real prince of a man," Bud said. "We remained friends all throughout the years. During my years as a pilot, whenever I would fly into New York, I would call him. He had an apartment, a whole floor in an exclusive apartment building overlooking Central Park. I would say, 'I just flew in,' and he would say, 'Come on up tonight, bring your friends.' We would go up and he would arrange dinner for us. My fellow pilots were always impressed that I knew Orson so well."

Bud told me Wells seemed to relish spending time with men of action, men outside of his industry. I surmised that there were deep bonds, difficult to understand, between these two: one spending his life in a make-believe world and the other having made an escape. When Bud spoke about Orson Wells, his demeanor softened and he smiled as if remembering good times.

Bud and I talked for a couple hours, with him reminiscing about his boyhood on movie lot. He didn't tell me about whatever it was that soured him on Hollywood and I didn't ask again. It was apparent that was painful to him. I sensed Bud had come to terms with whatever it was and that he was now re-connected with something he had put out of his mind for a long time. I felt it so strong that when we parted I called a friend who reported for the local paper, the Post Register, and told them that there was a human interest story here.

Bud and his family flew to Los Angeles. When he returned four or five days later, he was jubilant. He said that he had a great time. "I was chauffeured from my hotel in a limo to the studio where the party was held," Bud told us. "Everybody who was anybody in the movie industry was there."

Bud talked about conversations with Steven Spielberg and Ted Turner and he praised Charlton Heston, who he described as a real gentleman. He said Joseph Cotton was still alive and while frail, remained the life of the party. Bud received so much praise for his role in Citizen Kane that he almost couldn't stand it, or so he claimed. I knew Bud well enough to say with confidence that he could stand it just fine, as he was beaming with happiness.

The Sunday Post Register carried a front page story about Bud and his exploits. He had consented to an interview and a full photograph in color graced the cover. The story focused on his invitation to the re-release party and detailed his career as a movie star, Air Force pilot, businessman and detective.

Before the hoopla subsided, Bud was listed in "Who's Who in Idaho," along with such notables as U.S. Senators William Borah and Frank Church, something that pleased him immensely. It was obvious that Bud Swan was enjoying life.

Despite our differences, Bud and I learned to get along very well. I could tease him about things, such as his need to let me know where he was during the day, and he would let it roll off his back. Sometimes, those differences manifested themselves in odd ways.

I had invited Bud to come up to our ranch for a little fishing. For me, that meant being dressed in my jeans and an old shirt and grabbing a fishing pole that I usually left leaning against the lodge. I would abandon fishing quickly and take off on foot to explore the canyon or river bottom.

One Saturday, Bud and his lovely wife showed up at the ranch. He had not only brought her, but also his

Golden Labrador dog. Bud announced he was there to fish, and he was dressed to the hilt, right out of Field and Stream magazine: canvas pants, fancy wading boots, fishing vest adorned with dozens of pockets and every conceivable fly and lure and a sporty hat covered with whatever flies he had been unable to hook on the vest. Bud Swan was the very picture of outdoor sartorial elegance.

I revised my plan of a casual hour or two of fishing and decided to take him to a small lake, with a nice stream feeding it in the nearby Lemhi Mountains. Here was place of beauty with plenty of fish that was mostly unknown to the public.

The road to this place was rocky and it was not wise to try and get a car back there. I told Bud we would take my old pickup with four wheel drive and invited him and his wife to take a seat in the cab. "Put your dog in the back," I told him. Bud said the dog could not ride in the back and proceeded to load the big dog into the front on his lap. There was barely enough room left for me. But I'm game, so I crowded in and we took off toward the lake, bouncing around with the dog ending up mostly on my lap.

The lake, with the bright sunlight and clear blue sky mirrored in the blue and green water, was exceptionally beautiful on that day. The whole scene was ours as there was no one else around. We parked near a picnic table and Bud quickly jumped out, called his dog and took off to the stream at the head of the lake. He left us standing there, which was fine with me since we had a thermos of coffee. So, his wife and I sat down at the tableland and poured ourselves a couple mugs full.

She and I spent the rest of the afternoon sitting in the shade. We had a delightful time watching Bud cast and recast and throw fish back as his dog swam and splashed in the lake and stream. Ms. Swan and I shared stories and memories of younger days and I regard that day as one of the nicest I have ever spent. Everyone had a good time, especially Bud. That he insisted on loading his wet dog back on our laps for the trip back to the ranch did not make even a tiny dent in that good time.

Some stories have happy endings and others do not. Sometimes it's hard to know if it's happy or sad. Maybe all story endings are a mixture of both.

Bud talked with me often about how he was about to retire, as his wife was nearing the end of her working days. He said she was due to inherit some assets and they were planning on a comfortable life. He had his military and business retirements, had just signed up for Social Security and could rely on his investments.

He would bring real estate brochures into the office and excitedly show me prospective retirement homes - small villas with private sand beaches on small Caribbean islands; exclusive condos at Myrtle Beach; and beach estates in Florida. I would tell him I was glad he was looking at property in those places as we didn't want any more people retiring in our mountain communities and cluttering up the scenery.

As we joked, I sensed urgency in his statements. Instead of working, we would often sit around and talk about death and time and spirituality. Bud didn't have much tolerance for organized religion and it was evident he had not taken much time in his life to reflect on purpose and meaning of life. He said he had been busy living it, not studying it.

Bud said he had fought his share of demons – alcohol and anger being the most onerous – and that he was looking forward to quieter times. He suffered from an inability of the body to eliminate excess iron from his system. Every month, he would visit a clinic and have a pint of blood drawn out of his arm in order to maintain or sustain the proper chemical balance. He huffed and puffed a little when climbing the 26 steps up the stairway to our second-story office, but he seemed healthy for his age.

Bud was 64 when he took a plane trip to Denver to visit his daughter. After getting off the plane, he had a massive heart attack and died almost immediately.

We had a business relationship in the beginning but had become friends. I had not realized how good of friends we were until I heard the news of his death. I found myself grieving as if I had lost a family member. I felt so badly for his wife and children, whom he had expressed his love for so many times.

As I reflected back over our conversations, I realized that Bud knew he was not going to live a long life. I also knew he never would have been able to retire. He was one of those people who live all the way, all the time. He had not really needed to show up in my office that day. He could have joined the golf retirees that abound in our area.

But that was not Bud Swan's way. He went out living and loving and working at what he wanted to do. We should all do so well.

Four

One Thing Leads to Another

O ne thing about this business that attracts me is that every day can bring an unexpected experience and I'm always surprised at how one thing can lead to another.

Every town in America has someone that is seen as the principal source of illegal drugs. Idaho Falls was no exception. Local police believed the source to be an individual named Leon Lowman, who owned a place called the Farway Club, which was located on a street referred to as motel row. The street was the center of Idaho Falls' night life.

I had a long history with Leon, which dated back to when we were both young – I as a policeman, detective and state criminal investigator and Leon as an ambitious, under-educated entrepreneur trying to find his way in life and not having an easy time of it. He seemed to spend most of his time between lower class bars and upper class gymnasiums. He was involved in more than his share of fights in the bars and I always suspected that he worked out in the gyms to be in better shape to fight. I watched him grow and try to raise himself up from his beginnings and I had come to admire his spirit, if not his methods.

We became friends during those years as he worked his way up to becoming the owner and operator of a successful nightclub. I had become a detective and Leon would pass on information he thought would help me solve crimes. He declined to tell me about his own crimes as he knew I would go after him even though we were friends. It was a good relationship.

It has been a sore point with me to hear fellow detectives badmouth those who were helping them by sneeringly referring to them as "snitches," as if they only passed on information out of fear or for profit of some kind. Leon had no fear of anything, especially the police, and never asked for any favors in return. I knew him well enough to know he actively disliked police and took pleasure in their discomfort when he bested them, which was often.

I recall an incident that occurred after he became a major cocaine distributor in Idaho. Leon and one of his employees had flown to San Diego in the Cessna he owned and piloted himself. On that trip he visited the boat docks, making contact with a fishing trawler that had just returned from a trip to southern Mexico. The FBI had been tipped off that the boat was delivering cocaine and was secretly filming everyone coming to the boat. They had pictures of Leon and his man visiting the trawler and leaving with a large package.

They tailed him to the airport and alerted Idaho police that he was on his way with contraband. A few hours later, Leon and his employee landed at the Idaho Falls airport and were met by about 30 eager, excited and armed police officers from several different agencies. As they roared up to his plane, Leon casually waved them over and invited them to search. I later learned he had landed in a remote field in Nevada and passed his load to another confederate waiting for him.

I lost track of Leon after I retired from law enforcement and had no reason to think our paths would cross again. I was in a different kind of business and did my best to stay away from his kind of club. But as almost always happens, Leon reached out too far and allowed himself to get careless. One of his friends ratted on him and set him up to sell dope to undercover officers. It was a big case and he was represented by one of the best law firms in the area.

They, in turn, hired a nationally known detective to dig out the best defense possible for Leon. That detective, Woodward Beyers, sold them on the idea that he needed a local detective, me, to assist him. I told him I didn't work these kinds of cases, but he had evidently talked to Leon, who asked that I be involved. "The people we need to talk to will talk to you, not me, and Leon deserves his day in court," Woodward said to me. I felt obligated from my connection to Leon in the past and I do believe the law should work for everyone. I agreed, but from what I knew of the case there would not be much we could do for him.

It was a fun case, working with Woodward, who was a friend, and moving back through the sleazy barrooms, making connections with old acquaintances and underworld types. But things had changed. I arranged to have an individual I knew to be a scumbag meet with Woodward and I in a low-class western bar in town. After introductions I left Woodward with this fellow and went to use the bathroom. Two older tough-looking guys followed me in. I was preparing for trouble only to find the two had followed to warn me about having anything to do with the fellow we had sat down with, saying he was a liar and a phony that could not be trusted.

They knew me from the old days, though I had forgotten them. I thanked them and said I was well aware of that fact. Later we were to find that his information was worthless to our case.

As Leon's case was winding down and Woodward was about to leave town, he called to ask for help on another matter and asked to meet someplace quiet. I told him I was with my wife and together we would stop at a local restaurant we had used as a meeting place on other occasions.

Woodward said he had a client who was a very rich and well-known Texas businessman. This case involved setting up a private auction in New York City to sell jewelry his client had acquired.

In the late 1970s, when the Shah of Iran was deposed and the Ayatollah Khomeini replaced him, the Shah fled to America. He suffered from cancer and to pay for his medical treatments, which ultimately failed, he sold the queen's jewelry to a Texas businesswoman. She went bankrupt a few years later and the judge awarded the jewelry to Woodward's client. The set was valued in excess of $3 million.

Woodward said he was in the process of securing a private banquet room in New York and that lawyers he knew were putting together a guest list of wealthy buyers. The auction took the form of a swank dinner party with tuxedos and evening gowns, which ended with the jewelry being exhibited and sold either one piece at a time or as the complete set.

While in Idaho Falls, Woodward told one of the attorneys what he was doing. A few days later, the local firm objected to eastern attorneys being the only ones given a chance to have such a party and a chance to bid on the jewelry. Woodward reluctantly agreed to give them the opportunity and made arraignments with a local upscale restaurant for a secluded space and set a date for the event.

He told us that in New York an auction like this was kept private by everyone involved. It was taken for granted that everyone knew the risks involved when something of great value was in play and did not openly discuss it outside of their own crowd. He had assumed that everyone in Idaho Falls would be aware of that necessity. To Woodward's dismay, the word had gotten out and he was being contacted by persons who had not been invited and should not have known about the party.

He did not know how widespread the talk had gone, but realized he might have a problem and needed to arrange for security on short notice. The party was two days away. Woodward asked if I could help. I agreed. This was new to me and I wanted to attend that event.

An upscale event such as this needed to be tasteful with security as unobtrusive as possible. The party was designed to be a relaxed social event where guests would throw caution to the winds and spend money.

Woodward reached under the table and brought up a brief case. He opened so that we could see and examine its contents. I was astounded. I thought I had seen expensive jewelry before but this was in a class by itself. There were jeweled brooches, elaborate necklaces, immense diamond rings, bracelets and every kind of precious gem earrings. It was breathtaking. Woodward shared our awe of the beauty and insisted that Marilyn try on each piece as he explained what he knew of them. We noted the starting bid prices for each item; the lowest was $32,000.

Marilyn later told me she did not like putting on the jewelry and was uncomfortable with it saying: "It was gathered together on the backs of a lot of poor people who did without necessities in order to dress the queen up." I was proud of her. During the Shah's reign, my sister and her husband lived in Iran. He was a safety engineer and his company had constructed a large concrete dam in the northern mountains of Iran. They had shared experiences and observations with us and I knew the Shah was extremely unpopular with the general populace and that he spent lavishly on himself while many of his people struggled to survive.

Woodward then showed us the contents of a second briefcase, which contained exact copies of what had been in the first. He said they were paste and had very little value but I could not have told the difference. It amazed me that someone could have created something so similar.

I escorted Woodward back to his motel where he secured the briefcases in the office safe. I told him I would bring an experienced friend with me and we would bring our wives for cover. He told me the expense account would cover everything and not to skimp. I contacted my old criminal investigator partner, Jim Mason, who was head of security for a large laboratory doing nuclear research and still living in Idaho Falls. I thought he might like to get back into the action and I was right.

The night of the party we dressed "fit to kill" as the old saying goes, put extra weapons in our wives' purses and showed up early to set things up. The restaurant did not have a private room so a large part had been cordoned off with temporary floor-to-ceiling panels enclosing the rented space behind. Entry was gained by having left out a single panel against the outer building wall. It was ideal for us. Jim and I arranged to have a table placed just to the side of that opening where we would be able to see everything and everyone in that room and at the same time appear as if we were a part of the normal dining clientele. We ordered the filleted shark, a bottle of very good wine and prepared for a long evening.

The guests began to arrive and cocktails and appetizers were served as they circulated around the room visiting with each other. We noted much laughter and friendly chatter and the party was off to a good start. We enjoyed our meal and wine as we watched Woodward and the briefcase. It was like the old days, being on a stakeout waiting for something to happen and we could feel the tension rising.

Jim, Woodward and I have all known people who would kill for $30. Put $3 million in jewelry where they could get at it and they would wipe out a room full of people. There didn't appear to be anyone like that in the restaurant, but we didn't know how far word of this event had spread. We were on our toes.

The meals were served and a string of waiters and waitresses streamed back and forth by our table. Time dragged by with us trying to look nonchalant and concerned only with each other. We must have pulled it off as our waiter, who had been helping serve the party, stopped by our table. "Do you know what's going on in there," he asked us. Without waiting for a reply, he said, "They've got the Shah of Iran's diamonds in there and they are worth more than $3 million." We managed to look both surprised and interested and he said: "They really should have some security here!"

The briefcase had not been moved from its position and it was not time for the presentation, so now that the word was out within the restaurant, our focus had to include everybody, staff and customers.

We didn't have long to wait. A young man we had not seen before came out of the kitchen with a coffee pot in his hand. He passed our table and went into the party room, refilling coffee cups, working his way toward the center where Woodward sat. Jim gave me a nudge and nodded his head toward the young man. We were ready. It was almost humorous to watch. I caught Woodward's eye and he gave a slight nod. The young man had slowed down and kept looking down at that briefcase. The woman next in line held out her cup to be filled. He took another step, filled it and went to the next guest who had pushed his cup out also. Instead of filling it, he took another look at the briefcase. He was getting closer and had to bend slightly to see it.

For us everything stopped; he just stood there ignoring the coffee cup and staring toward Woodward. He gave a slight shake and his face and neck turned as white as one of the table clothes. He kind of wilted, turned around and came walking back past us with a totally beaten look on his face.

Our wives had seen us tense up and get quiet and one of them said, "What?" We told them they had missed the big drama. A young man wanted to grab the briefcase and run with it and that he lost his nerve and slunk out.

We speculated that even if he had gotten past us, which was quite unlikely, and got away from the restaurant, he would not have been able to get rid of that jewelry anywhere closer than Las Vegas and then he would have probably had his throat cut as they were being taken away from him. I wondered how many times in his life he thought back to the time he almost got fabulously rich and blew his chance. It was probably a good life lesson for him.

It was good to be reminded how temptation can push ordinary people to extreme depths. We stayed primed for something else to happen but it was all anti-climactic. The jewelry came out a piece at a time, with a lot of oohing and aahing and placed back before another item was removed. In the end it was all accounted for and later Woodward said it was good business to give the westerners a chance, but not a single item sold. We escorted him back to his motel where he made a big production out of having the briefcase put back in the office safe and accompanied him to his room.

He had put the paste set in the safe and he had the real ones with him. He was scheduled to catch the early plane out of Idaho Falls the following morning and I volunteered to stay the night for security. He declined but borrowed a weapon from me to be picked up before he left. We told him we hadn't enjoyed ourselves like that in a long time.

Leon eventually entered into a plea bargain and received a few years in the penitentiary. I was later informed that upon his release he said, "The best thing that ever happened to me was to get arrested. I was on a bad path." I was told by friends he moved to another state and was doing well. It did not surprise me.

The grand jury that indicted Leon had also indicted one of his friends. The same law firm asked me to help in his defense and although I didn't like defending dope cases, I had a feeling this man was not the bad actor he was being made out to be. His name was Howard North and I had known him almost as long as I had known Leon. He was a quiet and reserved man. What set him apart was his size. Howard was around 6-foot-7 and weighed maybe 260 pounds.

He had been charged with taking an active part in Leon's dope-dealing operation and it didn't fit the decent character I had known. I was anxious to sit down with him and talk. His attorney wanted him to have a polygraph test and wanted me to give it to him, even after I explained the limitations of finding questions he could give a definitive yes or no answer to.

I like to know as much as possible about a person before I test them. While Howard was quite willing to talk with me and there seemed to be some trust between us as we were talking, I had the feeling there was some part of him I wasn't getting. There was something he was hiding from me. The conversation was pleasant as we reminisced about the old days when I first knew him.

He told me he had been raised in a mountainous timbered area about 70 or 80 miles north of Idaho Falls. His Dad was a gypo logger. From my early years living in Alaska and having once worked in a sawmill I knew what he meant. That's a small, independent logging outfit that is always cutting corners, struggling and operating on the edges of success. He said his family moved around a lot in the woods and he was kept out of school until he was 7 or 8-years-old.

He told of having been a large kid and when he did get a chance to go to school he was put into a class of small, younger kids and he didn't fit in. As each year went by, his dad would take him back out of school for longer periods of time. When Howard was 12, his dad said he needed him to help full time in the logging business and he never went back again.

As he talked I began to get a sense of what I found puzzling about him. I asked if he was illiterate. I don't think he knew what the word meant, but he seemed to know what direction I was going. His jaw tightened and he paled, obviously struggling, looking up at the ceiling. Finally, almost in a whisper, he said: "I can't read or write."

I was astounded. I had been acquainted with him for 20 or more years, had many casual conversations with him and had observed him conversing and interacting with others. I have known illiterate people. Most fit a pattern and give clues to their condition, but I had never picked up on Howard as being handicapped in any way.

My personal philosophy is that human life is not supposed to be easy. Those who live protected lives can't grow and few really accomplish anything. We need to be challenged, the more the better. But to be challenged as Howard has, to live in our modern world and prosper and keep such a secret puts him in a world apart from the rest of us. How has he done it? What is his story? Why is he not embittered or socially clumsy? How can he laugh and smile and be at ease with others who can read and write? I feel a need to know and that becomes my focus.

I knew that Howard worked as a truck driver for a snowmobile distributor based in Canada. I had a friend in the company who told me Howard picked up snowmobiles in Canada and delivered them to western states. Howard drove solo everywhere. As I questioned Howard, I discovered he could not read road signs or maps. I asked him how he found his way to Canada on his first trip.

That question seemed to awaken him and maybe outside of his closest circle of family and friends he was able to share, perhaps for the first time, his remarkable coping skills. Howard had asked his closest friend, Leon Lowman, which way he should go to get to Edmonton. Years before, Leon had helped him get his driver's license and trucker's license. On each return trip either his wife or Leon helped him with his travel logs that truckers are required to keep.

On his first trip, he traveled east from Idaho Falls, across Wyoming and made frequent visits to the many truck stops along the way, where he would engage waitresses and other truckers in casual conversations, asking if they knew any shortcuts to Edmonton. Howard was always surprised at how helpful everyone was in pointing him in the right direction until he was lost again and he would go through the same routine someplace else. Once he had been someplace, he never forgot how to get there again.

He brought up Leon's name, describing him as a friend, and I took that as an opening to tell me how he had teamed up with Leon. When Howard was 16, he had a confrontation with his father, who was very hard to get along with and had treated him badly most of his life. From his look and body language, I assumed there was a physical altercation, which he had won. Howard walked out for good with no money and only the clothes he was wearing and hitched a ride to Idaho Falls.

When he got there, he had no idea what he was going to do or how he was going to get along, so he walked around the downtown area feeling hopeless and not knowing how he was going to survive. He kept walking through the evening and about midnight was walking down Broadway, the main street. As he passed Happy Jacks, a combination bar and café, the door flew open and a young man came flying out, followed by two larger older men, who attacked the young man. He walked up behind the two, grabbed each by their necks and slammed their heads together. They dropped unconscious to the sidewalk. The young man was Leon.

"We've got to get off the street before the cops come," Leon told him. As they were walking away Leon asked him who he was and where he was headed. Howard said when he told him his story and that he didn't have any place to go, Leon said, "You're coming home with me." Leon lived with his mother in an older house in a section of town scheduled to be obliterated by the first urban renewal project that came to Idaho Falls.

When Leon's mother heard the story of how Howard saved her son from a beating, she welcomed him into her home. Howard lived with them in that old house for the next couple years and moved with them when they lost the house. Leon became like a brother to him, teaching him how to live, getting him odd jobs and a bank account and managing it for him. Leon took Howard to his first movie and they partied together and sometimes double dated. While he talked, I reminded him that was the time I had first met him. He smiled and nodded. "Leon told me to stay away from cops, but you and your friend Blackie were exceptions," Howard said. "We knew you two ran the police boxing league for wayward kids."

When Howard and Leon were still pretty young, they had been out together partying and some cops had arrested him for being drunk in public. Leon protested to the police that he'd only had one drink and was not drunk. The police ignored that, so he asked what his bail was on the charge. He was told $300 and Leon said he'd get the money. Howard protested, knowing he didn't have any money. "I'll get it," Leon said and left.

In about 30 minutes, Leon was back with $300 and bailed him out. As they left the station Howard asked where he got the money. "None of your business," Leon replied. "Let's go home."

They had started the evening riding in Leon's car and now they were walking home. Howard knew Leon had paid more than $1,000 for the car and that he loved it. "You sold the car to get the money," Howard said. "You shouldn't have done that."

"It's none of your business," Leon replied. "I'll do what I want."

Howard stopped and sat there for a minute and then softly said to me: "How can you not be loyal and not stick with a friend like that, no matter what?" I didn't have an answer.

As time went by, Howard fell in love and was married. His wife took over handling his money and the household and life was very good for a long time. He would get together with Leon from time to time. They worked out together in the gym and Leon, who was in business by this time, would hire him to do odd jobs in his bar, mostly as a bouncer and doorman. He had a comfortable life when, without warning, the worst possible thing happened. His wife became very sick. He quit his trucking jobs to stay near home to care for her between times she was in the hospital. Leon learned of his circumstances and hired him as a permanent bouncer at the club, allowing him time off to run home and check on his wife when he wished and paying him enough to hire help when he needed it.

As he talked, Howard put his head in his hands, overcome with emotion. "Her death just about wiped me out," Howard said. "I went into a tailspin, drinking heavily and never leaving my house, sick with grief. I dropped out. I didn't go near the bar or my friends. I was in a terrible state for better than six months." He raised his head and looked at me with tears in his eyes. "My paycheck from the bar kept coming in the mail, every two weeks, just like I was there earning it," he said.

"You don't have to ask it again," I said. He was right. How can you not be loyal and not stick with a friend like that, no matter what?

"Tell me about why you've been charged with narcotic trafficking," I said. Howard told me he went back to work at the bar and started hanging around there a lot when he wasn't working.

"I can't say I didn't know what Leon was up to," Howard said. "He never talked of his business with me and when I would ask him what he was up to, he would say that it's none of my business and to stay out of it. Even though I can't read or write, I'm no fool. I could see the kind of people he had started to hang out with. I could see trouble coming. I tried to warn him and he would get angry and tell me again, 'Stay out of my business. I don't want you involved.'"

Howard continued: "I had two choices," he said. "I could leave and pull away and try to find someone else to help me get by or I could stay and try to look after my friend. It was really not a choice."

I couldn't think of a good reply. I was aware of Howard's reputation as a tough man and knew that anyone would have liked having him looking after them.

"I knew Leon trusted me and liked me to hang around and after awhile when he was going someplace he would ask me to come along," Howard said. "I could tell you about a lot of times we would take a drive to some of the surrounding towns and he would pull up at someone's house or farm, tell me to stay in the car and he'd take a bag of something in and drop it off."

When Howard asked Leon about what he was doing, the reply was always the same: "Not your business. You're here to keep me company."

"I made trips in his airplane with him and while no one ever told me what was going on, I knew," Howard said. "I have no excuses. The only thing I can say is that I wasn't ever there to sell or buy any dope. I was there to look after my friend."

Well, I'm supposed to be this expert on lie detection. I know the body language and the speech patterns and the physical giveaways and I have to say everything I heard from Howard was truth straight from the heart. As a polygraph examiner and employee of the client's attorney, the assumption is that the privileged communication the attorney enjoys extends to the examiner. If the client is lying, I'm not obligated to inform law enforcement. Many times I have found myself in the position of advising the attorney it would not be wise to allow this client to submit to an examination. In a case such as Howard's, the best thing a lawyer can do for the client is give him the test.

I put relevant questions together, reflecting his limited participation in the actual sales of illegal narcotics, and gave the examination. As I expected, Howard passed by a very comfortable margin. I was prepared to offer testimony on his behalf if it became necessary. My personal conclusion was that Howard was not a criminal, but rather a survivor in a world he had not been prepared to adequately cope with. My belief that education is an absolute must in our modern society had once again been confirmed.

The court now had my report and evidently felt the same way. Howard was eventually released on a strict probation rather than a long prison sentence. I ran into him again on another case as I was calling on a police officer I had admired in the old days. As he invited me in, Howard, who was sitting in a chair jumped up to greet me. It was like old home week, renewing friendships and being brought up to date. The icing in the cake was to discover that my old police pal had seen the same qualities in Howard and had taken it upon himself to befriend him. I left knowing Howard was in a good place and pleased about my little part in the saga.

This chain of events was over. But, while I'm on the subject of unexpected events, let me conclude this chapter with one more story.

Years ago, when I was a young policeman, I was working the night shift and driving around in a cruiser looking for a little action. My partner was also a fairly new policeman named Bill Anderson and I had already decided he was a good man to have around. Our town was somewhat rougher in those days, with all the lower class bars on one street and the crowds were made up mostly of construction workers, cowboys, sheepherders, drifters, bums, vagrants and colorful women of the tougher kind.

There were five or six cat houses scattered among the bars and every evening, except Sunday, there were fights and lots of drunks. In other words, this was a good place to break in a couple young policemen. That night, Bill and I had already broken up a half dozen fights, hauled several miscreants to jail and when 1 a.m. rolled by and the bars closed, we expected things to slow down.

About 3 a.m., however, we saw a very large man walking down Broadway by himself. He was covered in blood and looked like he had been beat up pretty badly. He had sobered up and said he was on his way home. He looked to us like he could make it so we let him go on his way. Before we did, we asked what had happened to him. He said there was a gang of toughs down the street at one of the bars and they had worked him over. He said they were still there partying. He didn't want to sign any complaints. We jumped back in the car and headed for the bar, as it was supposed to have closed two hours before.

We entered the bar and found nine construction workers drinking. They were all big, tough men, well known to the local police as brawlers and street fighters. They were also known to be contemptuous of the law and could be counted on to resist arrest. They were not totally outside of the law. When sober, the two largest ones, who were brothers, ran a concrete construction business and stayed busy.

The furniture in the bar was strewn around the dance floor and it was obvious someone had been fighting. The bartender was cowered down at the far end of the bar. He had a pitiful look on his face that clearly signaled his desire to be rescued. I almost felt sorry for him.

I've been in this kind of situation before and your senses warn that something bad is about to happen. Perceptions suddenly become clearer and in seconds you pick up on the little movements and glances that signal hostility. You see drinks being set down on the bar and hands clenching into fists. The only way I know to deal with it is to leave quickly or get aggressive, the faster the better. My background makes me choose aggression most often.

I quickly walked up to the boss of the group as he was the closest and the biggest. His name was Jerry Thorson. He was sitting on a stool facing the bar and had a drink in his hand. Bill was right with me. I leaned in and said: "What's going on?"

I had no illusion as to what his reaction would be. I knew his reputation. I had a lead-filled leather sap in my hand and had made up my mind to hit him in the temple just as hard and quickly as I could … hard enough to kill him, if necessary, as I didn't think there would be any second chances.

Everything got quiet. "I'm having a drink," he said.

"No, you're not, you're leaving," I said. "We're closing this place."

The room remained absolutely quiet; seconds ticked by. Jerry leaned back slightly, looked at me, shrugged, turned to his crew and said: "What the hell men, let's go."

We watched as they filed out the door. Bill had a grin on his face. "Damn you, you're going to get us killed," he said.

"I noticed you were right up there with me," I replied.

"That was before I started counting the bullets in our guns," Bill said. "We didn't have enough to shoot our way out."

We turned our attention to the bartender, thinking to chew him out for not closing the bar at 1 the way he should have. He read our thoughts. "They just took over the place and ordered me to keep serving drinks," he said.

Bill and I looked at each other and shrugged. He was a weak-looking older drunk who shouldn't have been there at all. We let it pass.

Suddenly the back door flew open and the whole bunch came stomping back in obviously worked up. Bill and I stood apart, this time with our hands on our pistol butts. They stopped and Jerry with a snarl said: "What are you guys gonna do about this God-damn vandalism out there?"

I couldn't resist. "What God-damn vandalism," I asked.

"Come out here," Jerry said, waving us into the parking lot. "We'll show you what God-damn vandalism."

I looked at Bill. He had a grin on his face and his hand still on his pistol. We went out expecting all hell to break loose. I was almost disappointed. Jerry pointed to his pickup. Lying on the pavement behind it was a large V8 motor with the transmission and gear case still attached.

"Look, some son-of-a-bitch has pulled that motor out of the back of my truck and dumped it on the ground," he said.

"That'll be somebody you were pushing around in the bar earlier tonight," I replied. "They came out here and got even with you. It's your problem. You know who you were fighting with."

The Thorson brothers grinned at each other. "You guys get that motor back in the pickup and head for home," I told them. "The party's over."

I was thinking between the nine of them they should be able to get it done. I was also thinking the thing had to weigh 800 or 900 pounds. Still grinning, the brothers walked back to the motor, one on each side, picked it up and gently slid it back into the pickup bed. They made it look like they were picking up a small sack of potatoes. Bill leaned over to me and said: "Now I know you are trying to get us killed."

We watched them leave. "Well, we got through that okay, but I think we can look for trouble with those guys from now on," Bill said. I agreed, knowing that these kinds of toughs don't like to be sent packing by a couple of rookie cops.

As the years went by, I heard about other police having trouble with that group. I had moved on and was working as a detective and was more concerned with felony crimes. As far as I knew, none were committing felonies. They seemed to confine themselves to brawls and disturbing the peace - having fun as they called it.

Then, out of the blue one day, I got a call from Jerry. He wanted to talk to me and asked me to contact him on a job he was working on out in the county. He asked me to come alone. By this time, I had learned to rely on gut feelings about danger and didn't sense any problem, so I went to the construction site alone.

He was operating a big bulldozer, digging a deep trench, and I had to throw a rock to get his attention, which made him laugh. He shut down and waved me into the ditch. He crawled down out of the cab and I, still being cautious, stopped a few feet away and asked: "What's the problem?"

After looking around, to make sure we were alone, Jerry told me about construction tools and materials being stolen from job sites. He proceeded to tell me names of those he was sure were responsible and where he thought the stolen stuff, including a commercial loader worth $100,000, could be found. I recognized some of the names. We had suspected them of being thieves in the past but hadn't been able to build a case against them.

I asked Jerry why he was telling me this.

"I like the way you operate," he said.

"I like the way you operate, too," I replied. "I'll keep your name out of it."

I picked up my partner and found the stolen contraband. It took a while to make the case and my partner and boss got mad at me because I wouldn't name my informant, which would have sped things up. I was in the game for the long haul. Once you burn your informants, you never get anything out of them again and I had a feeling this was going to be a good relationship.

I was right. Jerry and I remained friends for many years, right up to the end when sickness took him away. During those years, he dug out an enormous amount of leads for me to follow – all good, productive information. He also did a couple of constructing jobs on my place and when I tried to pay, he laughed and said: "Just pay me my costs. I'll swallow my wages and profit."

It's strange how one thing can lead to another.

Five

Reuniting Father and Son

When I started my investigation and security company, the plan was to hire others to work for me. Because I had developed my own way of doing things, I anticipated spending considerable time training and directing new employees. With that in mind, I purchased a long desk on which to stow my things and a big overstuffed chair to sit in.

As it turned out, I got lucky. Most members of my staff were natural investigators who hit the ground running. Outside a few bull sessions on life's oddities, they didn't spend much time with me in that office.

I wondered if I had wasted money on that long desk and overstuffed chair, dollars that could have been spent on surveillance cameras and electronic gear. But the chair was comfortable, even if being behind the desk was boring.

Each morning, I would come into the office, greet Geri at the reception desk, take whatever notes she had for me and head back to sit in my chair. I would lean back, relax and start planning the day. It was a nice time for me. That I never knew what would be happening each day was one of the perks of this business.

Far too often, however, my reverie was interrupted by the phone, which brought annoyances such as sales pitches for worldwide advertising, can't-miss electronic computer search services, the latest spy gimmicks and solicitations to order ball point pens with my company name inscribed in bold letters. No one warned me this kind of thing came with the big chair and desk.

Phone calls were not all bad, though. Almost every day, requests for our services came over the phone, so I took all the calls just in case. Occasionally a call came in that intrigued me so much I would work the case myself.

One of those involved a missing person named Derek Lander.

One day, I was relaxing in that big chair with my eyes closed and my thoughts far away on a beautiful high mountain valley in the Lemhi Range. Geri stuck her head in the door and brought me back to reality. "There's a woman from Salt Lake on the phone who wants to talk with you," Geri said, adding: "She won't talk to anyone else."

Almost reluctantly I picked up the phone. The woman on the other end began to speak in a soft, well-modulated voice that instantly caused me to like her. She had spoken with an Idaho Falls Police Department officer, who recommended me.

This was her story:

Nearly 30 years earlier, she had been an Army medic coming off a difficult divorce. She had an affair with one of the other medics in her unit, became pregnant and had a son, but did not tell the father.

"I had the feeling he would not be a good husband or father," she told me. "It was a good decision. Later I met a wonderful man with whom I have been married for many years and we have two children of our own. He accepted my son, born of that early pregnancy, as his own and has been a good father to him."

The problem was that this son, now 27, wanted to meet his biological father. "He is a nice young man, but is floundering a bit in life, not knowing what he wants to do, not holding a job very long, not getting serious about any girl," his mother told me. "He's just drifting. If finding his real father will help him get his feet on the ground, I want to give it a try."

I told her we often find people who had dropped out of families or relationships, but that we needed a place to start. "The only thing I can tell you is that the boy's father is named Derek Lander and he was originally from Rigby. I have no other information about him except a physical description. When he was in his early 20s, he was tall, blonde and good looking. I did not keep a picture of him."

That was something. Rigby is a 15-minute drive from Idaho Falls and I told her we would begin our search there. I explained our hourly rates and cautioned her that a search can be expensive. She said her finances were limited. Her husband had a modest income and she worked in a hospital to cover family expenses; but she needed to make an effort and thought they could borrow enough money to cover the cost.

I decided to work on her case myself. I felt that this was a good woman who wanted to help her son. If the case was simple, it would not cost her much. If not, I could swallow some of the expense. There are advantages to being the one sitting behind the desk.

I took her address and phone number and said I would call her as things developed. I didn't ask for the usual retainer as I felt this woman could be trusted. I thought I was looking at a simple case that would take a day or two at the most.

The next day I traveled the 15 miles to Rigby, a town of about 10,000 people who share the same values as most small western towns. The people are open and friendly. In the phone book, I discovered three families by the name of Lander. A simple case.

The first two families consisted of young people who had never heard of a Derek Lander. They had an uncle (the third Lander on my list) who knew more about the family and might be able to help me. I contacted the uncle, who said: "Yes, I knew of Derek Lander. He is a distant relative who was raised in the area."

But he had not been seen or heard from in 30 or 40 years. This man told me Derek's father died many years ago. He gave me the name of another uncle, also named Lander, who had been a real estate Broker in Boise. He knew nothing else about him. I had been hoping for more, but this was not a bad lead. At least I had information about a relative.

I called my client and told her a lead would take me to Boise, which was 284 miles away. She said she understood that there would probably be some travel expenses building up and her delay in answering indicated to me that she was mentally adding up the time it takes to travel to and from that distance, sifting costs of hours and travel time.

"It has to be done," she said.

"I know money is a concern to you," I replied and suggested to my new client that as I travel about on my normal assignments and find myself in a location where there might be a lead on Derek that I take a little time to investigate it there. That way I would not be making specific trips she could be charged for. She thanked me and said time was not so important that I needed to drop everything else I was doing. In the end, I was glad she agreed. I was under no pressure to get immediate results and she would not have a large bill to pay.

I had contracts with some national retail companies to supply them with shopping and investigative services. My contracts required that I, or someone who works for me, travel throughout the northwest to check and see if each outlet was following company procedures and investigating inventory losses, embezzlements and so on. At least once a month, we'd visit most major cities in the northwest. Sometimes, I would travel around doing the checking.

I didn't tell my client, but this was work I really looked forward to, a chance to get out of the office. I drove a big Cadillac that just floated over the road. I would throw in golf clubs and some clothes. If Marilyn was able to leave for a few days, she would accompany me. I would get in that big car, turn the stereo to the William Tell Overture, and soon would be floating over highways in Washington, Oregon, Wyoming, Utah, Montana and Idaho soaking in scenery with a sense of freedom that is difficult to describe. It filled my whole being.

As I traveled, I would sometimes think back to my police career and how much I had liked it, but it seemed stifling compared to what I was doing now. Not restricted by jurisdictional boundaries or state lines was heady stuff after all those years.

I had also obtained U.S. Government contracts to investigate backgrounds of perspective employees and check out backgrounds of existing government employees who needed to be qualified for secret government clearances with an occasional specific criminal investigation thrown in. I usually worked under time restraints and ever-changing bureaucratic rules and so did not feel the freedom that went with the private company contracts. I have often reflected on the differences in contracting with private companies versus government agencies.

After a few years, I found myself shying away from re-renewing or seeking new government jobs. Private companies asked for results and to be kept out of trouble. The government had procedural manuals that changed constantly, along with reporting formats that were guaranteed to be revised every three months, and I found myself bogged down in paperwork that I knew to be frivolous. The experience resulted in me becoming a strong advocate for free enterprise.

It was nearly a month before I made it to Boise. After completing my normal work, I checked into a motel and began searching area phone books for the name Lander. I got lucky and soon made phone contact with a man in one of Boise's bedroom communities who said he knew the man I was looking for. He seemed reluctant to discuss anything over the phone and, as was my practice, I asked him to meet with me. He agreed.

We met in a sandwich shop near his home. He was a nice-looking man in his late 50s or early 60s, graying but robust and fit. We ordered coffee and I told him why I was looking for Derek Lander.

"It may be that your client wouldn't really want to make contact with Derek," he said to me. He said Derek had become a "wino." Derek was his nephew, so he had maintained a relationship with him. Derek would show up every three or for years. He and his wife would buy Derek clothes and feed him. After a few days, he would move on. Derek, his uncle said, was not nice to have around. He described him as being about 45 but looking 80 as he had descended into a dissolute life, living from handout to handout and always on the hunt for something to drink.

His uncle had heard from Derek about a year before. At the time, he was apparently working as a cook in a mission in Walla Walla, Washington. He could not offer any more information about where I might look.

But he did give me greater insight into the man I was looking for.

The uncle told me Derek's father (his brother) was a good man but not well educated. His productive years were spent working for others and his income was modest. One of the highlights of his life was when he fell in love with a girl from Idaho Falls, who had been adopted by of one of the city's most prominent attorneys. At the mention of the attorney's name, memories flooded back to me. I had known him years before, when he was a senior member of a prestigious law firm. His firm had had often represented clients I had investigated and I had a high opinion of all the lawyers involved.

The attorney and his wife were unable to have children and their solution was to adopt a little girl. She turned out to be difficult and had given them a lot of

117

grief as she was growing up. She was headstrong and refused to comply with their rules. As a result, they were constantly bailing her out of trouble. Knowing what decent people the parents were, I pondered the age-old argument of genes versus environment, but came to no conclusion as Mr. Lander was continuing his story.

He said the girl and his brother got married and had a baby almost immediately. That was Derek Lander. The marriage was difficult, but Derek's dad tried to make it work. One day, however, he left work early, walked into his bedroom and found his wife in bed with another man. Even worse, she had stuffed the baby into the top drawer of the dresser among the clothes and shut it so his cries would not disturb the love making.

Derek's dad removed him from the drawer and walked out of the apartment never to return. He took Derek to his parent's home in Rigby and raised the boy by himself.

Mr. Lander told me Derek was in and out of minor scrapes as a kid but that they had no serious problems with him. As soon as he was old enough to go into the Army, he enlisted and left Rigby.

Derek would show up from time to time and it was obvious he drank heavily. Derek's grandparents had died and left him around $700,000. But his uncle told me it took about two years for Derek to drink up his inheritance. Soon, he was broke and living on the streets again.

In my police career, I dealt with hundreds of alcoholics who hit the skids and became pitiful people. I never saw them as just drunks. I would wonder: What was their past? Who and what were they when they were kids? How do their families deal with what they have become?

I shared my thoughts with Mr. Lander: "For a family it's hard," Mr. Lander said. "When someone you know and love has promise and fails, you feel sorrow and shame. You want to be proud of everyone in your family, but it can't always be. Derek has taught us to be proud of the ones who did turn out OK."

I thanked him for the time and information. I told him I especially appreciated him sharing something that many would have kept hidden.

"If Derek's son knows the facts about his father, he may not want to meet him, but will not be so disappointed if he does go through with it," he told me.

With those words, we parted.

A few days later, I shared with my client what I had learned about Derek. That he became a drunk did not surprise her. The signs were there many years before and may have had something to do with her decision not to involve him in her son's life. She said she would pass on to her son what I had told her, believing that he would not want the search pursued. She thanked me and asked me to send a bill for my services. Her check arrived a few days later and I thought that would be the end of it.

Within a week, however, she called and said her son still wanted to meet his father. "Maybe I can help him somehow," he said.

"You and I both know he won't be able to help," I told her. "Derek is too far gone for any help to reach him." She agreed, but thought it only fair that her son have his chance to learn on his own. She asked me to continue the search on the same terms. I agreed.

I spent the next couple of years on this search. It began again a few weeks later when I was scheduled to pass through Walla Walla on one of my contract tours. Marilyn was with me on this trip and I planned everything so that I would have a little extra time in that city. Like a lot of western cities I visited, I had come to love that place.

I had worked on a case involving a young girl in Idaho who had shaken her baby, causing its death. She was originally from Walla Walla and I had gone there to dig into her background to find mitigating factors that could be used at her sentencing.

She had been a member of a large Mennonite community that shares the area with several other religious faiths. I found these people so friendly, open and willing to share that I thought about putting Walla Walla on the list of places I would re-locate if my life ever fell apart. It's a mental game I play. In truth, I never expect my life to come apart and I have so many places now on my list I couldn't live long enough to work them all in.

In any event, Marilyn and I arrived in Walla Walla in early evening and checked into the motel where I usually stay. My plan was to take Marilyn to one of the good restaurants in town after checking out the rescue mission to determine if Derek had been there. As we cruised the downtown area, I failed to see anything that looked like the mission building that had been described to me. I did see an older hotel and from the street could see a few men sitting in the lobby watching television.

I parked, asked Marilyn to wait, walked inside and an elderly gentleman greeted me. I told him I was trying to find the mission that was supposed to be around here.

"You missed it by about two blocks," he told me. As he was giving me directions, I noticed the other men were looking at me. One stood and, with his hand reaching towards his back pocket, said, "Can we help you in any way?"

"No thanks, I have what I need now," I told him. When I got back to the car, I asked Marilyn if I looked like a needy person. "Those people in there just offered to give me some money." She laughed and said: "You look pretty good to me." Perhaps I was dressing a little too casually on these trips.

We proceeded to the mission – a large building with a sign on the front. I again asked Marilyn to wait a few minutes, assuring her I would be right back. From the look on her face I realized she probably had heard that from me too many times to believe me now, but she is a good sport about these things.

I entered and found myself in a foyer with benches along the wall. On the left, there was an old-time tellers' window. There was a large office behind the window and a young man was sitting at a desk with his back to me. Two connecting double doors directly ahead of me opened into what appeared to be a large meeting hall. There were several people, all shabby looking, standing around in the hall.

I got the young man's attention. As he turned, I realized that he was not as young as I first thought. He was near 40, still young to me, a nice and pleasant-looking fellow who smiled and said, "Can I help you?" I pulled out my card, handed it to him and said, "I'm trying to find a fellow named Derek Lander who is supposed to be staying here and cooking at the mission."

He had never heard that name but had been at the mission for only a year. He said they had many people coming and going all the time and even though he had not heard of him they might have his name in the file. He added, "I'll be glad to help you on this but I'm supposed to be preaching a sermon to this group in the chapel. We preach to them before we feed them. Why don't you come back here and you can search for his name while I'm busy and then I'll come back and help." He opened the door, waved toward the file cabinets and went into the chapel.

So, there I was, behind the window and apparently in charge of a place I didn't know existed a few minutes before. Well, I thought, I'm versatile. I can handle this. I opened a file cabinet and began searching for names beginning with the letter "L." I was soon disturbed by a woman rapping at the window, obviously wanting my attention. "Can I help you," I asked.

She told me a story about being out in the car with her kids and not having money to feed them or a place to go for the night. I told her the minister was in the chapel preaching and would help her when he was finished. She started to cry. I gave her a few dollars and told her to come back after she fed the kids.

She left and I turned back to continue my search, only to be interrupted by a couple fellows who needed help. I told them the minister would help them as soon as he finished his sermon. I gave them a couple dollars and told them to sit on the benches by the door and direct anyone who came in to sit down with them or join the group in the chapel. While I was searching, four or five more came in. I waved them to the benches and my helpers told them to be seated.

I had found no record of Derek and was relieved when the minister opened the chapel doors and the group filed out. He stood in the foyer, directing patrons to various locations, and then joined me behind the counter. I told him I was glad he was back because it was costing me too much to run the place without him. He laughed and asked if I found what I was looking for. I had not so he began searching the files with me. I told him why I was looking for Derek, which obviously piqued his interest.

He went back to the foyer and in a short time returned with a couple of derelict-looking men: "These fellows know Derek Lander and maybe they can help you find him," he said. These men were obviously suspicious of me. They were not used to cooperating with the law and they seemed to think I was connected with the police. It took me a while to convince them I was not a cop and that I meant no harm to their buddy. Then they opened up.

They said Derek was part of a group that moved around the skid rows of cities in Washington and Oregon. Neither had seen him in at least a year. They last they knew Derek had been sleeping at a mission in Spokane. They advised me to look for him in the Seattle and Tacoma areas, where he hung out a lot. If I didn't find him there, I was told to try Portland because Derek had talked about how he had been there.

The truth was that Derek Lander could be anywhere as the kind of lifestyle they shared had no patterns or constants. They speculated about how to find someone in their world and threw out all sorts of places and possibilities. Their use of language indicated some degree of education and they appeared to be reasonably smart.

Their appearances, however, indicated that life was bleak and downhill. The conversation gave me a small look into their world.

These people are probably the ultimate survivors. If a catastrophe ever occurs in this country, these are the ones who may get through. For a brief period in my younger days, working as a city detective in Idaho, I had been a radiological defense officer on a civil defense team and had spent many hours studying how our area could survive an atomic bomb attack. I could not help but think we should have had a couple of these fellows in those classes.

I found their descriptions and stories fascinating and could have listened for hours but remembered I had left Marilyn waiting in the car. I excused myself and thanked everyone for their help. As I stood, the minister said: "I hope someone like you comes looking for me someday."

"Why," I asked. It turns out that he married his childhood sweetheart and they had a little girl. He had a high stress job and began to drink to relax. He began overdoing it but thought he could handle it. As he told his story I watched the two derelicts assume far-away looks and nod to themselves. They understood what he was saying. He said that one day, when his little girl was 8-years old, his wife and daughter disappeared. He sobered up and started searching for them, hoping to make his life over, but could never find any trace of them. He said he stayed sober and in his grief studied for the ministry. Now he was trying to do for others what he wished had been done for him in his drinking days.

His simple statement was almost more than I could handle. His pain was so evident and his longing so genuine. I thanked the three men for their help and walked back to my car. I thought that perhaps when I retire and have time and a little income I could do more of this kind of thing for people in need. Marilyn could see I had been through some kind of emotional experience and chose not to give me a bad time for keeping her waiting.

It was a busy year. I managed to get all over the Pacific Northwest: Seattle, Tacoma, Spokane, Portland and Eugene – stopping at all the missions in each city and asking about Derek Lander. I ran across people who knew him, but hadn't seen him in quite a while. Some said a few months; others a few years. Most of the people I was talking to could not be considered good witnesses under any circumstances. I was handicapped by not having a picture of him. I had checked drivers license bureaus in each state but none had him listed. The different people who said they knew him gave me a variety of descriptions. The one consistent reply I got back when I described him as tall, blond and good looking when he was 20 was that each person would pause, and then say: "Yes, he could have been a good looking-fellow when he was young, but he's kind of wasted now."

Though I was not getting good information, I had the feeling I was close to Derek and it was frustrating me. This was the first time in my career I had gone all out to find someone. In the police world, where I had worked so many years, I had learned you don't have to go all out. You just put the information out that someone is wanted and sit back and wait. Usually whoever you are after will come in contact with the law someplace. Maybe he'll apply for a license or get a speeding ticket or have a complaint made against him for a minor violation. Then, "Zing," some agency notifies you where they are. There were no "Zings" in this case. I had set out to do something and so far I was failing. Failing went against my grain.

I had called my client from time to time to give her progress reports, or rather lack of progress reports. After the year passed, I shared my frustration with her. She graciously thanked me and said I had done more than she could possibly have hoped for and thought that maybe we should give it up as a lost cause. I agreed, but felt bad about my lack of results. That dissatisfaction was fuel to my decision to make some big changes in my own life.

Years ago I had met an individual who I had become friends with. He believed in a kind of eastern religious philosophy. One of our discussions revolved around reincarnation and the concept that you had better do everything you think you should do, or want to do, during this lifetime or run the risk of being sent back to do it next time. The theory stresses that all people are on a spiritual path and that it takes a lot of time to get to the path's end and you may not want to delay your arrival there by having to do part of it over.

I did not subscribe to this belief. Being a longtime detective, I require some evidence or proof on which to base my decisions. But I could see that if you adopted his premise you might have a more interesting life. With that in mind I decided to do a couple of the things I had wanted to do for some time. One was to involve myself in politics and the other was to open a western art gallery. Neither desire had good judgment behind it. I am a Democrat living in one of the most Republican states in America. Also, I had many artist friends who told me I lived in an area where people didn't put a lot of money into art. But both things I wanted to do.

An associate was now running my investigative firm, so I signed up to become a Democratic candidate for the state legislature, organized a political staff and was off and running. It was a heady and exhilarating experience and even though the Republican candidate beat me, I was glad I did it.

At the same time I opened, "Western Art Creations," a store and gallery featuring western art and rustic furniture. Marilyn and I had previously purchased the downtown commercial building in which my company offices were located. The street level of the building contained retail stores. We lost a tenant in one of the stores and I converted it into the gallery. I contacted my artist friends, accepted considerable amounts of artwork on consignment and opened the doors.

I kept the gallery open for a year and enjoyed every moment of the experience, giving it up only when a prospective new tenant offered me more money to rent the space than I was drawing through my cash register. And I was still running the gallery when Fate accomplished what my best efforts could not achieve.

One day, a year after I last spoke with my client, Derek Lander literally opened the door and walked into my gallery. The front of the gallery had large display windows that doubled as show cases for paintings and furnishings. It was difficult to keep all that glass shining and spotless and I was always looking for people to keep it clean. One summer day, the door opened and a stranger entered. He was scruffy-looking with shaggy hair and stubble on his face. He was around 50, a little less than 6-feet-tall, weighed about 180 pounds and seemed in fairly good health. He was dressed in casual work clothing and it was apparent that he was not a customer.

He spoke in a pleasant manner and asked if I might need my windows washed. He said he was good at washing windows and that he used newspaper to dry them, which kept them from streaking. I asked what he would charge. He quoted me a modest figure and I knew that even if he did a poor job I wouldn't be out much. I gave him the go-ahead and asked his name and where he was staying. He said he was staying at the Ross Hotel, which I knew to be a cheap hotel nearby, and said his name was Derek Lander.

I kept a straight face. "Derek Lander, huh," I said. He was a better-looking man than the one who had been described to me and in better physical condition, but everything else fit. "I know you," I said, and proceeded to tell him about his early life in Rigby, watching his face to see if he showed recognition of the facts I was telling him. He did. Here was the Derek Lander I had searched for so long. I continued to fill him in on his life and travels and he finally said, "Who are you? Am I under arrest or something?" I had thrown him for a loop. He had a dazed confused expression on his face.

I told him to sit down and filled him in. I told him I owned a detective agency and about his case. I watched his eyes for a signal of recognition and he said: "You must mean" … and then gave my clients name. He said: "I was pretty sure she was pregnant but she broke off with me kind of sudden." He paused for a while: "So, I'm a father," he said. "I have a son."

I told him it was actually his son who wanted to meet him and what I knew of him. I also told him that his son knew about his having become a bum. I had passed on the worst things that I had learned and he still expressed a desire to meet his father.

"How do you feel about meeting your boy," I asked.

"Damn, I'll have to think about that," he replied. I knew by the way he said it that he was interested.

We spent the rest of the afternoon talking. I told him of the places I had been looking for him and about some of the characters who professed to know him. He laughed about my descriptions of them and said that I was "right on." While he sat and talked, he obviously relaxed and responded openly to my questions. When I asked why he was in better physical shape than I had been told, he said: "The reason you have not been able to catch up with me is that I have been in prison for the last couple of years, in California."

Derek had been in the same prison as Charlie Manson and told me about the difficult life the cult leader had in prison. During his stay, three different prisoners tried to kill Manson. Inmates developed a sport of spraying Manson with lighter fluid and throwing a match on him. All three times they succeeded in burning him badly. Derek said prison policy was to keep Manson isolated from the other prisoners but that determined inmates can find a way to him and he didn't think the prison guards were worried about Manson's welfare, anyway.

Derek said that while he was in prison he ate reasonably well and worked out each day with weights and got himself in pretty good shape. He said he would not have dared to exist in that prison without being able to defend himself. He had been required to join a prison gang and fight constantly to ward off predators of the worst possible kinds. Derek said the best day of his life was when he was released.

I asked him how he managed to get into Bauchman Prison in the first place. Derek told me he had left Washington state to visit a half sister who lived in San Pedro, Calif. His mother had moved to Colorado, remarried and had a baby girl. Derek met them while he was in the Army. While he was at his sister's place, Derek was, as usual, drinking heavily and taking pills. He had only a vague recollection as to what happened next, but knew he got hold of a pistol from his sister's house and used it to threaten the neighbor who was a big ex-wrestler and had tried to intimidate him. He then asked his sister to take him to a store so he could get some more beer and she refused. He says he waved the pistol at her and she agreed to drive him. He got the beer and drank himself into oblivion. When he woke up, he was in jail. His sister had demanded that he be charged with kidnapping and attempted murder.

Derek had been assigned a public defender to represent him as he had no money and the lawyer advised him to plead guilty. He convinced Derek that the judge would take his lack of previous criminal convictions, along with his story of mixing alcohol and drugs into consideration, and likely release him with minor punishment.

Derek turned pale as he recounted that day in court. The judge did not want to hear his reasons or excuses. Glaring down at him, he said: "Eleven years in a maximum security prison." Derek said: "I knew I was of no value to myself or society, but I knew inside I was not a bad or evil man. I couldn't believe what had happened. I was just a drunk, not a criminal."

"It was hell in that prison," Derek told me. "I will kill myself before I ever go back into one. I soon learned how to survive and worked hard to avoid trouble. I suffered all kinds of indignities and was released after two years. The prison was just too full of really bad guys to keep someone like me in there 11 years."

I asked him about having received a large inheritance. He said it was true. "I think the lawyers beat me out of a big chunk of what I had coming," Derek told me. "You being a detective may want to help me recover what I was cheated out of for a percentage."

I said I wasn't interested in taking a case like that. He told me about being in an alcoholic fog in those days. He cooked up a scheme to go into New Mexico and buy up turquoise jewelry from some Navajos he had met while bumming around. His plan was to take the jewelry to Montana for re-sell for a large profit. Over time he managed to buy up quite a lot of jewelry and in the process was doing too much partying. He made it as far as Las Vegas, met a woman and continued partying with her. The next think he knew the jewelry, the woman and everything else was gone.

As a Scotchman, I have a hard time comprehending this cavalier approach to money. He described throwing away a small fortune as if it were a casual evening. I remarked to him about the possibility of looking after his future instead of the present. Derek said he knew better than to squander wealth, but it was not the first time he had done it.

I learned that after Derek had gotten out of the Army, he went to Los Angeles, met a woman and married her. She had a good job and he worked his way up in a freight company to a manager's job. They started to fight about his drinking until one day he stormed out of the house, jumped in their car - an expensive convertible - and headed north.

He left with just the cash in his pocket. He spent what money he had on gas and as he was driving through a forest just after reaching Oregon he ran out of gas. Derek let the car roll to a stop on the highway shoulder, left the keys in it, got out, started hitchhiking and never looked back.

I asked Derek about his plans. He said he wanted to stay in Idaho Falls for awhile and hoped he could find a little work to keep him going. I told him to stay in touch as I was going to see if his son still wanted to meet him. He said that he would and he kept his word.

Every day Derek stuck his head in the door to ask if there was any work I needed done. Sometimes I put him to work on the windows or cleaning but I knew he was really waiting to see what was going to happen about his son. Once in a while he would come in to talk and I could tell he was angling to find out what was going on about the visit, but would never ask directly. He was dirty and disheveled and his presence was probably not good for business in an art gallery. I noticed that a few customers looked at him with suspicion. I had little patience with snooty people and I wasn't in the business for dollars, so I tolerated his visits.

In the meantime, I called my client to tell her about finding Derek. She started to congratulate me and I was forced to tell her that he had just walked in on me. I didn't find him. She wondered if something was going on that was beyond our understanding. After learning what I knew about Derek, she said she would pass the information on to her son, John.

A few days later John called me. It was the first time I had spoken to him. He asked about his father and I filled him in. He was restrained but said he wanted to meet him and asked for a suggestion on how it should be done. I had not thought that far ahead, assuming somebody else would take over this function. It was not something I knew anything about. But not knowing had never stopped me before.

I asked John if he would come to Idaho Falls. He said he could come up Saturday. This was Monday. I gave him directions to my store and arranged a 9:30 a.m. meeting.

I scoured the town for Derek as I had not seen him for a week. I found him in a bar that serves as a place for workers and employers looking for day laborers to connect. He said he was waiting for somebody to come along with a job he could handle. So far that day the only employers to show up were ranchers looking for cowboys to work cattle. Derek said that was one thing he never learned to do. I kept my thoughts to myself about taking any job that came along when you are in need. Instead I told him his son would be in my store at on Saturday to meet him and if he wanted to go through with it he should show up. He said he would. I had done all I could do, or so I thought.

On Friday afternoon Derek showed up at the store. He was cleaned up and looked pretty good. He said he thought he better check in with me and find out what he needed to do.

"All you need to do is show up," I said.

"But what should I say," he asked.

I had no idea what he should say, but I saw no reason to show off my ignorance. So, I said in as positively as I could: "You don't have to worry, the right words will come to you. Things will work out OK." He seemed to accept that I knew what I was talking about, smiled and left.

The next morning, I arrived at the gallery at nine. As I opened the door, Derek appeared behind me. He had been waiting for me. Again he wanted assurance that he would know what to say. I again told him not to worry and that the right words would come.

"Well, I had better go get cleaned up a little and I'll be back right at 10," he told me. He already looked pretty cleaned up so I assumed he was going to get a drink to fortify himself.

At 9:30, a young man came in the door. I had been curious about what John would look like, thinking all kinds of possibilities. Suppose he was a little guy with bright red hair. How do we explain that? But I had no reason for concern. I was looking at a young version of Derek: same facial features; same hair, only darker; same build; and same height. It was almost uncanny.

I greeted him, introduced myself and set about making him comfortable. It was obvious when he walked in that he was in a state of high anxiety and it took a few minutes to get him laughing and talking. While we were chatting I saw him staring out through the front windows, at a couple grungy cowboy types who were looking at the paintings in the display.

"Neither of those is your dad," I told John. "Don't worry. He will be here in a few minutes."

He turned and asked: "What should I say when the time comes?" I offered the same advice I had given his father: "You will know what to say when the time comes."

He smiled, but I was thinking to myself: "Where do you get off telling these people they will know what to say? You don't know anything about this." By now I had stuck my neck out so far I couldn't back out of my position, but I was also curious about what was going to happen.

At exactly 10, the door opened and Derek came striding in as if he owned the place. He wore new clothes and a fresh haircut and looked pretty good. There were only three of us in the room and I went behind the counter and stood out of the way. Without a word, the two men walked toward each other, put their arms out and hugged each other. It was as if they had always known each other and were meeting after a separation. When they pulled apart, both started talking a mile a minute, as if to make up for lost time.

I couldn't help but get caught up in the moment. I knew I had witnessed something important. Later, I thought maybe my feelings had something to do with never having known my own father. But, for now, I was taking pleasure in seeing the delight these two men were sharing. I laughed with them as they compared bodies and features.

They turned to me and Derek said: "What about us going for a walk down by the river where we can talk and get acquainted?" It seemed they wanted permission. I nodded and said: "That would be a good idea, go ahead." They went out the door with their arms around each other's shoulders. I really did think it was a good idea, the river was just two blocks away and the park was an ideal place to talk in private. I wasn't real comfortable acting as a facilitator when I didn't know what I was doing.

After about two hours, Derek and John returned to the gallery and told me they were getting along great and thought they should go have lunch together. The idea was presented as a question, as if seeking approval. So, without hesitation, I told them it was a good idea and they should do it. They left again.

My day was a busy one. I had several artists show up with new works. The time was going by fast. It seemed like only a few minutes, but was closer to two hours, when Derek and John came back.

"We've been told there is a carnival set up in the Yellowstone Mall north of town and we thought it might be fun to go there together," Derek said to me. I again told them that it would be a good thing. I realized that I was serving as a connecting point for them and that I was somehow important to the process of their getting acquainted. It was a role I would not have deliberately sought but now was happy with it.

The day was over and Derek and John returned for the last time. It was apparent they had become friends. They thanked me for helping them get together. I thought about the time and travel that had gone into the search for Derek. It has been a worthwhile endeavor and I was happy to have been a part of bringing father and son together. I thought my part had finished. Again, I was wrong.

As the weeks went by, I kept busy running the gallery, politicking and taking back the job of running the investigation agency. From time to time Derek would stop by to say hello and tell me John had written him another letter and of plans they made to get together again. Derek was doing odd jobs around town and I gave him a little work. As winter came, I loaned him my snow blower so that he could clean sidewalks and make a little money. I knew he was drinking but it did not seem to be out of hand. He viewed me as a friend but there were too many differences and too much distance in our lives for me to reciprocate.

One day, Derek came into my office and said he needed to talk to me. "I hear you have a cabin up in the mountains," he said.

"Yes, I do," I replied.

"I don't know how to ask you this, but I'm desperate," he said. "I'm drinking too much and it's killing me. I don't want to go on and I need a place to get away and dry out. I don't have any way to pay you, but will you help me?"

I know people who are able to say no when a desperate man asks for help. I have heard all the reasons. The biggest one is that alcoholics are fighting a battle they can't win. An alcoholic will disappoint you again and again. But it's not my nature to turn my back, so I told him I would help.

When I first bought the ranch, it had a broken down one room log cabin on it and a couple of corrals. I bulldozed the cabin and built a two-room combination cabin and garage to stay in while I built the big house. I had long since moved into the new house and the cabin was empty. I told Derek the cabin had no amenities and that he would have to use an outhouse for a bathroom, cook on a wood stove and use a gas lantern for light. He said he would be glad to do that.

The next day, I picked him up with all his belongings in one small canvas bag. We went to a grocery store and picked up enough food to last about a week. (I wasn't sure he could make it beyond that). We drove the 116 miles to the ranch on a cold, rainy and miserable day. When we arrived, I showed him the woodpile and we started a fire in an old boiler that had been converted into a wood stove. I gave him an old sleeping bag and showed him the cooking utensils and silverware that were left in the cabin.

Derek piled up a big stack of wood beside the stove and told me that the next three days were going to be hell. Without alcohol he would soon start to shake uncontrollably and be unable to get warm or keep anything in his stomach. He had been through this before and within a few hours would be deathly sick. Derek said he knew how to handle it and would be OK in about three days. He was already showing signs of going into delirium tremors. I had seen drunks suffering from them many times and knew they were bad. I was almost afraid to leave him. It would not have surprised me to find later that he didn't make it.

If he couldn't keep the fire going it was cold enough to freeze him at night. The ranch is 6,000 feet and at that altitude it can get very cold. I told him I would see him in a week, checked in with the cowboy who runs the place for me, told him there would be a fellow staying in the old cabin who needed a few days to dry out and that it might not hurt to check in on him from time to time.

The week went by, and not knowing whether I needed to or not, I bought another couple weeks worth of groceries and drove back up. As I pulled into the drive, I saw smoke coming out of the little cabin stovepipe and felt relieved that I wasn't going to have to arrange for a burial. When I approached the cabin, Derek opened the door for me and I could feel it was nice and warm inside. He was grinning. He didn't look very good and it was obvious that he had suffered. His face was pale and haggard, but he was on his feet and taking care of himself.

Derek said my cowboy friend checked on him and what a nice guy he seemed to be. I didn't tell him my friend was totally blind and would not have been able to see him at all. He could learn about that later.

I spent the weekend working on the lodge, Derek came over and visited a time or two but said he didn't feel well enough yet to do anything and soon retired back to his cabin. I asked Derek if he felt like staying on and he said he needed to.

Throughout the spring and summer, I brought groceries each time I came up. As Derek improved, occasionally he would join Marilyn and me in the big lodge for coffee. I found that he had repaired a fence or fixed a gate and he would ask: "What needs to be fixed next?" I told him it was not necessary that he work on anything, but he said he wanted to, that he felt bad about not doing it.

It put me on the spot as I soon learned Derek was not a cowboy or farmer type. He knew nothing about livestock and had a healthy fear of horses. At that time we had about 40 head on the place, some from a wild horse herd that ranges in nearby mountains and that my blind cowboy friend was breaking to ride. Derek would watch from a distance, but there was not much he could do there.

As time passed, I saw something happening to Derek that happens to all of us when we live in a mountain area. He put on weight and started to look healthy. He was full of humor and moved around as if he felt good. He stayed through most of the summer. When we had guests at the ranch, they would ask about the guy in the cabin who seemed so friendly and I would tell them that he had been sick and was staying until he got well. It was true in a way and to tell them the full story took too long.

One day, Derek showed up in my office in Idaho Falls and said he had hitchhiked down and was ready to face the world again. And this time he was going to make it. I didn't see him again for a couple months. He came in to tell me he had a job, an apartment and a car. I congratulated him and encouraged him to keep on the straight line. He said he had made contact with a cousin who ran a small business in Idaho Falls and had been accepted into his family. Things were going well.

After Derek left, I thought to myself: "Well, that's that and this time it is really over."

But it wasn't.

One weekend, Marilyn and I were at the ranch and heard a car drive into the lane and up to the house. I looked out and saw Derek getting out of a big Oldsmobile. He was dressed nicely and looked good. "I'm here to take you and Marilyn to Salmon to a restaurant," he said.

We had eaten earlier and Salmon was 45 miles down river from our place, so I started to decline. As I was doing so I could see the look of disappointment on his face, so I stopped in mid-sentence and turned to Marilyn, who said: "Why don't we go?"

It was an interesting trip and we both felt good about it, but not as good as Derek. He told us he thought a long time about what he could do for us and there just wasn't any way he could pay us back. It was very obvious this was an important thing for him to do. It was like an affirming milestone he was passing. He said: "We've come so far. Here I am, an ex-con who lived on the streets and now I'm escorting a former police detective and his lady out to dinner. Instead of taking I am giving."

He paid for everything and would not even let me tip for the waitress. Even though we enjoyed the drive and the meal, there was still a wall between us that could not be breached. While we sat in the restaurant and chatted, we talked of different worlds. His intellectual and spiritual growth had been interrupted somewhere in his life. He didn't understand what made us tick.

We really didn't want to talk about the same things and it frustrated him. He talked of learning to hate blacks and Mexicans in the penitentiary and seemed baffled that neither Marilyn nor I could tell him we hated anybody. It really seemed to upset him when we talked about the need to care about other people.

He occasionally used foul language, would catch my glare and quickly apologize to Marilyn. On the drive back to the ranch he announced that "He had to piss" and parked along side of the highway and proceeded to do just that.

I didn't say anything but when he got back in the car and saw my angry look, he said: "Oops, I shouldn't have done that." It was almost funny because he was so unaware that his behavior might be offensive. I didn't want to spoil his important day, so I rolled along burying my desire to straighten him out on social graces. It was a real struggle for me to refrain from having him play better music on his radio as we traveled. He seemed so pleased that he could entertain us with hillbilly music.

At the end of the day, Marilyn and I discussed the many life experiences we shared and concluded that this day was a strange as any thing we could have ever imagined or experienced.

I wish I could say this story had a happy ending. But that wouldn't be real life, which doesn't have a happy ending. Like Marilyn told me: "It just seems to fizzle out."

Derek was doing OK by our standards and really well by his. He would stop by the office and fill me in on everything that was happening. He got a girlfriend, was making a little money and asked if he could use the old cabin in Leadore on weekends when he was not working, saying it was the one place in the world he found happiness.

I let him use the cabin a few times. After a while, my cowboy friend told me Derek was spending much of his time in town drinking and had shown up at the cabin drunk. I confronted him and told him that I was not interested in providing him a place to get drunk. He could find his own place and there were certain liability problems having a drunk around untamed wild horses and I wasn't going to run the risk. I told him never to go there again when he was drinking.

I chewed on him a while for drinking again. It always surprised me when he accepted criticism from me. He was like a child. He never argued or objected to anything I said. But I didn't see him for a while.

A few months later, his cousin called to tell me Derek had wanted him to tell me what happened and said I shouldn't do anything on his behalf. He just wanted me to know. The California Parole Board had not released him to leave California. He had jumped parole and came back to Idaho on his own. It had taken them almost two years to issue a warrant for his arrest and arrange to have him picked up and returned to California.

His cousin was quite concerned about Derek going back to prison. I told him not to worry. I had been around the system long enough to know California authorities didn't really want Derek back. They just did not want anyone challenging their authority and getting away with it.

"It won't be very long before he's back," I told the cousin.

I was right and a few months later Derek showed up at my office. He'd been forced to do a few weeks in jail and stay on a restricted parole in Los Angeles for four months and that this time they did release him. He showed me his papers. He said his job had been taken by someone else, his car impounded, his apartment lost and the lady he had been seeing had moved on.

Derek laughed and said it wouldn't be the first time he had started back up from the bottom.

This time it wasn't so simple. I didn't see him for a few months and then he showed up one day carrying a small oxygen bottle and breathing through a tube. He said his heart was giving out on him. He had suffered a serious heart attack and was limited in what he could do.

Derek eventually qualified for federal aid as a disabled person. He moved into a cheap hotel and each time I saw him he looked frailer and more unkempt. I have puzzled over whether his decline was caused by poor health or that he no longer had to use his wits and abilities to survive.

As the next winter set in, Derek disappeared and a few months later his cousin called to tell me he had been found dead in a cheap hotel in San Pedro, Calif.

I sometimes think back to the time I told my client: "We both knew, nobody could help him, he was too far gone for help."

Still I really didn't feel bad about having tried.

The New Lawman in Leadore

A n inordinate number of interesting people seem to connect with my life in Leadore. Something about this small and remote Rocky Mountain town draws unusual people away from the hustle and bustle of routine life in busy places. These people and I count ourselves among them, desire a quiet existence in a place of beauty.

That certainly was the case with Jack Stratton.

Again my point of contact was Sheriff Bill Baker of Salmon. My partner, Jim Mason, and I had been in Salmon investigating an arson case. We were wrapping it up and preparing to leave when Bill brought up the possibility, since we would be passing through Leadore on our way back to Idaho Falls, that we could check in on the town's new Marshall.

The sheriff had been asked to deputize the fellow and was concerned about giving deputy status to someone he knew little about. We figured there would be more to the sheriff's suggestion than he let on, but as it was important for us to know all law enforcement people in our assigned section of the state, we agreed.

I own property near Leadore and was familiar with the place. Leadore is an incorporated city of some 95 people and doesn't have much money to spend on law enforcement. The fire department, mayor and city council were staffed with volunteers. The going rate for the Marshall's salary was $50 a month. To my knowledge, they hadn't been able to find anyone who was worth that much.

Anyone who knew anything about enforcing the law wouldn't touch that job with a 10-foot pole. A job in law enforcement requires a decent salary and benefits and it would be crazy for anyone to take on this one. If you didn't know anything about law enforcement, somebody needed to tell you that in ranch country – where cowboys live near a town with two bars – trouble can appear in a second and you can get hurt badly if you don't know how to handle it.

Jim and I discussed our options during the drive to Leadore and concluded it was possible the town hired someone who is deranged or doesn't know any better.

Upon arriving in town, we stopped at one of the bars and asked about the new Marshall. He lived a couple of houses away in a rental home. We pulled over to the drive, got out of the car and knocked at the door with absolutely no idea of what to expect.

A man answered our knock. He looked to be in his late 50s or early 60s, was average size, 5-10 or 5-11 and around 160 pounds – not what you would call a striking build. He had blue, slightly bloodshot eyes and angular features. He was an average-looking man, except for his demeanor and aura. His eyes radiated an inner tension and my first thought was that this man is wound up tighter than a coiled spring.

Jim and I are fairly large men who look like the lawmen we are. Until we make friendly, open contact, we are used to being viewed with suspicion and even fear. There was no fear in this man's face, but a quizzical look that might be construed as suspicion.

I told him who we were and why we were there. I said our job entailed helping local police when they called and that we'd rather meet him now than later. My voice was friendly and he smiled and invited us in. I read his reaction as positive. He seemed to be comfortable with both our presence and explanation of why we were there.

He offered us seats and asked if we would like a cup of coffee "strong enough to pick a man up and throw him down." Jim and I declined and our new friend smiled as though he was pleased to have avoided making a new pot.

The ice was broken so Jim asked: "What made you take the Marshal's job? Are they paying more than they used to?" He laughed and replied: "I guess I've gotten a little bored. They wanted to pay me even less than before. When they heard that I had police experience they just kept throwing the job at me until I broke down."

Jack Stratton, it turns out, had started his career with the Los Angeles Police Department. He spent several years with LAPD, did some time in the Army and went to work for the police department in a small town near Santa Barbara.

"I had more law enforcement than I really wanted," Jack told us. In a few words, he threw half a lifetime at us and though we were there in a kind of unofficial inquiry, Jim and I wanted to know more.

147

Clearly this was no ordinary man. I had a strong feeling he would not allow himself to be interrogated and Jim must have sensed that as well. Without a nod or a word, we changed our approach. It is a real pleasure to work with someone who has the same instincts. It is also fun to get information from someone who is quite capable of withholding it. This was turning into something beyond a quick casual inquiry. As years passed, I marveled at where such an inauspicious beginning can, and did, take us.

We began swapping law enforcement stories. Jim and I, who have had more than our share of experiences, found ourselves being matched with anecdotes and opinions, which could only have come from real experience. Jack talked of cases he had worked in Los Angeles and the difficulties of working the streets.

He was obviously comfortable with our interest as he talked about his past. I had the feeling he had not been able to share his experiences in some time. Everyone has stories and thoughts they like to share, but some people will not open up unless a special opportunity comes up. It was as if we were meant to be there and this was Jack's special chance.

Later, when I got to know Jack better and saw his natural suspicion of almost everyone he met, it reinforced thoughts I've been having that there may be a bigger plan or purpose behind what we think of as routine, casual contacts.

Jack talked of beginning his police career, starting a family and how his marriage eventually fell apart. Jim and I understood. We both had friends in law enforcement who had suffered the same fate. Jack's solution had been to go into the Army and he found a home there. He had done a few tours of duty in Vietnam and thought his time there really screwed him up.

Jack told us his experience in the small town near Santa Barbara had been difficult. He was unhappy and unable to adjust. One good thing did come out of his stay there, though. He met and married a young woman who accompanied him to Leadore. She was working as a legal secretary in Salmon commuting back and forth the 45 miles each day.

Years before Jack had come to this area on a hunting trip and had been so taken with it that while he was in the military he dreamed about coming back, dropping out and getting away from people. He bought a four-wheel-drive, off-road International Scout and each day went exploring someplace new, realizing it would take a lifetime to make it up every little canyon. He was talking my language – exploring these mountains is my idea of recreation – but I mostly go on foot or horseback. Jim may be even more avid about this kind of fun than I am, so we both encouraged him to talk about what he'd seen so far.

Like all people when they talk about what they like best, Jack smiled and became animated. Maybe we did too. This is the reason we live in Idaho. These mountains are like a magnet that draws drawn us back again and again. The afternoon disappeared and his wife returned. She was a very pretty and likeable woman who graciously asked Jim and I if we wanted to stay for dinner. We declined with thanks saying we knew our dinners would be waiting at our homes if we ever got around to heading that way and that we were probably already in trouble for being late.

Jack stood. "Before you head out I'll show you my gun collection," he said and waved us toward a door leading into what may have been a spare bedroom at one time but now housed cabinets and tables filled with what looked like a small arsenal. We had already established ourselves with him as being familiar with and conversant about guns. He had five or six rifles of various calibers and four or five shotguns, including a sawed off twelve gauge that is generally used for close-in fighting. I have one myself and know them to be deadly. Jack had swords, hand grenades and some stuff he brought back from Vietnam.

He showed us a couple of land mines and small sharpened sticks he said were used by the Viet Cong, who would soak the sticks in human feces until they became infected. They then place them upright at the bottom of pits they dug in trails. Jack said that when Americans came along the trail, with their eyes scanning the jungle for the enemy, they sometimes fell through the pit cover and were impaled on the sharpened sticks.

He had an automatic machine gun, which I was interested in looking over, but I knew that Jim is a real rabid gun nut and if we got started it would be the next day before we got out of there. I told Jack we looked forward to coming back but that we had 116 miles to go before supper and we had to get started. Jim reluctantly agreed and we said our goodbyes.

Two weeks later, Jim and I had occasion to pass through Salmon and we stopped in to see Sheriff Baker. After the usual kidding around with the group hanging around the department, he motioned us into his office and asked: "Did you guys check on the new Marshall in

Leadore?" We said that we had. He frowned and said: "Well what?"

"Here's the deal, Bill, this fellow Jack Stratton is a tough man," I told him. "What we are predicting will happen is that some young cowboy is going to get liquored up, start trouble and when Jack shows up to slow him down, the cowboy may not have enough sense to realize what he's up against and Jack will end up killing him. Jack's not the kind that will allow himself to be pushed. When that happens, he is going to fade back up one of those canyons and wait for someone to come after him. When that happens, don't call Jim or me because we're not going after him."

Bill laughed. "Well, I guess he'll have to stay up there because I'm not going up there after him either," he said.

Months rolled by and my prediction did not come true. I was not ready to say I was wrong, only willing to concede that circumstances had not developed to fit my scenario. But they came close. Later the folks who ran the Silver Dollar Bar filled me in. There had been a fight one night in the bar between a logger and a young cowboy.

The cowboy lost. He was a big fellow, weighing about 220 pounds and standing 6-feet tall. The cowboy regained his feet and went outside.

The Marshall was called. He only lived half a block away and was at the scene in a few seconds. Bar patrons went outside to see the action. The cowboy went to his pickup and retrieved a chain saw from the rear box and was trying to start it as Jack approached.

"What are you going to do with that chainsaw," Jack asked.

"I'm going to cut the tires off that guy's truck," the cowboy replied.

Jack spread his legs, crouched slightly with his hand near his pistol and with a little grin on his face said, "Go ahead."

Everything stopped and it became very quiet. There was no question that there was going to be a shooting. The crowd started backing away. The cowboy stared at Jack. "Ah, the hell with it," the cowboy said and put the chainsaw back into the pickup.

"Go on home and sleep it off," Jack told the cowboy.

My guess was that even though the cowboy was drunk, he wasn't so drunk he couldn't see the same thing in Jack that Jim and I had seen. When you are staring at someone who is willing to kill you, it shows on his face.

My plan had been to take an early retirement from my state employment and start a private investigative business. In addition, I wanted to become an outfitter/hunting guide at least during the fall hunting season. Why not? I had been doing it for years for my own pleasure. I owned horses, saddles, packing gear … all the things I needed. That's the reason I bought the ranch at Leadore and was building a lodge as a base for the outfitter's business.

The outfitting part of my plan didn't work out. Once I got serious, I discovered it was no longer fun. To get my foot in the door, I started small. As I attended various law enforcement and polygraph conventions around the country, I lined up folks to come to Idaho for elk hunts. Some of the hunters were wonderful companions, but many were out of their element.

I had to teach them to ride and look after themselves in the mountains. They needed waiting on and I quickly learned I wasn't the one to do it. A whole book could be written about my packing and outfitting experience, but I'll pass on it. The interesting thing that came out of the experience was that I soured on hunting and gave it up altogether.

But I didn't give up horses and trips into the mountains with family and friends or by myself; so I still needed the lodge.

While I was building the lodge, I became closely associated with Jack Stratton. On weekends and holidays I would travel to Leadore and work on my ranch house. It took me a couple years to get it done. Marilyn had a busy life of her own running a hospice program and she had no desire to come with me when all I was going to do was hammer and saw. Most of the time, I was alone.

My place was not far from town and one day Jack drove by, saw my vehicle and stopped. I needed a break and invited him to sit with me on a pile of lumber and share a sandwich. He declined the sandwich but spent a couple hours sharing police stories and thoughts about the people and places he'd known.

I thought Jack came across as an angry, bitter man and it was hard to get him to laugh or even smile. However, I've spent a half a lifetime dealing with angry and bitter people and I found it easy to keep a conversation going. It turned out to be a pleasant visit, at least for me. I have a natural curiosity about almost everyone and felt a need to figure out what was eating Jack.

The visit must have suited Jack as well, because he started coming by every weekend. Before the summer was over, it had become a kind of ritual I looked forward to. Jack told me he was going to keep an eye on my place while I was gone. I said that wouldn't be necessary as I had a cowboy who took care of my horses and was there most of the time. Jack said he was going to do it anyway. The cowboy told me Jack did come by from time to time. He would drive in and around but never say anything.

By this time I had learned that not many people in the community liked Jack. He was not a friendly man and I began to suspect that some may have feared him, though nobody told me that directly. It was just the aura he carried.

Jack and I became friends. He would watch for my car or truck to show up and drive down to the house. He usually had a bottle of vodka in his car. I would furnish the glasses and he would pour us a drink as we talked. He was a real drinker and I am not. I can enjoy a drink or maybe two at the most and I limit how much vodka gets in my glass by mixing it with soda or something. Jack drank his vodka in a large glass - straight. He often told me that's the sign of a real man. I would counter by saying that's the sign of a real drunk, which almost always got a smile out of him.

Sometimes we would be joined by an old rancher named Dick Tyler. I met Dick at an auction and we became instant friends. He was full of humor, stories and down-home wisdom. There was no way you could dislike this man. How he and Jack became friends I never found out, but he was a welcome addition to our get-togethers.

Dick was a lanky Western rancher who claimed he was broken down because of age. I never saw any evidence of it. When you spend your life in the sun and freezing cold, you get a weathered look and I couldn't tell if he was old or weathered.

His son and daughter-in-law had taken over running the ranch, so Dick had time to spare. He would have a couple drinks with us, start telling stories and jokes and I would forget all about the work I was there to do.

I was never sure what to expect from Jack. While he was a lawman, he more often than not acted on what he thought was right rather than what the law commanded. A case in point occurred one day while we were sitting in the shade on the north side of the house. The lodge backs up to a pond and directly beyond that is the Lemhi River. It was a pretty place to sit with a view of the river, hay fields and mountains dominating the backdrop.

Jack, Dick and I were sipping our drinks when, all of a sudden, Jack jumped up and shouted: "Where's your pitchfork?"

It took me totally by surprise and I had no idea what was going on. Dick looked baffled as well. I waved over to the corrals and said: "It's in the haystack where it belongs."

Jack took off running toward the haystack. Dick and I sat there and exchanged comments such as: "He's gone off the deep end at last" and "I don't know if we should drink any more of this stuff. It looks like Jack's seeing snakes."

Jack came running back past us, headed down to the river and jumped in. The water was about three feet deep, crystal clear and so cold it took your breath away. I learned that the hard way trying to get a rope on a mean mule as he dragged me through the river and out the other side.

"Let's check on what he's up to," Dick said. "He can't be sane and jump in like that."

We started toward the river and met Jack coming back with a big smile on his face and carrying a salmon that was about three feet long. "You fellas can come by the house tonight for barbecued salmon," he said.

Dick grunted and said: "God damn-it Jack, you're going to get us all arrested and thrown in jail. These waters are closed to salmon fishing."

Jack kept grinning and took off with his fish. "I'll see you fellas tonight," he said. I hollered after him: "You won't see me."

"I'm not coming either," Dick called after him. "They're going to have to hang you by yourself."

It didn't slow Jack down.

I felt bad about that incident for some time. In fact, I still do. Someone once told me those salmon had a 1,400-mile trip up river, over dams and past anglers, nets, natural barriers and rapids, from the Pacific Ocean to the small river where they spawned and then died. The last 20 miles of river had been closed to fishing to give them that chance to concentrate solely on propagating and starting the cycle over again. I thought they deserved that chance after running that fantastic race against almost insurmountable obstacles.

Winter arrived and I didn't make it to Leadore often. It was a hard winter. I had been there in January and my thermometer read 60 below zero. I had been in the cold before, but nothing like that. As I walked around the place, the corral poles and posts would pop with a strange startling sound. Someone explained to me that though the wood looked dry, there was a tiny bit of moisture inside and as it froze it exerted pressure on the inner wood breaking it from the inside.

I couldn't hear that sound without thinking about how much moisture might be in my bones and how I should get more layers of clothing around them. The horses grew a thick layer of hair, but you could tell they were affected because they ate more and didn't move around much.

And though their breath was steaming, when you laid your hand against their skin they seemed to be putting out a lot of heat. At times like these, I was particularly aware of how the animal world endures changes in weather as a matter of course and of how inadequate we humans are. I had tried to gas up my truck and none of the six pumps in town would work. When they were turned on, they made a mechanical groan and nothing came out. Luckily I had some gas stored in cans and was able to get back to Idaho Falls, where it was a balmy 20 below zero. Fortunately the winters have been steadily moderating and we now complain when it's 10 below.

During that winter, I got a call from Jack's wife, who said she was in Idaho Falls and wanted to meet. She had left Jack and was working for a local lawyer. She said she loved Jack and wanted to stay with him but was not going to spend any more time in Leadore. He refused to leave, so she decided to get a divorce.

After that winter, I could not blame her for wanting to leave. She was a California woman unused to extreme winter weather. After the divorce she was moving to Boise, which was somewhat warmer. I wished her luck.

As soon as the winter began to break, I renewed my building project. I contacted Jack with the intention of giving my condolences about being divorced. He shrugged as if it didn't matter and changed the subject by telling me he had filed a claim up one of the local canyons and thought he might find a little gold.

He showed me a small rocker he had built to recover bits of gold from dirt. I kidded him about how mining was hard work. Jack replied that he had no intention of working hard. He figured his friends could do the work and he would reward them with a small portion of the gold they recovered. As far as I know, everyone shied away from his offer, especially me.

As before, Jack watched for me and came down if he saw my vehicle. He always brought his bottle of vodka and seemed to be hitting it pretty hard. It was obvious he wanted to talk, so I encouraged him, sat back and did a lot of listening. He wanted to talk about his Army experiences and over a period of time I got his story.

His first tour of duty was in the early 1960s, when he ended up in a special tactical infantry unit. He said it had a fancy name, but was essentially an assassination team. He worked with six others and their job involved standard guerrilla warfare. He said they would be given the information that a particular mayor or leader of a village was sympathetic to, or aiding the Vietcong, and their job was to get rid of him in a way that frightened the other villagers.

They were all trained as snipers and in pairs would sneak into position to get a shot at the leader. They were told what hut or house he lived in and given a general description of the individual. There were lots of palm trees and Jack said he liked to climb into the top foliage, which offered a good view and concealment. There was no indoor plumbing, so each morning the occupants would come out and look around before heading to relieve themselves. When the target came out, it was like shooting ducks. They would kill him and fade back into the background while the villagers were demoralized and taking cover.

On another occasion, Jack talked of being with his team on the Ho Chi Minh Trail in Cambodia. He said they weren't supposed to be in Cambodia, but the Vietcong were ferrying supplies on a jungle trail from North Vietnam to South Vietnam and they would slip over and set up ambushes to intersect the supply lines. The jungle was thick and they could hide easily. Jack said most people think at night the jungle would be a quiet place. He said it was actually full of noise from the sounds of a million insects, rustle of small animals – and sometimes large ones – bats and an incessant rain that beat on the broad fronds like drums.

Here was more than enough background noise to mask the killings of careful men. Jack said the Vietcong would usually travel in groups of 11 and would be loaded down with unbelievably heavy loads … walking slowly with their heads bowed forward and pulling against a head band that stabilized their packs.

The groups were spread out to avoid too many being wiped out at once by the heavy bombing by U.S. Air Force pilots, who also were not supposed to be there. Jack said they used special sniper rifles equipped with silencers. They picked spots where the jungle gave way to a clearing and would allow the group to pass by. When No. 11 passed, they would start shooting them from the back. He said you could usually get seven or eight before the ones in front realized what was happening. They would throw off the packs and run. If the clearing was big enough, you could get a few more.

We talked of strategies, hardships and living each day thinking it would be your last. We discussed the ease in which you could take lives and about losing your way and it became clear to me what Jack meant when he said his last tour in Vietnam had screwed him up. How could it not have? His solution was to retreat to the mountains in Idaho, hold himself apart from most people and drink a lot of vodka. I had watched him allow a loving, beautiful and smart woman get away because he wouldn't give that up, but after hearing his story I cut him some slack.

Looking back on the day Jack revealed his demons, I marvel at the contrast between what he described and where we sat as he described it.

Sometime that year, there had been a killing in Salmon. A young man was visiting from another small town to the south and as kids do in every town in America on weekend nights, he cruised up and down the main drag and parked in a grocery store parking lot on one end of the main street to watch whoever else was cruising. A Salmon boy, the son of a local logging family, drove up to him at the parking lot and said: "Your car looks like a pile of shit." The fight was on and the out-of-town boy won. He stayed in the parking lot and the loser drove away.

The loser soon came back with two boys and two girls. He asked the out-of-towner if he wanted to have another go. And this time to drive out in the country where nobody could stop it. Young men can be foolish. The out-of-towner accepted and followed the carload of kids a couple of miles out on a country road. Both young men got out of their cars and the Salmon boy walked over and stabbed the out-of-towner in the chest with a hunting knife.

He left him lying in the road and went back to his car to drive away. The two girls said they ought to take the kid to the hospital, so they loaded him into their back seat, drove back to town and made a pass through the local hospital parking lot, rolling the body out on the pavement as they sped through. It was a while before anyone found him. It was to late to save his life. He had lost too much blood.

Jim and I were assigned to investigate the case and we ended up charging the Salmon boy with first degree murder. The trial was held in Challis, about 50 miles south of Salmon. Challis is a small town with a small courthouse and when the trial was about to begin the boy's family showed up and attempted to take charge, threatening prospective jurors and trying to intimidate attorneys and the judge.

The judge was not prepared for this. He brought a young law student to act as the bailiff, probably to give him a little experience and a taste of what he might encounter in his budding career. The student was totally overwhelmed and unable to act at all. So, Jim and I were pressed into service to clear the court and maintain order. After 28 years in law enforcement, I was still running into new experiences. We got things settled, the jury was selected and the trial started. All witnesses were excluded, meaning they couldn't sit through the trial and hear the other witnesses testify. I was a witness, so I had to sit in the hallway until my testimony was needed.

There were several of us out there: the two boys and two girls who had been in the car, various police officers, the coroner who examined the body and a psychiatrist,

Dr Atchley, from Idaho Falls, who conducted a mental evaluation of the defendant on behalf of the state.

I had a nodding acquaintance with the doctor and during the three days we waited out in that hallway we became better acquainted. What normally would have been a dull and tedious wait turned into a fascinating exposure to another world. Without naming anyone he gave accounts of the various patients and illnesses he was treating, including those who "scared the hell out of me." That experience taught me there were even more screwed up people running around than I already suspected.

One of the areas we talked about was the mental condition of returning Vietnam veterans. He said that his practice included a variety of veterans, from WWII, Korea and Vietnam.

"War changes people into something just opposite of what they were," the doctor told me. "We take nice young men with fairly healthy outlooks on life and teach them to be eager killers. Then we put them in positions where they use the skills they have been taught. There is nothing clean or honorable about killing under any circumstances, but if you ask these young men to kill women and children, as happened on many occasions in Vietnam, and to look into the faces of those they'd killed, they become something other than what they were."

He described them as having developed a coping personality. They turn inward and become what he called "pure survivors" in that they lose their moral anchors. The doctor said they are dangerous people and they know it and are in a constant struggle to get a grip. Often they become alcoholics as a way to cope. They can be extremely anti-social and many times suicidal.

The doctor lamented that we create these people and turn them loose in society and pretend they are not there. We leave it up to them to find their way back and hope they make it. Many don't. As he talked, I thought back on all the senseless acts of violence I had seen in my police career and how often it had been caused by a returned veteran who couldn't "get it together."

You may guess who I was thinking of as he talked. One afternoon when Jack came down to the ranch, he said he couldn't have a drink because his stomach hurt. He was leaning forward with his arms around his stomach and a pained expression on his face. He had been hurting for some time and suspected he had stomach cancer.

I never knew where Jack was coming from when he opened a subject, so I had become cautious about giving flippant comments, as I liked to do with friends.

"Have you been to a doctor to check it out," I asked him. I didn't know it, but Jack was about to open a dark recess and show me the demon he kept asleep with Vodka. He didn't answer, but straightened up and changed the subject by looking intently at me and saying in a deep, harsh voice filled with tension: "You don't know anybody who needs killing, do you?"

Forgetting my caution, I replied: "Sure, there are some pimps down in Los Angeles we'd be better off without."

Jack didn't smile. "What are their names," he asked. I didn't like where the conversation was going, so I laughed and changed the subject. I knew, however, that I had a glimpse into his inner soul.

One month followed another and I retired from the state and started my investigation company. Life was good. I was busy, but managed to make it to Leadore from time to time and stay in touch with Jack. On one of those occasions, he told me he was getting married again.

Gwen worked for the U.S. Forest Service's ranger station in Leadore. I knew her reasonably well, having met her a few years before when she was going through some difficult times coming out of a bad marriage. She was in her late 30s and a very attractive woman. A better description might be that she was a sexy woman with blonde hair, good curves and an open attitude.

Men flocked to her. She probably could have had her pick and I don't know why it surprised me that she selected Jack, but I'm always being surprised by the men women choose.

I asked Marilyn what she thought of Jack and she described him as a good-looking and well-mannered man that most women would find attractive. After that I kept my opinions to myself.

Jack and Gwen got off to a good start. One of our friends had built a nice log home in Leadore and they bought it and moved in. They were planning an open house and wanted it to be a big deal. Jack borrowed a fancy saddle to place on one of the large log beams in the living room ceiling. They had other saddles scattered around and lariats and spurs hanging on the walls. It looked pretty good.

The open house was a big success. They served barbecue with all the usual accompanying foods and had beer and wine at a small bar in the yard. All the local town people were there, as well as ranchers and their families from up and down the Lemhi valley. The Salmon newspaper sent a reporter and a photographer and gave them a full page in the local paper. Everybody had a good time.

I took it in from the vantage of a comfortable chair on the porch. I suppose that, based on my background, I find myself watching people more often than I should and I noticed a large young man pacing back and forth in the road across from the house. It didn't look right to me. He seemed agitated and I saw him speak to a young cowboy who I hired from time to time to help me with horses, and with whom I was quite friendly. I sought the cowboy out when he returned to the party and asked him the story on the young guy out in the street.

He said the fellow was a former beau of Gwen's and that he was upset over getting dumped when she took up with Jack. He wanted Gwen to come out and talk to him. I sent the cowboy back out to tell him that he better leave before Jack discovered him out there and killed him, adding that if Jack didn't do it, there were others at the party who would. The cowboy gave a big grin and went back out. I could see him arguing with the big guy. They turned and the cowboy pointed in my direction and I thought: "Well, the trouble is about to start." It didn't happen. The big guy got in his pickup and drove away.

Later I asked my cowboy friend what he had told the fellow. "I told him I had seen you shoot that big pistol you carry," he said. One of these days I'll have to learn to mind my own business. I hadn't carried that big pistol for some time, but I do credit myself with saving that young fellow's life that day.

I liked Gwen and as time went by I could see that she and Jack fit well together. She had a mind of her own and petty rules didn't affect her any more than they did Jack. Once she told me about getting stopped for speeding on a trip to Idaho Falls. She seemed offended that the state trooper who stopped her was so rude.

"I know him and I have never heard of him being rude to anyone," I said. "What happened?"

Well, Gwen was driving her big Chrysler and met the trooper coming the other way. She gave him a wave as they passed each other. The red lights flashed behind her, so she pulled over. The trooper rushed angrily up to her window and shouted: "Where in the hell are you going?"

"I'm going to town," Gwen replied.

"You're going to jail," the trooper shouted at her.

I stopped her and asked: "Just how fast were you going, Gwen?"

"Well, I was doing a little bit over 100, but it was a straight highway and I could see for the next five miles and the only two people on the road were us," she said.

Gwen calmed the trooper down and did not go to jail.

Once I was sitting shooting the breeze with them when some sort of animal came up from under a hide on the opposite end of the couch and raced up my arm and across the back of my neck, taking a swipe at my head as it passed. It went behind the sofa and disappeared.

I jumped to my feet and reached around for something to hit it with. Jack and Gwen were doubled over with laughter. "What the hell was that," I asked.

It was a ferret that had been declawed but still had its teeth. I can appreciate that they saw humor in the ferret attack, but I was not comfortable and planned to avoid any later confrontations. I learned that almost everyone in town was, sooner or later, set up the same way.

The summer rolled along and when the first snow fell in the fall I buttoned up my building project for the winter and planned to spend more time with my new business. I was in my office in Idaho Falls one afternoon when I got a call from Gwen.

"I need your help," she said. "Will you help me?" Without thinking I replied: "Sure, what's happening?"

At some point in my life, I'm going to start reflecting before I agree to things, but I wasn't there yet.

"Jack is in the hospital in Missoula," Gwen told me. "He's in bad shape and we need to get him into a treatment center and we need your help to do it."

"That's not really my kind of thing," I said. "I don't know how I can help you."

"Please, we need you," Gwen replied and I had not heard her speak like this before. There was urgency in her voice that told me she did need help, only I didn't know how I could possibly do her any good.

Gwen wanted me to drive to Leadore the next day, pick up her friend, Barbara, drive to Missoula and meet her at a motel at 6 p.m.

I was full of questions. She was asking me to drive more than 250 miles. She cut me off: "Barbara will be waiting for you and she will fill you in," she said. Then I heard the dial tone.

I made arrangements to leave the next morning. My first stop was the Sagebrush Bar in Leadore, where Barbara was waiting for me. I knew Barbara and liked her. She was a woman of about 60 who owned and operated the bar. She once ran a roadhouse in Alaska and made some money, which she used to buy the Sagebrush Bar and settle down. I never knew exactly what running a roadhouse meant and didn't ask. I cut Barbara slack because she was a kind woman.

Just across the Bannock Pass in Montana there was a man who worked as a janitor for a small backcountry school. It was not much of a job and he struggled to make a living. He was a fair piano player and singer, so Barbara hired him to come across the pass on Friday and Saturday nights and play and sing in her bar.

He was a transsexual and wore a floor-length gingham dress and an unkempt brown women's wig. He might have been considered a fair-looking man, but as a woman he didn't look so good. I'd heard the description "God awful" used a time or two. If any strangers came in and said anything about his appearance, or what he was, Barbara gave them hell. The locals all liked him and looked after him; woe to the occasional redneck hunter who made any off-color remark about him. It was not what you would expect to find in a western ranching community, but you can find good hearts and tolerance everywhere.

Barbara, it turned out, didn't know any more than I did. It didn't matter; we were on our way. There are interesting people everywhere and Barbara was no exception. We talked about Alaska and our experiences there. In my early years I had been a commercial fisherman working out of Sitka. She spoke about the difficulties of being a single parent and we talked of the good times we'd had in different places. As I got to know Barbara better, I liked her more. The next thing I knew we were driving into Missoula.

Before we could get checked into the motel, Gwen met Barbara and I in the lobby and ushered us into a small conference room. I recognized a couple of the people there out of the eight or 10 present: Scott Tyler, rancher and construction man, who I knew to be a good, solid citizen and a friend from Leadore; and Bill Breen, a longtime FBI Agent from the Idaho Falls office.

I began to understand what we might be doing there as I knew Bill was an alcoholic who had struggled to overcome his addiction and won. Many years before, when Bill and his wife had just moved to town, I invited him to our house for a good Mexican meal. Bill was from Texas and had complained about the lack of good hot Mexican food in Idaho. He never reciprocated that invitation, but we moved in different social circles so I was unconcerned about it.

We got along fine in the work arena. Many years later, he sat down with me in a restaurant and asked: "Do you know why I never had you come over to my house for dinner after you were kind enough to ask my wife and me to join you?"

I told him no and he continued: "A week or so after that dinner, we both attended a crime conference in Nevada and following the meeting everyone had retired to the hotel lounge for a drink. It was happy hour and everyone soon had four or five drinks sitting in front of them. I watched you drink one drink and then get up and excuse yourself and leave the group with those four drinks untouched. For an alcoholic, that kind of behavior was unthinkable. I had to drink everything I could get my hands on. I knew you and I could never socialize. I have wished so many times I could walk away just as you did."

Bill overcame his addiction and like many alcoholics spent much of his time helping others fighting the same battle. I assumed he knew Jack and was there for that purpose but I didn't have time to ask as Gwen stood and introduced a woman she described as a "facilitator" and nurse who would explain everything.

She began by thanking us for being there and had each of us introduce ourselves. I was surprised to learn that two of the young men were Jack's sons, whom I had never met. He did not often talk of them and I assumed he walked away from them after his first divorce.

A doctor and second nurse were present. The facilitator said: "The purpose for which you are here is to participate in, what we call, intervention. Jack is a very sick man and if he does not stop drinking he will be dead in a few months." The doctor nodded and she continued: "We will all be in a room together, formed in a circle and Jack will be brought in to join us. He does not know any of you are here. You must pick a leader and that leader's job will be to greet Jack and get him to agree to a contract. The contract will be to allow each of you to have your say before Jack speaks. He must agree to the contract."

I didn't much like what I was hearing but kept my mouth shut. I knew Jack well enough to know that, even sick, he wouldn't agree to anything he thought he was being pushed into. She continued: "Our purpose here is to get Jack to agree to check himself into a treatment center where he can combat his addiction. No one else can check him in. He must do it himself. If he agrees to the contract, the leader must make the first statement and then each take a turn. When it gets back to Jack, the leader must ask him if he is willing to agree to check himself in as everyone has asked him to do."

This meeting was set for the next morning. "I want each of you to be thinking through the night about what you will say to Jack to convince him he has to give up alcohol," this lady told us. "It may be difficult for you to do, but you must be harsh. You must tell him that, while you may like him, you will no longer be willing to associate with him if he continues to drink."

This was getting heavy and I was starting to feel uncomfortable about being there. I could see in the faces of the others that they felt the same way.

The facilitator continued: "You were asked by Gwen to come here today because she thinks each of you has some influence on Jack. If you fail, then Jack will fail. He will surely die. His body has reached its limit of absorbing alcohol. If he agrees, there will be no time to waste. We do not want to give him any chance to reconsider. The doctor will immediately get him checked out of the hospital. One of you must have a car in front of the hospital building and two of you must rush him to the car and he must be driven as fast as possible to the center, which is located several blocks away. There he must be rushed inside where someone will be waiting with a form, for his signature. Speed will be of the essence. Does everyone understand?"

I spoke up: "We may be getting ahead of ourselves a little bit as I don't think it is going to work so simply. Suppose Jack does not agree? What do we do then?"

"The longer it takes and the more arguing with him that you do, your chances to succeed go down proportionally," the facilitator replied. "A lot will depend on your leader."

Gwen looked at me and said: "I want Steve Watts to be the leader."

Her words and the plea in her look caught me by surprise. I was still thinking I didn't belong there at all, much less take the lead.

"You know Gwen, I know nothing about this kind of thing," I told her. "Someone else may do a better job, someone who knows what they are doing."

"Steve, you're the only person I know he will listen to," she said.

I looked around the room and all eyes were on me. They seemed to have a look of expectation and approval and I felt shaken. I didn't like it. I'm supposed to be a tough guy who doesn't think on an emotional plane. It was quite a compliment to say I was the only one Jack would listen to, but I didn't want his failure and eventual death dependent on me. I couldn't look at Gwen – that plea remained in her eyes. I looked at the ceiling and finally said: "Hell, there doesn't seem to be a lot of choice does there?"

Early the next morning, we all had breakfast at the motel coffee shop and traveled to the hospital. I was driving my big Cadillac Brome, which had a lot of room for extra passengers, so I parked adjacent to the hospital entrance. We were taken to Jack's floor and into a small meeting room near the nurse's station. The table had been removed and several chairs brought in and set in a circle.

I had given much thought to the assignment I had been handed. I remembered how for many years I had been an interrogator and taught the art of interviewing at the police academy. Though this was new territory, I was well qualified and was going to use those skills to the best of my ability. I had resolved during the night that if we failed Jack, it wouldn't be because I didn't give it my best.

Above our heads was an intercom. Every few minutes it would blare out, calling for a doctor or wanting

172

to know who owned the red Ford parked in the emergency entrance driveway.

"We can't have that noise interrupting us when we get into this," I said. "How do we get it turned off?" Someone called the head nurse and she said it could not be turned off. It had no switch and hospital policy did not allow any of the systems to ever be turned off. I could see she was defensive and we were closing in on 10 a.m.

I pulled a chair underneath the speaker and pulled out a wire that led to it. The nurse seemed agitated and left in a huff. I've never been able to deal with people who make rigid rules which are never to be broken.

We took our places and watched as the clock moved to 10. As it did, the door swung open and our facilitator entered, pushing Jack, in a wheelchair, into the spot next to me that had been left open. She took her seat in the middle of the circle. Jack was pale and obviously weak but still had the familiar, sardonic and dignified look that always characterized him.

I saw him look around the room, taking everyone in, and his eyes slightly widened with what may have been surprise. You would have had to know him to see it. I marvel at that kind of self-control. Not a word had been said during those few seconds but I could also see Jack's guard come up by the way he stiffened and set his jaw.

I began by telling him it was good to see him alive, that I figured he wouldn't last as long as he had and that he should have been dead long before this. I heard a slight rustle from the group, which could not have been expecting that kind of a greeting. But I knew Jack and that's how we talked to each other. It worked. He smiled and the ice was broken. I told Jack everyone here had come because they cared about him and they had

Stephen T. Watts

something to say to him about how they cared. I wanted him to hear everyone before he said anything and asked if he would agree to that.

He shrugged and said: "Sure." So far so good. Now for the heavy part!

I began: "Jack, one of the great pleasures of my life has been our friendship. I have looked forward to being able to talk with you about things neither of us would dare bring up to other people. I like being able to sit down with you and have a drink and talk. The problem is, I can drink and you can't. And you know it. It's gotten away from you. I've been watching you kill yourself with that vodka. Jack, nobody wants to see a friend killing himself. We are all here to ask you to check into a treatment center and get through this. If you don't agree to do this I'll be drawing away from you. I'm not going to sit around you and watch you kill yourself."

I felt terrible, like I had committed an act of betrayal. And I had. The world Jack and I lived in was one where friends stuck it out to the end. I didn't give Jack a chance to remind me of that. I turned away and motioned to Barbara, who was seated beside me, to take it from there.

Like the trooper I had come to believe she was, Barbara came through. She included an oath or two in her remarks so Jack would know she was genuine. There was nothing condescending in her approach. She was like a mad mother. Barbara said that she was speaking for the City Council.

She said Jack had become a fixture in the town and no one wanted to give him up. There was no way they could ever get another Marshall of his ability and caliber. She said that, despite his ornery ways, they liked him and it would be a damn shame if he let himself be beat down

174

by booze when he knew better. Her honesty and sincerity came through, even though her language was a bit rough. Barbara talked for a few minutes more in the same vein and concluded with the admonition: "Jack, check yourself in. We want you back."

One of Jack's sons sat in the next chair. He was a good-looking young man in his early 30's and was obviously in distress. This had to be a very difficult time for him. He began by saying: "Dad, I love you very much and I want to share in your life and I want you to share in mine and with my family. When you came out to Oregon last year to visit us, you were drunk every day that you were there. I know you didn't mean to but you created terrible problems between me and my wife.

She told me she did not ever again want our kids to be exposed to that again. Dad, I have to tell you that if you continue drinking I don't want you ever again to visit my home. Please give up drinking. Check yourself into the treatment center so I can welcome you back. Make it work."

Damn, this was getting heavy. I stared at the ceiling thinking how difficult it had to be for this young man to tell his father he is no longer welcome in his life. I never had a father to interact with, but could imagine his emotions. I looked around the room and saw tears being wiped away and knew others felt as I did.

Next was our friend, Scott Tyler, and I knew that Gwen had made a good choice in asking him to come. Scott had grown up ranching in the Lemhi Valley. He was a big man in his early 40s and looked exactly like what he was: a working rancher who ran a construction business as a sideline. Cowboy boots. Stetson hat. Large belt buckle. He was not wearing these things to look like the real thing; he was the real thing.

Scott exuded a quiet strength. In a quiet, measured voice he spoke directly to Jack, telling him he was needed in the Lemhi Valley. He was speaking for all their mutual friends and that included his own father, Dick Tyler, who was unable to come. His quiet certitude was powerful and he ended by telling Jack that every one of them wanted him to get treatment, get better and return to Leadore whole.

The facilitator told Jack about what alcoholism does to the mind and body and how it affects the people who share that alcoholic's life. She reminded Jack that those in the room cared for him and had gone to some trouble to be here. "You must get treatment, or you won't live very long," she said.

The doctor looked directly at Jack. "Mr. Stratton, your liver is in very bad shape," he said. "You have abused it for too long. Its collapse is what brought you into this hospital. We are able to stabilize it for a while with drugs. I can guarantee that if you continue using alcohol you will die within six months and maybe much sooner. We will not be able to help you after a certain point. If you accept treatment and stay with the program, you may have several more years of life."

I thought of the phrase, "The tension is so thick you could cut it with a knife" and thought it fit this situation. Everyone was absolutely still, waiting for Gwen.

The full weight of what had been happening was evident in her slumped shoulders and tearful face. I realized that I was holding my breath. We were all suspended in time as we waited for her to gather herself.

And she did. Straightening up in the chair and taking a last wipe of her eyes, Gwen began to speak.

Looking directly at her husband she said: "Jack, I love you so much. You have brought me so much happiness and life has been so good since we got together." She paused and continued: "But Jack I can't live with you if you are going to be a drunk. Please, please check yourself in for treatment. If you don't, I won't be there when you come back." Tears came into her eyes and she slumped back.

I nodded to Bill Breen, sitting next to Gwen. At the same time, I was thinking, "God, what a hell of a spot for a wife to be in, to have to give an ultimatum like that." I don't know if Jack believed she meant it, but I was convinced she did.

Bill is a class act — a super-intelligent man full of humor with an easy-going manner that instantly puts people at ease. Tall and lanky, he was just the opposite of the FBI agents portrayed on television. I had kidded him about not being anal enough to be a typical uptight FBI man. I was glad he was there.

"Jack, you and I know each other," he began. "You know that I am an alcoholic and I know that you are one, too. In fact, you know you are one. There's nothing you are going through that I haven't been through myself. I went through the treatment program. I can tell you it works. I haven't had a drink in several years and my life is good again."

He ended on a positive note: "Jack, if you agree and go through the program you will be glad you did. You have nothing to lose by agreeing and everything to lose if you don't."

177

Jack's second son was next. We heard again a son speak of his love for his father and then issue an ultimatum. Emotion twisted his face and his voice. It was twisting my stomach, or maybe my heart, and I forced myself to look around the room at the other participants, whose faces indicated they were being twisted also.

Sitting next to Jack, I could neither see his face nor hear his breathing. His silence was unnerving. I kept thinking that if I was in his place I would have jumped into this conversation long before, but Jack said nothing, just as he had agreed to do.

And then it was time for the last speaker, the second nurse. Her voice was calm and soothing and I could understand why she had positioned herself last. She was obviously experienced and in a few short statements brought every thing each person had spoken of together. I felt my breathing becoming normal again and realized that my shoulder muscles were relaxing and a feeling of relief passed through me.

But his was no time for me to relax. I had to speak again and the difficult time was still to come. Then the nurse smiled at me and nodded, indicating I was on again.

I turned again to face Jack and we looked at each other. There was no expression on his face – no hostility or acceptance – just watchful waiting. "This is going to be tough," I thought. There are physiological tricks and moves that will help an interrogator get his target to agree and I was going to have to use all of them.

I opened with: "Looks like you have some people who like you Jack," nodding my head up and down slightly as I spoke. He didn't nod back, as I was expecting, or answer, but he did raise his eyebrows in a manner that I took to mean he agreed. And then the direct approach: "Will you check into the treatment center?"

"Well, I'd like to know more about it," Jack replied. In interrogator's language, this is called "the stall." I looked across the room at Bill Breen and he nodded. "You don't need to know anymore than what Bill told you, that it works," I said to Jack and nodded to Bill. For the next 10 minutes, we went back and forth, first to Bill and then back to me, steadily increasing the tempo and intensity of our questions and demands and watching the frustration build in Jack's demeanor. Finally Jack gave in, "Hell I guess so," he said.

It happened suddenly and I thought that Jack probably was in agreement from the beginning, but it was not his way to go without putting up a fight.

His words were magic. Everyone jumped to a task. One son wheeled Jack from the room with the doctor. I grabbed Gwen's arm and pulled her out the door, joining the facilitator and heading for the hospital entrance.

As we were moving down the hall, Gwen stopped me and asked: "What was going on in there?"

What do you mean," I asked.

"You know, between you and Bill."

I wanted to play it down. I said: "Gwen we were just using some old police interrogation methods. I'm surprised Jack fell for them."

"I knew it, it had to be something," she said. "Jack just does not respond that way normally."

It struck me that all those things that Bill and I learned over the years had not been wasted.

In a couple of minutes, Jack was wheeled out the door. We got him to the car, put the wheelchair in the trunk and were on our way. The facilitator made some small talk but I was holding my breath. Jack could still change his mind. I wasn't the only one worried. One of Jack's sons was out of the car almost before I got it stopped in front of the center. I popped the trunk and he had the wheelchair under Jack as quickly as Gwen pulled him from the car and stood him up.

They raced to the door and disappeared inside. I slowly followed, allowing myself to breathe. When I got inside, Jack had already signed the form and they were transferring him to a center's wheelchair. I leaned over and said: "See you in a few weeks, Jack, stick with it." He didn't answer, just glared at everyone and was wheeled away.

We arrived back at the motel around noon. It had only been two hours but it felt like a lifetime had passed since we left there that morning. We gathered back in the conference room and everyone was subdued. The facilitator had a big smile on her face. "I want to congratulate everyone," she said. "You have pulled it off. To tell you the truth, we didn't think you would be able to do it. Jack is one of the toughest people we've tried to work with. He wouldn't even talk to our staff."

She pointed to Bill and me: "As for these two, we're going to ask them to come to every one of these we conduct from now on." Everyone started to clap.

"You won't get me back," I said. "I wouldn't be able to take but one of these in a lifetime."

We learned that Jack would be at the center for 12 weeks, undergoing a rigid program, and not to give up on him if he stumbled a time or two in the future. It was over.

Life returned to normal for me. There was a lot of work coming into the agency and I was struggling to find enough time to work on the lodge. When I did get to Leadore, I too often succumbed to the lure of the mountains, thinking: "A short horse trip won't hurt anything." The next thing I knew, I had to return to Idaho Falls and no work had been done on the building.

One day I saw Jack driving toward the house. I wasn't sure what his attitude might be. I remembered the hostility in his glare as he had been wheeled into the center months before.

He had evidently gotten over his anger as he greeted me as casually as he had in the past. I invited him in for coffee, saying: "That is if you can take it. I make coffee that picks a man up and then slams him down." He grinned and followed me inside.

I asked him about the treatment center and his face darkened: "It was a hell of a place," Jack said. "Those bastards had me sit in a chair and scream out about how I hated my mother."

"I've heard of that," I told him. "It's called primal therapy."

"Those sons-of-bitches wanted me on my knees to pray to God," Jack said. "Here I am, the biggest atheist in the country; can you imagine me on my knees?"

He went on in this vein for about 10 minutes and I interjected with: "Well, it looks like you got through it OK. You're still alive. Have you given up on booze?"

"Maybe," he replied.

I could see defiance in his eyes, so I changed the subject. I didn't think he needed an argument from me. I was to see later that I was right.

"They're expecting me back at the house," Jack said. "I'll talk to you later."

The next week I returned back to Leadore and had not been there but a few minutes when Jack drove in again. "I've got a little present for you," he said. Immediately my guard went up. A person like Jack does not use that kind of phrase unless he has something on his mind, such as,   "Here are a couple bullets" as he shoots you."

Jack must have seen my face cloud over because he grinned and pulled his hand from behind his back and handed me a bottle of vodka. As I took it, I could see the contents were down a couple inches.

"The first thing I did when they released me from that center was to go buy this bottle," Jack said. "I thought I needed it. I had a couple of drinks before you came up last time. I don't need it. I will never take another drink. You can use this bottle, I can't."

Later, I thought about all the things that could have been said in that moment, but down inside I knew nothing more needed to be said. I felt good about the part that I played.

As time went by, it was apparent that Jack meant what he said about never taking another drink. I saw less of him and when I did see him he talked of the things he and Gwen had been doing together. It was obvious his health was improving. I concluded that Jack had come to grips with whatever it was that had been eating on him when Jim and I had first met him.

He spent less time chasing around by himself in the mountains and more time socializing around town. It did not come as a surprise to me when one day he stopped by the place to visit with Marilyn and me and announced that Gwen had been promoted and they would be moving to Las Vegas.

As Jack was leaving, he turned back and said, "What about the saddle?" It came back to me that I had lent him that saddle to decorate his house. "The saddle is yours," I said. It was one of the best sudden decisions I ever made. Jack nodded and left.

The next day he pulled back into our driveway pulling a flat bed trailer loaded with building materials. "I can't take this with me and maybe you can use it," he said. We unloaded lumber, kegs of nails, spikes, electrical wire, paint and enough 12-inch inch knotty pine to completely panel the great room in the lodge. The things he dropped off were worth thousands of dollars.

"Jack I've got to pay you for this," I said. "How much will you take for it?" He refused to take anything. "I'm giving it to you," he said.

I knew better than to argue so I thanked him. "I'm not through," he said. "I'm also giving you my camp up on the mountain."

It wasn't really his camp, he just called it his. It was at the very top of one of the nearby mountains nestled in a grove of pines, actually on Forest Service ground. It consisted of an outhouse, picnic table and a fire circle lined with large stones. To get to it you needed a good four-wheel drive vehicle and a certain amount of guts. The last few hundred yards you had to encircle the mountain peak tipped sideways with a thousand foot drop on one side and then drop straight down onto a knife ridge that gradually widened and led you to the grove of pine.

Jack had discovered it years before and shared it with me. Later I was to call it mine and took great delight in taking family and friends on that spooky drive. Everyone was always glad to be there as it was a beautiful and serene place where it seemed you could see 100 miles of close and distant mountain ranges.

Jack and Gwen had moved on with their lives and like most people I found it hard to stay in touch. Jack called me from Vegas and gave me his new number. We talked a couple times a year. On one of those calls, Jack said he had decided to pass on to me his knowledge of a hidden gold mine where miners had left a couple of kegs of wire gold to be picked up later and never got back.

Wire gold is essentially strings of gold imbedded in quartz. It was supposed to have been mined back when gold was worth $32 an ounce. It was now near $400 and worth looking for. He said he thought he knew generally where it was and had planned to come back and continue his search. He realized that his days of poking around the mountains were over and was content to sit back and relax in Vegas. He gave me a detailed description of where he thought it might be. One of these days, when I get some time, I will take up the search.

Jack stuck by his word and cut liquor out of his life totally. I heard that not only from Jack but also Gwen. On one of their calls they said the Las Vegas City limits had extended out to their place and they had been offered an "ungodly" amount of money to sell and couldn't turn it down. They were getting a small place closer to town. It looked like life had taken a good turn for them.

I didn't hear from them for about six months. One day Gwen called to say that Jack had died from a heart attack near his 70th birthday. Even though time and distance had separated us, I found myself grieving over the news. Not a bad grief though. Jack got it together.

When I'm up in what is now my camp, I think about him and how far he came and how knowing Jack was also good for me.

Jack had served his country with exceptional bravery and loyalty; convinced by his commanders that he was on the front line of holding back the "tide of communism." Only years later had the doubts crept in and finally the realization that he had assassinated hapless men who were caught in circumstances beyond their control. The village leaders knew that the communists would behead their entire families if they didn't cooperate and Jack would kill them if they did. The human mules that carried backbreaking loads on the Ho Chi Min trail had little choice, either. They could be shot as traitors or take a better chance with Jack. After all, he only got a small percentage.

Damn, this thing we call life, and this place we spend it in, has so many lessons to teach us.

Seven

A WORLD IN NEED OF BEAUTY

The first time I met a Russian came when I was a young soldier, in the early 1950s. The "Cold War" was in full swing and people feared communism would take over the world.

The meeting was not what I expected. My Army unit was stationed in Germany. The Soviet forces instituted a three-mile security zone throughout Europe. They moved everyone living in that three-mile zone, including entire villages, away from their side of the border.

They began extensive patrols to prevent citizens on their side from escaping to the west. I was assigned to an armored reconnaissance battalion and for several months we patrolled our side of the border, and when possible we assisted citizens able to slip through their patrols.

In Army terms, our assignment was regarded as good duty and particularly so when we compared our conditions with those of our enemy. We conducted patrols with six men in two jeeps and, being mobile, we were able to return to our base where hot meals were served in our mess kits and shelter.

Like most armies, both ours and the Russians were comprised of mostly young men who ached for action. In addition, we were still young enough to believe what we were told: that the enemy was made up of very bad people who had a strong desire to wipe us out. I had no reason to doubt what I was being told. In those conditions, friendly contact should have been very unlikely. The officers in charge constantly warned us to be alert and avoid the inevitable firefights that would ensue if we spotted our counterparts on the other side.

And still, because we were young men who liked to think for ourselves, we paid little attention to the admonitions. I recall three separate occasions when we instituted contact and found the enemy was as curious about us as we were of them.

Once, our six-man team drove to the point where our road crossed into the Soviet zone and parked on the berm that had been bulldozed up to stop any vehicle traffic. Looking back, I think that in our boredom we may have been trying to start a little trouble. On the other side, we observed two Soviet soldiers sitting on a rock and looking at us. They showed no sign of hostility and one of our group waved for them to join us.

It took a couple waves and some wary looks but they walked over and greeted us in German. They couldn't speak English, we couldn't speak Russian and we conversed by speaking what broken German we could conjure between all of us. There was a lot of hand waving and frustrated groans in trying to get our ideas across.

We learned that they made five-day patrols on foot and were expected to cover considerable distance during that time. They carried all their provisions in a bag hung around their shoulders and slept in the great overcoats they wore even when it appeared to be much too warm to be wearing a coat at all. We concluded that it was easier to wear the coat than carry it as they were also required to carry their weapons in a position of readiness at all times. It appeared their food supply consisted of several loaves of a dark brown bread that was supposed to last the five days. They shared some of that bread with us and all six of us liked it.

In return, we gave them some of the emergency C rations we always had in our Jeeps. We traded cigarettes for their engraved buttons and insignias and when we parted they looked longingly at our Jeeps, but giving them a ride was not on our agenda.

The word must have spread among both sides that we didn't have to shoot at each other, so we all started carrying extra cigarettes and C Rations to trade when opportunities arrived.

Well, here it is nearly 45 years later. The Cold War is over, we have moved on with our lives and most of the things that happened to us in our youth are distant memories. I've been through a couple different careers and am now leading what I think is the good life, one that I could not have dreamed of in those old Army days. The detective agency allows me to do the things I like to do. No one makes decisions that affect my life but me. I spend much of my time in the beautiful Idaho outdoors and am always thinking: "It doesn't get any better than this."

My friends have also moved on with their lives. My former law enforcement partner, Jim Mason, left the

Idaho State Bureau of Investigation and went to work for Argonne National Laboratory at the atomic energy site near Idaho Falls: first as security director and then as Argonne's representative as a part of the US. Department of Energy's team to help the former Soviet Union countries catalog and secure the vast nuclear arsenal and material leftover from the Cold War.

Steve Chatterton left the state bureau to become the head of security for Idaho State University in Pocatello and the three of us have maintained our friendships since those challenging days as state criminal investigators. We see each other often and share stories of our new lives. I had been especially intrigued with Jim's descriptions of his travels and experiences throughout Russia and his interactions with our former enemies.

One summer day, Jim stopped by and said he had a proposition for me. He was bringing eight Russians to Idaho for two weeks of classes on nuclear security. He was responsible for their care and comfort while they were guests in our country. Jim said they had treated him very well while he was in Russia and he wanted to see that they had as good a time as he had.

He planned to house them in one of the nice motels on the banks of the Snake River, where they would have access to the greenbelt, water falls and good restaurants. Jim told me their days would be full with classes and activities and that his problem was going to be weekends.

He said they knew nothing of the United States except what they had seen in old movies. They were delighted to visit the American West, though he suspected they thought of it as the pile of rocks Gene Autry and Roy Rogers used to chase the bandits around.

The first weekend, Jim planned to take them to Jackson Hole, to show them the "New West." They could be like American tourists and wander through the art galleries, watch the mock stagecoach holdup in the town square, see the ski lodges, golf courses and magnificent homes and view the wonderful mountain scenery.

The second weekend was where I would come in. Jim wanted to show them the "Old West." Steve Chatterton was to hike them up to one of the high mountain lakes in the Lemhi Mountain Range, where they could fish and spend time in a place unknown to most people. In the meantime Jim, Marilyn and I would prepare a western dinner for a party that evening. Prior to the dinner we would show them around the Leadore area.

I agreed that if you wanted the "Old West," Leadore was the place. There is nothing but cattle ranches. When you visit either of the two cafes, The Silver Dollar Saloon and Café or the Sagebrush Restaurant and Bar, you may see cowboys wearing spurs and chaps, and not for show but because they took a few minutes off from the job to grab a cup of coffee or a beer.

The cowboy who looked after our place had a side business of breaking horses. We had constructed a standard round corral for that purpose and visitors could watch him breaking and training horses and sometimes being bucked off. It was like being at the rodeo.

Jim said interpreters would accompany the Russians because they spoke no English. The group consisted of ex-KGB agents and a couple Army colonels. When he mentioned KGB agents, my first thought was that they were thugs or brutes. But then I realized that I'd been conditioned to think that way by Cold War propaganda.

The weekend arrived and Marilyn and I drove up to the ranch. Steve had taken off with the group for the hike and Jim was setting up to cook. We barbecued elk steaks, baked Idaho potatoes and boiled fresh sweet corn. I saddled a couple gentle horses for the guests to ride. We were set for their return.

In the late afternoon, they drove in and we got our first look at them. They looked just like the people who live down the street from us. I don't know why I expected them to look different. Maybe I had been conditioned more than I thought. They were looking up at Marilyn on her horse and seemed to approve. Marilyn is a good-looking lady and she really looks good on a horse. Jim told me later that they had never seen a lady on a horse before; in fact, they had seen very few horses at all.

As we were being introduced, there was a lot of smiling and laughing as everyone stumbled over words. It was obvious they wanted to tell us about their day and how much fun they had and the two interpreters couldn't keep up. Steve said they were like kids exploring, pointing the sights out to each other and enjoying the beauty of the lake and mountains.

They had been especially delighted to discover mushrooms in the woods. They gathered up a backpack full of various kinds of mushrooms and asked that we cook them for the coming meal. "If we had this many mushrooms in Russia we would all be rich men," one said.

I had once become interested in wild mushrooms and learned enough about them to know that for every type that was good, there was another that looked just like it that was poison; some so poisonous that you hardly had

192

time to say goodbye. I had become extremely cautious and told our guests I did not plan to eat any of their mushrooms. The Russians, however, assured us that they knew mushrooms and insisted these were all good. We cooked them and served them with the meal. The Russians ate them with gusto and nobody keeled over. Later Jim told me he was worried about having to explain how all the Russians ended up dead.

We have a large dining room table I made out of old bridge timbers. Sanded down and varnished, it looked very western. Best of all, it can seat almost 20 people. We all sat together and enjoyed one of the most memorable meals I've ever attended. These people were cultured with good manners. They laughed and expressed delight at the food. There was friendly repartee between them and us as the interpreters struggled to keep up and eat. We would all laugh when the exchange didn't come off quite right. I had the feeling that even though these people lived on the opposite side of the world, I had known them for years. Too soon the meal was finished.

Jim brought out the customary bottle of Vodka and glasses for everyone. He had warned us that toasts could run a little long, but had not told us of their eloquence. Jim began with a simple toast to the day and the events and thanked us for our participation. We all took a sip in response. Then the Russians took turns, each with a different theme. They toasted America and all the wonderful people they had met; they toasted peace and cooperation between our countries; they toasted the brotherhood of man and the future of all peoples of the world; they toasted their countries within the Russian Republic and promised to live in peace and pursue justice.

Each time, we would take a small sip out of our glass and I was glad Jim had warned us not to drink deeply. They toasted us individually. There was warmth in the room and finally the interpreters ran out of steam declaring they needed to rest their voices.

I ended up out on the deck with three guests and one interpreter. They were full of questions about everything, but mostly wanted me to tell them about myself. I told them about being in the Army and assigned to the East German border; of being told we needed to be constantly ready for the Russian Army to invade the American sector at any moment; about meeting Russian soldiers and exchanging cigarettes for bread.

Our guests said they had been told we were preparing to attack. At the common soldier level, none of us wanted war and were able to get along. Those who don't have to do the fighting are always the ones who look to war as a solution. The three said that though they were military men, they never had a quarrel with the United States and didn't want war. They didn't think any of their countrymen did either and were baffled by how close the United States and Russia had come to annihilating each other.

It was a great evening with the interpreter and I trying to explain how things worked in our society. It was probably good for me to explain how in the American system you could start out with nothing and build yourself a good life doing whatever you wanted to do. I sometimes forget to appreciate that. They had not had that experience and it was obvious they hungered for it.

Later Jim told me how suspicious they were about how things worked in America. When he first picked them up at the airport, Jim had stopped with them at the local Albertsons to pick up a few things they would need. They gathered by the meat counter, looking it over and talking in low tones. When he left them at the motel, they asked him through the interpreter: "Where can we go?"

"You can go anywhere you like," Jim replied. They seemed surprised at his answer. In their country, a secret police guide would have been required to accompany and direct them everywhere. I think they learned more about the free enterprise system by experiencing it than what was taught at the school they had came to attend.

I could have never met another person from Russia and it would not have mattered. I now viewed them in a favorable light. But maybe there is a special destiny that directs people to each other. As happened so many times, I was sitting in my office shooting the bull with one of my investigators, Jay Gentle, when the phone interrupted us.

The man voice on the other end had what I suspected to be a Russian accent. The caller said a couple of his neighbors were threatening to kill him over a property dispute. I advised him to call the local sheriff and report the threats because we did not involve ourselves in these kinds of matters. The caller said he had already done that and the sheriff's deputy had laughed and said he couldn't do anything. He thought the deputy and neighbors were friends.

I was anxious to get out of the office and the caller had pushed one of my buttons. I find it difficult to abide policemen who can't or won't do their jobs. When a person's life is being threatened, he is entitled to more than being laughed at. I got directions to his place and said I would come out and take a look.

Jay said he'd "come along with me for the ride." We had been friends for many years. I had suspected he would make an ideal detective, though he had no background in the field. I was not wrong. Jay started solving cases the day he began and never slowed down. He made the company money and with his sense of humor created the kind of working atmosphere that made it a pleasure for the rest of us to spend time with him.

He was a good-looking man, about 6-feet-tall, slim and carried himself well. He was in his early 50s and I suppose because he had been a salesman for large corporations most of his life, he had an easy-going and positive air about him that people responded to. Jay could get information out of people when the rest of us could not. I was always happy when he accompanied me anywhere.

We found the caller's house and discovered an area of small farms and wooded areas with an occasional house or trailer home set back in the woods. While it was a pleasant area, it could not have been considered an upscale housing site. The gate and the high wooden fence were elegant for the area and stood out like a sore thumb. It looked like there was about a 25-acre plot of heavily wooded property crisscrossed with a couple large canals behind the gate.

As we passed through the gate, Jay and I found ourselves on a drive lined with fruit trees that circled back through the cottonwoods to a large log house in the rear of the property. The house was also out of sync with the neighborhood in that it was a large two-story structure with gables on the roof and what appeared to be tower glistening in the sunlight.

We parked in the drive circle at the end of the lane and the owner appeared at our car to welcome us. This act also was out of sync with the general practice of people living in these parts. As a general rule, a visitor was required to go knock on a door or search out whoever he was looking for. We introduced ourselves and learned that the caller's name was Aleksei Khristolyubov, a Russian artist who had escaped from behind the Iron Curtain and made his way to America.

He showed us to the house where we declined the offer of refreshments as graciously as we could. He introduced us to his wife and three children. Later, when we were alone, Jay said it appeared this man's wife had been a little more interested in us than would have been expected under the circumstances, flashing her eyes in a coquettish manner and gripping our hands and arms slightly longer than necessary. As we both see ourselves as men women are attracted to, whether true or not, we were able to shrug it off as having no particular significance.

I asked Aleksei to show us where his problem was. We crossed one of the canals on a small foot bridge, passed through some woods and entered a pasture that ran the length of his place. The outer fence was brand new. On the opposite side of the fence sat a couple trailer homes in the woods and a house - all having access to the road beyond. Aleksei pointed at one of the trailer homes and said that was where the threats had come from. I looked toward the house and saw two people in the yard watching us.

I recognized one as a man named Chester and recalled that in my days as a police detective I had arrested him a couple of times on bad check charges. I started toward them and when he saw me coming, Chester and the other fellow quickly disappeared around the house. I heard a car start and watched them drive out of the driveway.

I figured that he recognized me and probably was still up to his old tricks. He would likely spread the word among his neighbors that we were there.

Aleksei appeared totally unaware that he, as a foreigner, and particularly one who came from a country that had until recently been an enemy of America, might not be welcome in the neighborhood. I had been around long enough to know that wherever a person might go, they would find pockets of old-time residents who were clannish and narrow-minded. Based on Chester's presence, my guess was that Aleksei had inadvertently stumbled into one of those pockets.

I asked him how he came to be in Idaho. It turned out that he and his brother had studied art with an artist who had established a school in Idaho. Both had been so taken with the natural beauty of the surrounding area that they elected to come back and establish their own studios where they could paint in privacy. This particular piece of land was for sale at a good price and fit his needs.

I was familiar with this artist and had met him years before during a state investigation, where I was searching out cult activities relating to animal sacrifices that had become a phenomenon throughout the western states. I had discovered that he was an extremely popular artist of national stature. In fact, I had pictures of him with some of his patrons, including actors such as James Cagney and Ralph Bellamy. He was based in Los Angeles and during the summer conducted the artist school in Idaho. I had found no evidence that he was involved in any kind of cult activity and noted that he professed a belief system that seemed to be mostly agnostic with no religious convictions. I concluded that his neighbors had turned him in as a cultist because he did not fit into the extreme religious community that dominated the area. Local police said someone had seen him painting a picture of Christ being crucified upside down as evidence that he had to be a Satan worshiper.

The report didn't check out. I had learned long before that most people are very suspicious of anyone that does not fit their standard concepts and patterns of living. Someone different is always suspect.

As we were walking back to the house, Jay laughed and said, "That guy recognized you, didn't he?" I speculated that there would be no more threats and told Aleksei to call if he had any more problems. He politely shook our hands and we left. I viewed the incident as a pleasant outing while thinking it was nice to meet someone with good manners.

In any event, I was not surprised when I received a call several months later from Aleksei. He wanted to talk about a personal matter and asked if I could come to his place. When I arrived the next day, I was met with the same courtesy I had witnessed on my previous trip. We entered his studio, took opposing seats on a sofa ensemble and sipped fruit drinks.

I could not help looking around. One of my hobbies is oil painting and I have been around other artists and their studios, but I had never seen anything on such a grand scale. His studio had a vaulted ceiling with large skylights situated so sunshine shone down into the room in shafts of light toward a very large easel with a painting he was working on. In the shaft of sunlight, the brilliant colors shimmered and drew my eyes back to it each time I looked away. In the middle of the studio sat a stout table loaded with jars of paint brushes of every conceivable size and type.

It was difficult for me to focus. I wasn't there to look at paintings, so I opened the conversation by asking him to tell me about himself and whatever problems he was having. As was my habit, I asked him to start at the beginning.

We began with his early life in Russia. His father was the principal artist for the Bolshevik Opera Theater in Moscow and painted the backdrops for the productions they staged throughout the years. Because his father was good at what he did, he was held in high esteem by Communist Party officials. Aleksei said his family enjoyed a better lifestyle than most Russians because of that association. His father passed on his skill to Aleksei and his brother and life in their home was pleasant. He was surrounded by educated people, classical music, good books and a cultured lifestyle.

In spite of his father's connections, Aleksei was required to do a mandatory enlistment in the Russian Army. The Cold War was the focus of his country and Aleksei said the Russian people were being told America was getting prepared to attack and each citizen had a duty to defend the homeland. Aleksei said the two years he spent in the Russian Army were the most miserable time of his life and that soldiers were treated like dogs. Living conditions in the field were harsh and the food was terrible. Much of his time was spent freezing in the bitter cold and being constantly hungry.

He said a soldier's pay was inadequate, so they were unable to purchase extra clothes, food or medicines. He recalled his unit being required to cross a river during flood stage and some of his close friends drowning. The soldiers knew that crossing under those conditions was unreasonable, but the Russian military demanded absolute obedience.

I thought back on my own experience on the opposite side when one of my friends was crushed to death between two tanks our company was loading on railroad flatcars in Austria during maneuvers designed to make us tougher. That soldier's scream rang in my ears for a long time. I thought about the Russian soldiers we met and how they must have perceived us with our abundance of vehicles and equipment and casual attitudes about cigarettes and C-rations. Maybe those contacts had been the beginning of our message being spread throughout the Communist countries that things are better in a free country.

Aleksei said he and his family concluded that life was not good under a dictatorship. He and his brother made their escape through Bulgaria to Greece and, after some difficulties, ended up in Hollywood.

It was interesting to draw Aleksei out about this portion of his life. It was as different as possible from his previous existence. His abilities as an artist quickly lifted him to new opportunities and he was offered employment as a backdrop painter for various movie and television producers.

He told of being required to join a union and finding himself in trouble. He was working too fast and doing too much - creating a standard the other union members could not meet.

Aleksei was living a kind of fast lifestyle in Hollywood and was not prepared for it. A rising artist is required to attend a lot of social activities and make promotional appearances and move in social circles with people he does not always relate to or understand. His parents taught him that the only alcohol a person should consume is a very moderate amount of good wine - that any kind of narcotic is unhealthy and therefore taboo and that a person should eat only healthy foods. Life in Hollywood was not generally in compliance with his lifestyle.

One night, Aleksei attended a party, met a girl, fell in love and, after a quick courtship, married her. He had by then established himself as an artist and needed to get away from the hectic Hollywood life so he could devote himself totally to painting. He and his new bride moved to New Mexico and rented an apartment and studio. He spent almost all his time painting in the studio and she managed the household and what little social life they had. He turned what money he was making over to her. Things rolled along pretty well and he was putting out a lot of work when one day he was served with eviction notices for his apartment and studio.

His wife, Aleksei said, had been leading a double life. Most of the money had been used to buy cocaine, marijuana and expensive booze. During the many hours he was occupied in the studio, she had been partying and neglected to pay the bills. In addition, they had a baby and within a couple of months after its birth it died. Aleksei blamed his wife's lifestyle for the child's death and he divorced her soon after the burial and moved to Idaho.

Eventually, she showed up and moved back in with him. I interrupted him. "Explain to me just how that happened after what you had been through," I said.

He shook his head. "She just moved in," he said. "She said she had changed, that everything was going to be all right now."

For a while it was. They had three children. As they grew, however, their mother reverted back to her old habits. They had several confrontations over her behavior. Aleksei told her not to smoke in the house, stop feeding the children junk food, to cut down her drinking and that the children needed exposure to good music as opposed to some of the modern rock music with filthy lyrics she favored. He wanted her to clean up her language in front of the children, promote education and values and to be preparing them for a good future and to be ready to enter good colleges when they became of age.

His wife, Aleksei said, struggled to accept her role as a parent and was letting herself go with drugs and booze. She started hanging out at a seedy beer bar and neglecting the children. They argued often and the situation grew steadily worse. It finally ended with her telling the State Department of Health and Welfare that she was abused and that Aleksei was a threat to her and the children. They bought her story and furnished her with housing and welfare payments. They issued a restraining order against Aleksei to prevent him from seeing his children.

"I need your help," he said.

My first question: "Did you hit her during one of your arguments?"

"Of course not," he answered softly.

During my years as a young policeman, I worked on what seemed like thousands of cases of spousal abuse.

Like all policemen, I learned to be wary of accusations. I had never been answered quite that way when I asked the same question so many times before. "Of course not," he had said, with a disapproving and hurt look. He seemed to be as gentle a man as I had met in a long time. I also knew that passions can be enflamed when family situations are falling apart. There must have been some reason Health and Welfare officials thought he was dangerous.

My second question: "What did you tell the state child protection representatives that make them see you as a threat to your wife and children?"

He looked baffled. "I didn't say anything," he said. "No one has ever been to see me. No one has ever asked to talk to me. No one has ever been to investigate me."

Aleksei told me he had hired an attorney, Robin Dunn from Rigby. I knew Robin to be a good lawyer. He was the Jefferson County prosecutor and also had a private practice.

Dunn had helped convince a judge to allow Aleksei to see the children every other weekend. His wife was supposed to meet him with them every other Saturday at 10 a.m. at a grocery store parking lot. Sometimes she wouldn't show up and other times he had to wait a few hours. Some of Aleksei's friends told him she was drinking and partying heavily and neglecting the children.

He complained to Health and Welfare Department and they ignored him. Dunn told Aleksei he needed to get some independent evidence that this was happening so they could get him custody of the girls.

I thought back over my career and of how many times I had found myself at odds with the Child

Protective Division of the state Health and Welfare Department. My contemporaries from other states had the same problems. We had come to view many of these people as a part of the problem as opposed to being part of the solution. They too often hire people who lack experience and knowledge. Even worse, they sometimes hire people who bring a personal bias to the job.

Aleksei again asked if I would be able to help him. I told him I had good people and could almost guarantee we would get what he needed. I told him that he would not have to pay me, but that if he hired people who worked with me he would need to pick up their fees. I was willing to help him without charge, but I couldn't ask the staff to do the same. My agency would be taking a loss on this case.

I have had a lot of fortunate things happen in my life. One was meeting a woman named Teresa Stilson. We got to know one another when I was running my art gallery. Teresa is an expert welder who created art works from metal. I had set up a small shop in the basement of the gallery where she and a friend kept their welders and torches and created works for me to sell in the gallery.

In addition to being an intelligent and good-looking woman, Teresa had a broad range of interests and she often participated in the bull sessions that always seemed to materialize when friends and fellow investigators stopped by. She had a varied background, mostly in sales, and had developed an easy ability to communicate and read people.

One afternoon, Jay Gentle had stopped by to discuss a case he was working. He was having difficulty getting a man to give him information he needed. Teresa heard us discussing how we should approach the man. She interrupted us. "Why don't you just let me call him," she said. "I'll bet I can get your information in just a few minutes." Jay and I looked at each other and he said: "Why not, he won't talk to a man."

I handed Teresa the phone, Jay told her what he needed and we sat back and watched, confident that no inexperienced woman was going to obtain what we skilled, polished and experienced males could not. Her voice took on a honeyed, flirtatious tone as she chatted with Jay's nemesis and within minutes she had the names and addresses he had been looking for. That man had given her the information without ever asking her name or who she represented.

From that moment, I was a believer. I asked her to consider working with our group and within a few weeks she was on board. It was one of the smartest things I did. The next several years she successfully worked hundreds of cases while attending school part time until she completed her degree in psychology.

We eventually reached a point where I was ready to move on and asked her to take the company over. After a couple years managing the agency, she elected to go into social work and make better use of her education. I regretted losing her from the agency but we remained close friends throughout the years.

It was Teresa I went to with the Aleksei case. I knew that she had to feel she was on the side "that was in the right" before she accepted a case. That was one of the reasons I admired her. I took her to meet Aleksei and watched as she questioned him and sized him up. When we left, she said: "He's got his problems, but he's OK with me." She took the case.

A few weeks later she had verified and documented what I considered to be horrific behavior on his wife's part in caring for the three children. She was living in a fairly large apartment complex and her neighbors were willing witnesses to her behavior. Teresa learned that she appeared drunk much of the time and partied until late in the night with a variety of what the neighbors described as undesirables. It was winter and the neighbors observed the children unsupervised outside in the snow without shoes or enough clothing and complaining of not having been fed.

Teresa was able to video many of the violations and obtained written statements from the witnesses. Complaints to the Health and Welfare Department were not answered or ignored and none were investigated.

Teresa and I took this information to Robin Dunn at a time Aleksei was in custody of the girls. He advised Aleksei that he should not return the children to his wife's custody, pending a return to the court to reverse the previous order. He filed a motion for a hearing, citing new information that constituted an emergency situation.

While that action was pending, Aleksei's wife complained to her friends at Health and Welfare that had been championing her case and reported that Aleksei was refusing to return the children to her. The case officer immediately went to the local prosecutor and asked him to provide an order to have the children picked up by the police on the grounds that they were in great danger. She took the order to a local magistrate, who knew nothing about the situation and he signed it based solely on the case officer's testimony.

While Teresa's investigation was going on, Aleksei contacted me almost every day to find out what was happening. We started going out to lunch together and I enjoyed his company immensely. He taught me about art and I found myself astounded that he not only could name all the great masters and tell of intimate details of their lives but also that he knew all of their paintings and where they were now.

His eyes would light up as he spoke of various paintings and sculptures while describing what those artists were trying to portray with light and color and the techniques they had developed. He became animated and very alive as he spoke. When he found out I liked to paint, he gave me a paint box and invited me to paint with him. I was totally unaware of the value of his offer. In fact, I never got around to doing it.

I later observed painters from around the world showing up at his place to spend a few days with him in his studio. I also heard more than one local painter say that "They would kill for a chance to study with him."

No one likes to see families break up. In this case, though, it looked like some good would come of it. The children were back with their father. It was a good home in every sense of the word. Aleksei had been befriended by a local couple, Paul and Elna Johnson. Paul had contracted to do some of the construction work on Aleksei's place and they became friends.

Elna was a wise woman who had raised a family and volunteered to take on the job of mothering Aleksei and the children. I took an immediate liking to her. She was a striking woman with a warm and open personality who advised Aleksei on how to provide a stable and organized home for the children. Aleksei hired a live-in nanny who soon became a part of the family. Aleksei now had the freedom to paint in his studio throughout the day and night.

The children started school, were served healthy meals on a regular schedule and received tutoring from their nanny. The household became a special place that I liked to visit when I passed through the area on business. The children would greet me with squeals of laughter and show me projects they were working on or beg me to go with them on a tour of the woods, showing me where the fox had his den or which hole they thought a skunk lived in.

Teresa sometimes accompanied me on these visits and after working through her natural skepticism of men, she concluded that the children were in the best of all worlds. They had a wonderful living situation and a promising future ahead.

She and Aleksei became good friends. Sometimes, Teresa and I concluded, detectives can make a difference.

It was touching to watch the interplay of affection and love between the children and their father. I watched Aleksei try to give strict orders to the kids, that it was time to go to bed, and they were all over him, romping and laughing while he tried to keep a straight face as he gave the order four or five times. Elna would step in and take charge. They loved her but knew she meant business.

No seasoned detective would ever describe any situation as being "a fairy tale come true," but this was the closest thing I had seen. It was not to last. There is an ogre in most fairy tales and in this case it had several heads: the Department of Health and Welfare, the county legal community and the local sheriff's department. That's not to say there wasn't an occasional shining knight who showed up, but they were rare.

It began with Aleksei's ex turning to her family in California for financial help. They hired an Idaho Falls Attorney, Bill Barnes, in an attempt to recover custody of the three children. I couldn't fault her parents, who wanted their grandchildren in their lives. Teresa and I knew Aleksei was sympathetic toward their position but no one ever approached him to ask him if some sort of visiting arrangement could be worked out.

In any event, I knew we were in for a fight. All logic and reason was on our side, but Bill Barnes, who was a longtime friend of mine, is an excellent attorney. I knew that no matter who he represents, Bill pulls out all the stops. We could only wait.

Bill arranged for a psychiatrist to conduct a mental evaluation on his client. He also asked Aleksei to submit to an evaluation. Aleksei readily agreed as he perceived himself a stable, rational and decent person and thought an evaluation could only help. We perceived this particular psychiatrist to be a kind of "hired gun" expert who was often used to bolster the cause of any client that hired him.

We were wrong! To give the psychiatrist credit, his evaluation of Aleksei's ex was a disaster for her chances of regaining custody of the children. He described in detail all of her issues and recommend she not be given custody of the children. In the same report, he wrote that Aleksei would not be a good father, because he was from a different culture and too rigid in his beliefs of how to raise children; his strictness would be harmful to the children.

Armed with the baseless opinion that Europeans are too strict with their children, the Health and Welfare employee assigned to this case convinced the local county prosecutor to draft an order placing the children in foster care, pending a hearing. She took the order to magistrate judge for his signature. It was forwarded to the local sheriff's office for service.

Having been a police detective for so many years, I have firsthand knowledge of how our justice system works. Once it gets cranked up, it can roll over people with a force out of proportion to reason and good judgment. This was to be one of those cases.

I was at my home in Idaho Falls one Saturday afternoon and answered the phone to hear a terror-stricken female voice telling me I needed to help the nanny Aleksei had hired to take care of his children. Between sobs she said: "The police are here, there are seven or eight cars, they've got the house surrounded, they've all got guns."

"Why are they there," I asked. "What do they want?"

"They want to take the children," she replied. "They're demanding that we open the doors; they're threatening to shoot us.

"Where are the children now," I asked.

"They're upstairs hiding under their beds crying."

"Where is Aleksei?"

"He's in the studio. He won't come open the door."

"Does he have any guns?"

There was fear in her voice. "I think he's got a shotgun."

I gave a small groan and heard her gasp. "Don't worry," I said. "I think he's got a cool head. Sit tight and I will get some help out to you."

I quickly dialed the sheriff's office, thinking there might be a chance to scale back or defuse what the nanny was describing as a major assault, shock and awe raid. In my day as a young cop, it took two people, one man and one woman, to pick up children on court orders. I had done it by myself on a couple occasions. Thoughts were flashing through my head: These are U.S. citizens. They're gentle, well-mannered people that have never been a threat to anyone. What has gone wrong with police in America?

The sheriff's dispatcher told me there were no command officers around and she didn't have any authority to interfere with an ongoing raid. I didn't waste my time and quickly dialed the judge with jurisdiction over this case. He was a longtime friend whom I admired. As I filled him in, he told me he had signed the pickup order and had been told the children were in danger. I called Robin Dunn, who was much closer to the scene that I was.

Within moments Robin was there. By the time I was able to join him, it was over and he gave me the details. I already admired this man, but after his description, his approval rating with me jumped to the very top of the scale.

He said the standoff was still on when he arrived and deputies, while hostile, had not gone into the building. The nanny had done a good job. Robin took charge, having the police wait while he and the nanny comforted the children and brought them to their father, who was disturbed but was not threatening in any way. Robin explained to them that the court order required the girls be taken into custody and delivered to the home of volunteer foster parents. He assured Aleksei that they were not to be handed over to his ex and that we would be back in court to set things straight again.

One of the few shining knights in our story was a young deputy who stepped forward to volunteer to have the three children ride in his vehicle together along with the nanny to comfort them and allay their fears. He did this without first checking with the command officer.

Time was taken to pack some clothes and dolls and he drove away with the little children, followed by the long line of police cars. I started to remember why I had become discouraged with my police career and had been ready to move on. My thoughts took me back through my classes on Sociology and Human Behavior.

People have never mixed well. From almost the very beginning, people who are alike gravitate together. Anybody different immediately comes under suspicion. Suspicion quickly grows into fear and then hate. Those people are somehow a threat to us. And so fear grows and grows.

I watched the police world change. After teaching my courses, I stayed over at the Police Academy to hear younger instructors give their classes. They were telling rookies how much danger they were going to be facing, about all those people out there who where against them. And police seeing themselves as being from another world, only talking to each other and buying into their own bull until it takes the whole swat team to go out and pick up three small helpless children. And police all over

America are killing people at any slight provocation. I was reminded again that fear makes a poor master.

It was time to go back to court and get those children back to their father. We were ready. Would the Child Protection Division of the Health and Welfare Department be as ready as we were? Our nemesis, the case worker, had conned the judge into thinking there was a possibility the children were in danger. I didn't fault him. In a perfect world, he could count on her to be educated and competent. In the real world ... not so much.

The court date was set. Our case had been assigned to a good judge and we had an excellent attorney. Aleksei, not knowing the system, was worried. I did my best to set him at ease, but knew how much of his life was riding on what we were about to do. An artist does not need the kind of turmoil he was about to be put through. This good and gentle man was about to be tested in a way most of us could not fathom. I assured him that we had the advantage. Half a lifetime in and out of courtrooms giving testimony teaches one something.

I knew that our best witness was going to be their only witness - our nemesis at Health and Welfare. The hearing began. It was the nemesis's job to present the complete state case alone. She had the psychiatrist's report and her own opinion. This was a woman who, we had been told, made a statement to her co-workers that she had her children taken away from her once and if it was in her power she was going to see that it never happens to another woman.

As we were to observe, it is possible to be hired as a caseworker based on educational background with no calculation of competence or ability. She exuded an air of arrogance, seemingly ignoring the fact that a competent attorney was about to challenge her assumptions. The state attorney tried to save her, to get something of substance out of her, but she was having none of it. It was Robin's turn for our defense.

There were so many questions available to challenge her premise that Aleksei was too strict. What exactly does that mean? Is it insisting the children be fed wholesome prepared food? Is it limiting trash television, exposing them to classical music and fine art early in life? Is it wrong for him to want his children to grow up to be knowledgeable and sophisticated? I had the impression that this was not a very sophisticated woman. She tried to parse her answers, weakening them into irrelevance and all the while bristling with resentment that her opinion alone was not carrying the day. Could she be so blind as to not see what she was doing to herself and her case? And, of course, we all should know by now how blind anyone who has staked out a position on anything can be, especially in a strict, religious community.

The Mormon religion is based on women being mothers. They are denied not only the main leadership roles in the church but also the family. The father is supposed to be the leader in the family. The mother position is held in reverence. They can't do wrong, can they? The man must be to blame. And so in this tight-knit point of view, the local justice system propagates the continued abuse of these children. We have a long way to go.

But for now we were carrying the day. Robin did his usual good job and the state attorney could not resurrect the nemesis' credibility. Robin called me to the stand. My job was to put a human face to Aleksei for the court. To show he is not some foreigner who set down in their midst to corrupt their children, but that he is their neighbor and a good man. I was uniquely able to do that. Robin took me back through my background as a lawman working throughout the state and as someone who has built a reputation and been accepted as one of them long before Aleksei arrived in Idaho.

Robin gave me a free hand. I spoke of how I met Aleksei, was impressed, and that we became friends. I talked about the time he and I spent together, meeting often for lunch and discussing everything under the sun, of the frequent visits to his home and watching his children grow up. I also spoke of how he had asked for my help when his wife left him with the children and how I learned of her behavior through the efforts of my staff.

I've been told I'm a natural story teller and I've given a lot of testimony in courts over the years. As I spoke and watched those in the room, I knew I was connecting. Robin picked the right time, thanked me for the statements and turned me over to the family attorney, Bill Barnes, to be cross-examined. As I have already said, Bill is a very good attorney and his job was to try and find a way to discredit me. This kind of exchange is usually where the real courtroom drama begins. It could be called a duel and wits and abilities are the weapons.

He made a good beginning that might have worked in a normal case, but this was anything but that. With a kind of contemptuous sneer, he stood before me, rolled his eyes and loudly said: "Mr. Watts, how much money have you been paid to investigate this case and give this testimony here today?"

I put on my most offended look and with a trace of a smile said: "No money at all. What I have done for this family was without compensation, except to be a part of an injustice set straight."

"You mean you work for nothing," he said, rolling his eyes.

"With another slight smile, I replied: "Sometimes I do." Bill rolled with the punch and changed his approach. Even though we knew each other well, he did not know of my interest in art. He has known me as a lawman and lawmen do not normally talk about these things. So he again rolled his eyes and with a slight sneer said,: "Mr. Watts, when you say you go to these lunches with Mr. Khristolyubov here, pointing to him at the defense table, "What do you talk about?"

I was waiting for him and replied: "Much of the time we talk about art. I am an amateur painter. You may have been aware that the gallery, Western Art Creations, located on Park Avenue in Idaho Falls, in the same building as my detective agency, was a side business of mine for a few years. Really good art fascinates me. But we don't just talk about art. We talk of politics and world problems and religion. And sometimes we even talk about women." That little remark elicited a laugh from at least all of those within my sight in the courtroom. I knew I was connecting.

Bill knew it, too. There was no place for him to go and he was wise enough to cut his losses. After a few more desultory questions, he looked around with a feigned look of satisfaction and announced: "No more questions for this witness your honor." The hearing came to a close with the judge announcing he would be taking the case under advisement and would have a decision within a few days.

Robin and I both knew we had won and that Aleksei would be regaining custody. I joined Aleksei at the table to cheer him up. I could tell he had not liked the judge taking the case under advisement. We walked out of the courthouse out onto the big front steps. I realized while I had been comfortable in that courtroom, even maybe having a little fun, it had been a terrible time for Aleksei. So much of his life was riding on the outcome. He turned to me with a very sad look and said: "I guess we lived through Stalin. I guess we can live through this, too." I had a hard time answering and for a moment I was ashamed of America.

It didn't help when Bill came up behind me and poked me in the ribs joking with me, as we often did, about how we performed that day. We parted with smiles. Aleksei turned to me and said: "How can you even talk to him?" I could only say: "He's a good man and a good lawyer. He's doing his job. He believes everyone should get equal treatment in a courtroom and he was giving the other side his best. Sometime we may want to talk him in to defending us." I knew that didn't fly with Aleksei.

The children were returned to their home and reunited with their father. They had been gone a long time. Our court machinery runs on slow. They had been exposed to other lifestyles with foster parents. It was time for healing. They returned to local schools, which reflected the area community standards and the home environment where Aleksei's high standards prevailed. In the back of my mind I saw another duel coming up and at the same time my optimism landed on Aleksei s side.

My optimism may have gotten the better of me. Things don't change that fast. There was another police raid. This time it was even screwier. It was a sunny summer afternoon and Aleksei and the children were alone. Aleksei was gardening and the two oldest kids were swimming in the canal. Aleksei needed to go into town to buy groceries and didn't feel he could leave the youngest child, so she went with him.

He returned to find six police cars at his home. They had called a locksmith to get into a locked closet and had already searched his big house and studio. They showed him a warrant and told him they had been investigating his case for a long time and were looking for contraband. We never did figure out what the contraband was supposed to be, but it was evident somebody had told them something was there. I have reached a point where nothing can surprise me. Aleksei had a small safe in the closet and they asked him to open it. He declined, saying he had personal papers in. He said it surprised him that they didn't seem to know what to do next. He kind of laughed as he told me of the raid. At the end, three deputies approached him with tears in their eyes and apologized to him and said that they had never seen such a clean and nice home.

Around this time, our nemesis approached Aleksei and asked him if he would sign up for anger management classes. He declined and her pleading did not reach him. We saw it as an attempt to save her job. On another occasion, a man and woman showed up at the house representing Health and Welfare. They had been told Aleksei was not feeding his children. He immediately took them downstairs to his storage pantry, which he kept well-stocked with a large variety of wholesome foods. I had seen that pantry and been impressed. He said he could not help but be a little bit rude to them.

There was to be another time when a long line of deputies' cars with blue lights flashing came down that lane. He said it was probably the one time he became angry. He discovered that the two older children were mistreating the younger one. Without going into details he perceived it to be unjust and was not going to allow it to continue. He and the children stayed up through most of the night discussing that and other issues. As dawn came, he announced that because of the lack of sleep for everyone that the children were to stay home that day and not go to school.

He told me he had trouble sleeping, especially when he was upset over things and kept over-the-counter sleeping pills for those occasions. In this case, he took a couple of them and set about making sure everyone got to bed. He noted that one child seemed reluctant to go to their room and was acting strangely. When this child did get in bed, he went to sleep.

He was to surmise later that the two older children had, behind his back, made an arrangement with a neighbor to have Health and Welfare called if he showed any anger. Aleksei later described the next morning to me. He hadn't slept long when he heard noises outside the house. He said he was in a sleep fog, but went to the window and saw the long line of police cars, blue lights on, going out his driveway. When he checked on the children, they were all gone. He felt devastated.

Word had somehow gotten back to him that the children were up waiting for whoever was supposed to come and pick them up. The youngest broke away and ran to the nearby canal, raced across a narrow and dangerous foot bridge and took refuge behind a bush, terrified and screaming, "Don't shoot my father, don't shoot my father."

I later got the full version from this child, who had been awakened soon after she had gone to bed. Her siblings had her go outside and the police cars raced in. Officers rushed around the house, carrying automatic rifles. It was a horrible time for this child and it took a lot of coaxing and promises to get this child back across that bridge.

Eventually the authorities allowed the children to come home. Aleksei continued his busy life. He painted constantly, showing in galleries across America and attending art shows and promotions. I had not realized the complexities of an artist's life. Sometimes both patrons of his art and gallery owners seeking his paintings visited his home. He invited various artist to come and stay and study and paint with him.

He had traveled a lot, taking the children with him when he could, but it was not often practical. He went through a series of nannies that mostly ran the household. I met most of them and they all liked Aleksei, maybe a few of them too much. I was aware of at least one who wanted marriage. Aleksei was maturing and learning and making progress in the art world. There wasn't ever enough time in his private life, especially when he had unknown enemies diligently working to undercut his efforts to raise his children as he thought best.

Aleksei's ex-wife slipped back into the mix without his knowledge. Even though she was not living nearby, she had arranged for the oldest child to have a hidden cell phone and devised a method of passing letters back and forth.

Aleksei discovered the phone and we found the letters hidden in one of the bedrooms. It was a bad time for him. The power of the court had dealt her out of the picture. The two oldest children, now teenagers, were being influenced to embrace her way of life and bad habits and they were responding to her.

Aleksei shared with me his memories of life in Russia. He said that the people not connected to the government were solid, kind and hard-working with good values. There were not a lot of corrupting influences in their lives: no illegal narcotic trade, no terrible music with rotten lyrics; everyone had a job and family life was important to them. I had heard a bit of this from my friend, Jim, who traveled throughout Russia during his nuclear security mission. While I like my American life, I couldn't argue with his memories. In my travels, I have learned there are good people everywhere. But I did wonder why Aleksei would often bring the subject up.

I didn't have to wait long for the answer. Aleksei could see the two older children drifting away. Rather than lose them he made one more try. He broke his property up, setting a portion aside and took loans on the house and remaining land. After making arraignments with a school in rural Russia, he moved the eldest children there to get a new start.

He told me things were working well for a while, until one day a school administrator called to say the kids were unmanageable. Things went downhill fast and they returned home from Russia. Within a few years, they left to live with the kind of friends of which no parent would approve. Reconciliation seemed impossible.

There was sorrow, but Aleksei and his youngest child had formed a close bond. I was able to see how good genes could work. This child had grown into a delightful young person, intelligent, disciplined and with an interest in the arts, literature and everything else in life that was positive. They started painting and working together.

Aleksei had good friends. Robin Dunn stood by his side throughout every arrow shot his way. His other attorney friends pushed back against a giant financial firm, one of the biggest in the world, and beat them back. Big-money collectors of his art helped him recover his property. Commissions started coming in. It was a very happy day when one of my investigators, Keysha Denning, and I were visiting and saw that Aleksei had regained his old spirit. He and his youngest child made plans to fix up the old studio and put it into use and create a healing center with a large greenhouse to grow healthy foods. Keysha and I had started collaborating on screen plays about all that happened during our detective years. We started discussing a screen play of Aleksei's story. After all his trials and tribulations, I was so very proud to be sitting with a former Russian soldier who was more than that. He was a winner with so much to contribute to a world badly in need of beauty.

Eight

TAKING ON THE SYSTEM

I had taken a psychology class and the professor had asked us to describe each of our classmates using one word. We found it very difficult to do with any accuracy. It was not, however, difficult to find one word to describe Darwin: "intimidating."

He had to duck his head to come in through the doorframe of our detective agency, which was six feet, eight inches of the ground, and he must have weighed between 350 and 400 pounds. But weight and height alone does not equal intimidation.

We have all seen tall and heavy men who are not threatening and only present a problem if they sit on you; or, recalling my early police career, if you have to load a falling-down, fat drunk into the backseat of your squad car by yourself.

Darwin had a thick chest, broad shoulders and muscular arms and didn't carry any of that weight in his belly. He was in his late 40s or early 50s. Maybe the best way to describe him is to say what he was not. He was not the pretty-boy type who works out daily in the gym and dresses to enhance his looks. Darwin had a beard and dressed casually, giving off an air of not caring if you liked him or not. But more than that, he had a tough hard look about him that made the hair on the back of my neck go up.

He was busy looking us over just as I was looking him over, and wondering where this visit might go. I let a few seconds go by and Geri, maybe not liking the building tension, smiled, greeted him in her most professional manner and asked if we could help him. He didn't smile back. In time, he and I become friends and in thinking back I can't remember a time when I ever saw him smile or laugh.

As a matter of fact, I think anyone seeing him smiling at them might have had cause for concern. He carried a look of controlled violence and I was to later learn that, among other things, he was an esteemed gambler in big-time poker circles. I could visualize players sitting in the game with him, seeing his smile as a portent of disaster coming their way.

Teresa and I had been in the foyer when he came in and I could see she was intrigued as well. If there was a case here, I wanted her in on it so I invited him back to my office signaling her to join me. I asked him to tell us what was going on and about himself.

Darwin said he had an attorney, who I knew to be street-wise and a fighter for his clients. His attorney told him his problem required professional investigative help and he had looked us up.

"We can get to the case in a moment or two, but we like to start by knowing who you are," I said to Darwin.

This seemed to please him. I assumed that like most people he didn't get to tell his story very often.

Darwin was born and raised in this area but left at an early age to join the military. He completed several tours of Vietnam and after his discharge settled in Las Vegas, working mostly as a professional gambler. He met Diane, who was to become his wife, and she was employed as a pit boss in one of the casinos. She had two children, a boy and a girl, by an earlier marriage. When they married, Darwin elected to change his profession and got into the semi-truck business.

Some of his financial backers wanted him to continue gambling. They had been providing the funding to get into the big games, betting on him and taking a percentage of his winnings. They did well financially and so did he. I made a mental note that at some later date I was going to find out more about his poker playing, particularly at the level he was describing. The $100,000 front money was something I was totally ignorant of, in spite of my law enforcement background.

The lifestyle he and Diane were living in Vegas was not good for raising the children, who were in their teens at that time. They elected to return to his home in Idaho. They settled into a home in an Idaho Falls suburb and Darwin established an independent truck sales business in a nearby community. His stepson, Steve, wanted to work with him so when he graduated high school, Darwin took him into his business and the boy prospered.

Darwin said he and Diane were doing OK, and had a reasonably comfortable life, with one major exception. His stepdaughter had taken up with the wrong crowd and ended up marrying a local hoodlum named Steve Anderson and soon the young couple had a daughter they named Kylee. Steve had a long history of criminal behavior, such as arrests for aggravated assault, property damage, hit and run, cruelty, burglary, DUI and possession of a controlled substance. In addition, through their daughter, they knew him to be a serious alcohol and drug abuser. Darwin said that in his conversations with local police, they described Steve in very derogatory terms.

When Kylee was 4-months-old, their stepdaughter killed herself, shooting her self in the head with a shotgun. I have had considerable experience investigating suicides and have long been aware that it is unusual for women to use a gun for suicide and very unusual for them to shoot themselves in the head when they do.

I brought this up to Darwin, who said there was considerable emotional trauma associated with her death. The sheriff's office investigated it as a suicide and at that time the family did not question it. Darwin told us he came to suspect that Steve was somehow implicated in her death, but he had no direct evidence of it.

Darwin and Diane assumed custody of little Kylee as Steve disappeared and would have been incapable of caring for a baby at that time. Within a few months of his wife's death, Steve married a girl named Lisa, who had a 5-year-old daughter from a previous marriage. Steve and his new wife were allowed to keep Kylee every Friday through Tuesday.

Darwin said Steve was on probation relative to the cruelty charge. On one of the visitations, he was drunk, became enraged, smashed Kylee into a wall and severely damaged her face. The child's injuries were ignored and she received no medical care for a three-day period. Lisa's sister happened to stop by, saw the injuries and insisted that Lisa take Kylee to the Hospital. Doctors reported the injuries to police and Steve was arrested.

Darwin and Diane were designated as foster parents relative to that incident. Darwin said things went pretty well for a few years. Diane placed Kylee in pre-school as soon as she became of age and enrolled her in a private school. Darwin and Diane were very attached to their granddaughter and had big plans for her future.

And then Steve decided he wanted his daughter back. He was able to get a law firm to take his case. Darwin said he has no idea how Steve came up with enough money to hire a lawyer because he only worked sporadically as an independent sheet rock installer and handyman.

His lawyer arranged for the local Health and Welfare office to enter the case on Steve's behalf. Darwin said the thrust of the social welfare system was to place Kylee in her father's care, without any apparent concern for the environment that exists in his home.

Darwin and Diane grew extremely frustrated with the system and the social workers' inability to see Steve's behavior as critical to the child's welfare. Steve failed numerous blood tests for alcohol and drugs, which was contrary to the terms of his probation. Darwin said that each time the probation officer cited Steve for violating his parole, the head of the child welfare system, a woman named Sharon, testified that she is working with Steve and is confident he is doing well and Kylee will be safe with him.

Darwin said he confronted Sharon, telling her of the problems he knew about. He said Sharon not only ignored his pleas but also became quite combative with him. Darwin said he thought there was something personal in her refusal to hear him out.

I interrupted Darwin at this point to clarify his dilemma. We knew state and national child protection agencies believed the best policy was to always return any child to its natural parents. The policy was adhered to in spite of a vast amount of evidence that it had caused great harm and in many cases had resulted in severe injury and death. We had encountered this policy in many cases and had, in our files, dozens of reports of children having suffered because of that misguided policy.

It's difficult to express the depths of frustration that comes with fighting a bureaucracy whose members can be so willfully blind or fearful of losing their jobs they willingly go along with policies they know to be wrong. "It looks like I came to the right place," Darwin said.

I told him the case would not be easy and it was going to cost him some money, both for his attorney and our services. When I told him how much money he could expect to spend in taking on a government agency, Darwin didn't bat an eye. I was to learn as time went by that this man not only looked like a fearsome fighter, he was one.

Teresa took the lead in the case. Her investigative plan included surveillance of Steve's activities and to make discreet inquiries of those who knew him, to establish a pattern of behavior on a day-to-day basis. Knowing that a major surveillance needs different vehicles and agents, we made plans to have those things available to her. As always, Teresa knew what she was doing.

Within a few days, she established that when Steve left his job he stopped at a store to buy at least two six packs of beer. He would then leisurely drive around the foothills east of Idaho Falls as he drank the beer.

Because of his furtive movements in the sparsely traveled hills, I was amazed how much she learned without giving herself away or arousing his suspicions. She had statements from the clerks at various stores, telling how much and what kind of beer he was buying and witnesses willing to testify to his probation violations. She had the empties he discarded at hiding places in the hills.

Teresa had also noted from her surveillance of Steve and Lisa's trailer home that the curtains were always drawn and they had little contact with others. Steve had been seen driving away from home at a high rate of speed, leaving Lisa and the children by themselves and staying away until late in the night. While Lisa was alone, she would not answer the phone. From our past experiences with dope dealers, we suspected he was involved in the same or some other nefarious behavior.

Darwin took to dropping by the office to, as he would say, "touch base." He and I had hit it off pretty well and would go to lunch together or have coffee in the deli across the street. I'm a person who, when I meet unusual people, can't let things alone. I want to know more, who they are, how they got that way and the story behind them. I seemed to have developed the talent to learn these things, to draw people out without offending them.

Having been a detective all these many years taught me much. One of the things I have learned is that people like to talk about themselves, and will, if they're made comfortable. So, even this big intimidating looking man who seemed fearless and unfriendly would open up.

Darwin talked about his youth. Because of his size, he did not fit in well with his contemporaries and found himself hanging around with an older crowd. This was not necessarily good for him, as he was gambling, drinking and fighting. While in his teens, Darwin learned of a poker game that floated around town. It was played for big stakes by businessmen, bar owners, farmers, car dealers and so on. As he named some of them, memories from my past flooded me. I knew these men and of the floating game.

In fact, while I was a young police detective in Idaho Falls, I had worked an embezzlement case at a local bank. One of the young loan officers had made some hefty unauthorized loans and promptly lost all the money in that same floating game. It was a fun case for me, interviewing all those so-called big shot players who did their best to profess their ignorance about where this young man's money came from.

A private poker game of willing players being conducted in private premises is difficult to prosecute. Knowingly accepting stolen money is a different story. They told me they didn't know it was stolen and I couldn't prove otherwise. They may have been right, but I called their bluff telling them, they could their story to the jury. I learned later that they had difficulty deciding which one had won the stolen money, so they all agreed to contribute equally to the check going to the bank.

Darwin told me he had been invited to play with that group. Evidently, they believed young men were easy touches. He said he played in three games, winning all the big pots in each. One of the older players told him he was no longer welcome because he didn't really know how to play poker.

"If I didn't know how to play, then how did I win all the money," Darwin asked. The player, while refusing to look him in the eye, answered that his winning was just a fluke. Darwin said it didn't matter because the Vietnam War had started and he was anxious to get in it.

This brought up a subject I had been wondering about. His attitude, demeanor and little statements he unconsciously dropped fit what I had learned over time about personality changes that result from too much military combat. My psychiatrist friends told me how combat changed people. They described many of returning veterans as quite dangerous with some never really regaining complete control over their emotions and destructive urges.

I was guessing that Darwin might be one of those veterans. When I had asked the psychiatrist how to heal these people, I was told one of the first things that must happen is to get them to talk about their experiences.

Darwin seemed almost eager to talk and said he was in the thick of the fighting, in a unit where body count was a big thing. Dead enemy bodies were stacked after a fire fight to be counted and photographed. He and others took great pride in having a bigger stack of bodies than other units. Darwin realized that he had begun to like killing and took pleasure in screwing with the minds of the command officers.

Command officers, particularly lieutenants, were replaced pretty often as they were getting killed at a rapid rate. New ones, direct from the states, were always a little squeamish about how enemy dead were treated. He described how on one occasion they had a large stack of bodies after a firefight and the new lieutenant was obviously uncomfortable with the casual way the bodies had been thrown on the stack.

Darwin said he pulled his rations out of his pack and climbed up on the pile of bodies, eating a can full of cold beans with a smile on his face and acting like he was having a good time. He took pleasure in watching the lieutenant turn away and retch. Darwin volunteered for extra tours, knowing he had changed and feeling he couldn't be comfortable in civilian life.

Darwin said that following his discharge and his return to the states he struggled to reorient his thinking. I could see where that controlled violence look originated. He told me he was unaware of it and that he really looked like a kindly old man. The look on his face was as close to a smile as I ever saw from him.

One afternoon Darwin asked if I knew of a good place to hunt deer. He said his father still lived in the area and had suggested to him that maybe they could get together on some sort of hunting trip. Darwin was trying to reestablish a good relationship with him.

My experience as a hunter taught me that spending quality time together in a wilderness setting is good medicine for the mind. As I look back at my hunting career, I realize I did it mostly for the experience of being there as opposed to killing anything. I happened to know where the largest mule deer in America hang out and I told Darwin I'd be glad to show him how to get to them.

We made arrangements to meet the following weekend at our place in Leadore. When he arrived, I told him we would use my older four-wheel drive three-quarter-ton pickup as we were going to be climbing up some rough terrain. Darwin insisted we take his almost brand new pickup truck, even after I told him we might bang it up a little bit.

I really did know where the big deer hang out, in a remote deep canyon in the Bitterroot Mountains. I directed him up a series of knife-like ridges until we came to a high place where we could look down into the canyon.

My plan was to point out from our high vantage point the thick forest areas and rock ledges that those big bucks used for concealment and tell him how he could come up to those places from the bottom on foot. He didn't give me time. When we stopped and got out he slid down the cliff toward the bottom, which was about a half mile down.

I like to think I'm a pretty tough fellow, but there was no way I was going to follow him down off that cliff, knowing I would have to just turn around and come back up. I sat down facing the sun with my back against a big rock thinking to take a short nap, until I thought about the possibility of him breaking a leg down in that canyon. He had been sliding recklessly before he disappeared.

My thoughts were now on how I would get him out. There was no help within 20 miles and no good trail into where he had disappeared. Also, it would be dark and cold in a few hours. Every so often I would get up and take a look down to see if I could spot him, thinking this wasn't such a hot idea after all.

I shouldn't have been concerned. After about two hours I heard a noise and saw him clawing his way up over the rocks to the top. He had shed his jacket and was covered with perspiration and had an excited look about him.

"This is the place," he said. "There's tracks all over the canyon." He pointed back down and across telling me where he had been during those two hours. As we made our way down off the ridge, my thoughts were that I knew this was a formidable man. I decided if I ever went hunting with him I was not going to try and keep up with his pace. His style was to go full bore at whatever he did.

A few weeks later, Darwin and his father went back up that ridge, got a big buck and had a great time. They had gone just after a snow storm and the going was even tougher. We went to lunch and he insisted on buying me an $80 bottle of wine, which I didn't need but appreciated. I saved that wine for a special occasion. It turned out that Marilyn and I had opened $12-dollar bottles that tasted better. I didn't tell Darwin that, though.

We were at lunch one day and I asked Darwin about his poker-playing career. He said the big games in America were mostly private affairs held on ranches, big estates and large hotels. The games always had a sponsor, someone who would provide a gaming area large enough to accommodate up to 50 players, comfortable tables and chairs, bathroom facilities, snacks and refreshments, including hard liquor, although Darwin said the smart players avoided booze during games.

"Probably the most important thing the sponsor provided was security," Darwin said. That meant a guarantee of no police and no outside interference.

"It could vary, but the game was scheduled for 48 hours of straight play and if it was a $50,000 game, each player entered with his fifty and played straight through. The sponsor took up to a 10-percent fee for expenses. I mentally did the math. Ten percent of $50,000 per player with 50 players was a pretty good chunk of money for a 48-hour game.

"Think of the conditions," Darwin said. "Gambling is a cutthroat business. Those who are running successful gambling operations, like the big casinos, don't like missing out on any of the massive amounts of money spent in just this country on gambling. They see these independent games as robbery of money they should have been entitled too. They not only would turn you in but would actively seek information about the games so they could take action against them. These are tough people, there could be danger, secrecy is paramount to security and everything costs money."

Remembering my own career in law enforcement and how diligently I and my fellow investigators had sought information about this kind of thing, I told him: "I believe it."

I guess what intrigued me about his descriptions was that, even though I'm not a gambler, I like playing poker. I play only in small games with close friends for peanuts, but I see it as fascinating the same way others might see playing chess. So many possibilities; a real mental game. I mentioned this to Darwin.

"It's all mental," he said. "You put everything into it and beyond constantly calculating odds, you are constantly measuring your opponents, probing and pushing, looking for weaknesses you can exploit and most of all making sure they can't read you which means show no emotion of any kind, ever."

Teresa was getting as frustrated as Darwin about the probation officers' reluctance to act on all the new violations she was digging up on Steve. She said that unless something major came along, we would be unable to act.

We rose to the challenge. At this point, Steve had no permanent job and was drawing unemployment checks. But we knew he was doing odd jobs. He was required by law to report his earnings and our inquiry revealed he had not. We knew the Labor Department would take that violation seriously.

With undercover cases we often traded services with another agency located in a city 100 miles from Idaho Falls. We borrowed a house from a friend and set up two of their agents up in it, acting as carefree bachelors who needed a small sheetrock hole repaired and didn't know how to do it themselves.

They contacted Steve, who agreed to do the work. They offered him a beer, but he refused, saying he was on probation and tested. Steve did say he could smoke a little dope as he knew how to beat that test. He knew of some herbs that cleaned his system before each test.

He told them his uncle was a local drug dealer, a main supplier for the area and offered to go get some marijuana and methamphetamine at a good price. The investigators said Steve laughed about how ignorant the probation and health and welfare officers were and how he had them wrapped around his little finger and that nobody could touch him.

They laughed with him and made a deal for him to come the following day with some good dope.

Teresa called one of her contacts on the police department, a young narcotics agent, and we set things up so he would be present when the dope deal went down. I called Darwin to tell him what we were up to and that we were spending his money pretty rapidly. He was excited and said: "Spend whatever it takes." I told the staff: "You don't get many clients like that in this business … or any business for that matter."

To make a long story short, we ended up making two felony meth buys from Steve the next two days and paid him a little money for a half-baked job of repairing the hole. We filmed and recorded everything.

Our narcotic officer friend was ecstatic. He had been trying to get a case on Steve for a long time. He arrested Steve and booked him into the local jail telling us: "He won't be able to make bail on this one."

A few days later, Steve was arraigned before the same judge who had been complicit in ignoring his past behavior. Steve's protector, Sharon, head of local child welfare, came to court and berated the prosecutor and judge about Steve's arrest, saying he had been illegally set up by police and that he was innocent and should be released immediately while her department completed an investigation.

She had no business at that hearing. Witnesses told us it appeared the judge had lost control. The arraignment was postponed and Steve was released pending her report. The bailiff told us that during the tirade, Steve sat and smirked and grinned at his friends who had come to court with him.

I should not have allowed Darwin to hear that remark. He joined us the following morning to discuss where we were and what our next move would be. I could see his face tighten and he was not able to conceal "that look."

"Maybe I should just go over and blow that whole God-dam building up and kill all those bastards in it," he said. He was referring to massive concrete state building that housed the child protective division of Health and Welfare.

I had been expecting this eventuality, even planning for it. I have been dealing with violent people most of my life. You expect that sometimes they will act violently.

Also, a big part of my career has been dealing with city, county and state bureaucracies and they don't often work very well. The causes include lack of oversight, incompetence and the fact that people who have been given authority don't handle it very well.

When the case was first opened, I asked one of my friends who worked with Health and Welfare about Sharon. What I heard is that she is disliked by a lot of people, pushy, arrogant and not as smart as she makes out to be. "Somebody should check her out," my friend concluded.

That statement had been bouncing around in the back of my mind. It was now time to act on it

I picked my words carefully with Darwin, telling him it wasn't time for blowing anybody away yet. We were going to turn what had happened to our advantage. This time Sharon had gone too far. Those were the right words. Darwin had risen from his chair, but hadn't started for the door. My plan was to try and stop him, if necessary, though none of us in the office had that capability, short of shooting him, if he didn't want to be deterred.

I breathed easier and asked Darwin to take his seat back, which he slowly did. I knew I had his confidence. "Just leave it to us," I told him. "We're going to focus on investigating Sharon. Don't be going over there and screwing up our case yet."

Later Teresa and I talked about how we knew immediately that he not only had decided to do it, but had the ability to carry it through.

"What the hell is going on," Darwin asked. "Why is the judge going along with this crazy woman?" We gave him our standard explanation, which we had observed from long experience.

The criminal justice system – and maybe all kinds of systems – are for the most part made up of good and decent people who are trying to do the best they can, I told him. Everyone, judges, prosecutors, police, parole and probation officers, takes ownership in that system. They want it to work. They want it to be admired for how good it works and often that desire to give the perception that it is working well blinds them to any possibility it may be flawed. When any kind of attack comes along, there is a tendency to draw together and ignore the reason for the attack and show a united front.

To have to admit that maybe the system is not working very well is often very difficult for those in it. It's easier to just go along pretending everything is still all right."

"Sounds like the Army," Darwin replied.

Our emergency had passed and it was time to start digging in.

Our focus was now on Sharon. It didn't take long to unearthing facts about her that should have been known to her employers had they vetted her properly. We started with her credentials.

Her position required someone with a doctorate degree in social work, preferably in child care. We needed to find out where she went to school and that can be difficult coming at it from the outside.

Our small firm took pride in our agents. They make friends easily and I am always surprised to find out who they know and where they can go to dig up information that should not be in the public arena.

In this case, we had three agents, as well as me, who knew employees in the Health and Welfare agency. Employees in the trenches, much to the chagrin of their managers, are always a good place to find out what you want to know.

The employees we knew were honest and smart people who didn't feel they had anything to hide. We soon came up with the name of the university Sharon was supposed to have graduated from.

We could not find out anything about the school, other than it was located in Pasadena, Calif. All detective agencies have contacts in other states and ours in California just happened to live in Pasadena.

We gave him a call. He said he'd get right on it and call back as soon as he could. We thought we may have to wait a few days, but he called the next day, laughing while he explained that the school was a well-known diploma mill.

Any person can obtain a doctorate degree by giving them $800 and writing a short essay on the subject they wanted the degree in.

The school was located in a small office and had no standing or credibility of any kind," our friend in California told us. "Calling it a legitimate school would be like comparing a crap game in an alley to the MGM Grand Casino in Las Vegas and even that would be a stretch," he said.

I began to think this case may be easier to bring to a close than I had thought, but when you're making an attack on the "System," nothing comes easy.

I knew the manager of the Seventh District Health and Welfare Department, which had jurisdiction in this case. My impression of him was that he was a nice man, well educated and probably knew much about psychiatry and sociology.

But like many academics I've run across, he seemed to be a bit of a wuss. My suspicions were confirmed. After we had provided his office with information about the phony diploma, our friends in the agency told us what happened.

The manager had told Sharon to come in and bring her diplomas. Sharon showed up at his office without the diplomas, instead accompanied by her attorney. She told her boss the diplomas were impeccable and proceeded to threaten him with a sexual harassment lawsuit. The supervisor quickly backed away, assuring her he had not meant to create any problems and that everything was okay.

Plan B entailed going over the district supervisor's head to Boise, the capital city, with our complaint and information. We had no way of knowing how things were handled there, but I later learned that we created a lot of turmoil.

From experience working for state and federal agencies over the years, I knew they keep a tight wrap around internal troubles as they like to present a competent image to the public. I didn't expect to be told anything and that we would have to wait for results. They weren't long in coming.

I left the office one afternoon and as I stepped out onto the sidewalk I was hailed by a long-time friend, an attorney who was walking on the opposite sidewalk. I crossed to greet him while observing he had a serious look on his face.

As we spoke, it became apparent that he was angry. He didn't waste time, but shot a question at me. "Is it true that Sharon's doctorate degree is phony?" The question didn't totally catch me by surprise. My attorney friend was a well-respected state senator and one of the committees he headed up had jurisdiction over the Health and Welfare agency.

It appeared the agency had been unable to keep our complaint totally under wraps. I told him what our detective friend from Pasadena said. He appeared to get madder. I told him if he would like I would get him a written report detailing our findings.

"Thanks, I won't need it," he said and took off at a fast pace. At that point I knew that not only did we win this round but that the case would be coming to a close.

Things moved fast. Within the week we learned Sharon had been fired from her job and was leaving the state. The same judge took Health and Welfare off of the case and awarded Darwin and Diane total custody of little Kylee. Steve went back to jail.

When it was over, as was our practice, we critiqued the case. While Darwin wasn't smiling, it was obvious he was pleased. He told me that he might have to recommend us if he ever ran across anyone needing help. By now I knew him well enough to know he had given us a very high complement.

Teresa joked that the "System" was probably very happy with us also as we had saved them from their own mistake. There was no telling how much trouble Sharon would have caused had she had been allowed to continue on. Any day now, we would be receiving a letter from them thanking us. We all had a good laugh and broke up the meeting

I really felt good about the case. For us it had ended well. But I have learned simple fairy tale endings are rare. During the next year Darwin came in to bring me up to date. He said Diane was divorcing him.

I asked about Kylee. Darwin seemed pleased. "Remember me telling you I took Diane's son into my business and he was doing okay," Darwin said. I nodded. He said the boy had married and the young couple had a child and were doing great. They had approached Darwin and Diane about adopting Kylee and raising her as their own.

"I love that little girl, but I know I'm not the type to make a good father," Darwin said.

Later I told Teresa of the visit and she said that as a woman she saw Darwin in a different light than I did. She could both see and feel the turmoil in him and viewed him as potentially dangerous and thought the split inevitable.

"You women should not be so hard on us men," I said and we both laughed.

Time went by. I saw less of Darwin and after a couple of years realized I hadn't seen him in a long time. I had written a book about my law enforcement career and was promoting it around the state. One of my young friends had arranged a book signing in our local Barnes & Noble and Darwin came in accompanied by a very attractive woman.

When he saw me at the table, it was apparent he was pleased and took his lady friend's arm and brought her over. After hellos, he introduced her, telling me she was the reason he had been spending so much time in Salt Lake City.

He grabbed one of my books and told her she should read it as there were no other detectives of my caliber. I was impressed with her and told him it looked like he was doing alright for himself. He bought the book and we had a good visit.

Before the year was over, I got word that Darwin had a heart attack and was dead. He was still a fairly young man and it shouldn't have happened. I didn't think it was fair. I thought back to the first time I saw him and how I had picked the single word to describe him: "intimidating."

Remembering our last visit at the bookstore, I thought I'm going to have to pick another word or two to describe my friend, Darwin: "Big heart."

Nine

TRYING TO GRAB THE BRASS RING

Investigating interesting cases was not the only purpose in starting the Idaho Protective Specialist Company. I had always done the kind of work I liked, knowing the pay and benefits were not that good. From time to time, I've been reminded that the American way is to make money and the more the better. I've heard so many times that life is not complete unless you make a grab for the "brass ring."

Like most kids, I was fascinated by the rides at the carnivals. Often, a brass ring would be hung just out of reach. You rode your pony around and around with the music playing and the excitement building. When you thought you were positioned right and had worked up the nerve to risk a spill, you would lean way out and make a grab for that ring. If you got it and were still straddling your horse, you won a prize.

It was not easy and grabbing the brass ring was a rare achievement for any kid. Now, in our overprotective society, we no longer allow kids to take risks like that.

Also, now that I'm no longer a kid, I made the decision to do my brass ring-grabbing on a larger scale.

I think it is likely that most people throughout the ages have struggled with this dilemma. Are we working to enjoy life or do we work to make money, which for many people equals power? My feeling has always been that if your power lies within and is a part of your being, you should be content. I was about to test my theory.

The company was doing OK and I didn't need to spend all my time on routine stuff: providing security for businesses, special events and sales and even an elk ranch near Salmon. An animal rights organization slipped out to the ranch at night and opened the gates, allowing the elk to escape in the surrounding mountains. This coupled with poachers shooting elk from the nearby highway made security a necessity.

After being released, those elk gathered in the high mountain meadows. Had they been ordinary elk like the ones I hunted during my lifetime, they would have had to be killed to bring them back down. But these elk had been spoiled. It didn't take long for the thrill of freedom to wear off. They filtered back down to the ranch and were standing by the feeder eating cut hay. They watched while the gate was shut behind them and the lock replaced.

Every time I looked at those elk after that, I thought about people I have known who have sold out for a little comfort.

Once in a while in life, opportunities to sell out for money come along and I was seeing one approaching. To the west of Idaho Falls is what is referred to locally as "the desert." It is not a desert such as you will find in Arizona or New Mexico, with cactus and prickly plants, but a high-mountain desert consisting mostly of sagebrush and ancient lava bed formations.

It has a beauty of its own, but was considered worthless for settling in by the early pioneers as there was no available water for irrigation. Cattle and sheep were grazed at first. Now the land belongs to the federal government, which used it as a gunnery range to test cannon and shells for Navy battleships prior to World War II.

And then as the Atomic Age arrived and the Cold War began, America needed a remote place to develop the new nuclear industry. Our "desert" was an ideal place, sparsely populated but near towns large enough to provide comfortable living space and amenities for the scientists and their families.

Idaho Falls was the closest and largest city and the local Chamber of Commerce was determined to beat out other places in the west vying to attract what would surely be a growth industry.

When I came along, the site was well into its development stages and would eventually go through several name changes, finally deciding upon the Idaho National Laboratory. At its busiest time, there were more than 12,000 employees commuting back and forth from Idaho Falls and nearby small towns to their desert worksites.

As I completed my transition into private work, one of my first jobs was to do background investigations on site employees who needed secret clearances to allow them to work on highly secret and protected experimental work. This required that I get a top secret security clearance, which allowed me to roam freely throughout the various laboratories and support facilities. After a couple years, I had a pretty good working knowledge of operations.

This was also my first real encounter with pure government bureaucracy. I used to think police departments were the epitome of a bureaucracy with their military structure and overloaded command systems, but nothing in my life had prepared me for a large government operation. It began with getting my clearance. My timing was good because I was needed quickly and within two weeks I had been investigated, vetted and was on the job.

Naturally, I thought this a simple process. Almost everyone hired for the various positions at the site had good work backgrounds and were educated, solid citizens. Checking out their qualifications for secret clearances was child's play for a former criminal detective. Within a couple weeks, the investigations were finished and submitted to Washington for the issuance of the document.

Six months later, those I had investigated would look me up wanting to know why they weren't getting their clearance. I would tell them it was sitting on some self-important bureaucrat's desk. In the meantime, I found myself often escorting new hires to their desks and workplace. These folks were not allowed to move within the facility unless escorted by someone with a top-secret clearance. They were given nothing to do until the clearance showed up, but still the pay checks came.

As a taxpaying citizen, this waste bothered me. But what really made my teeth grind was to discover that everyone in the system seemed to accept this way of doing business as normal.

It wasn't my job to change the culture. It was just to see that the work was done and collect the money. Before long, I had expanded my government contracts to do special investigations and background checks for six other federal agencies. I began to suspect that government contracts were like sitting under a money tree. So far it was still-small time stuff when, out of the blue, a real opportunity presented itself.

Over the years, I had watched two or three large and well-known companies obtaining contracts to provide the security for the whole site, as well as peripheral operations in town. The Department of Energy renewed the contracts every four years or so and I was baffled about why they changed companies so often. From my perspective, security did not seem to be a big deal. We were way out in the west, in a sparsely populated state with little crime, and everything was separated by miles of space with controlled entry. This was probably the easiest site in America to protect.

However, the mindset of the site managers I interviewed was that they were in constant danger of attack from terrorist groups and that there were subversives everywhere waiting for a chance to foul up the works.

I had been asked to do some polygraph testing for a couple laboratory contractors. I laughed when I was told of the problem. In one of the business offices a note had appeared on the bulletin board, obviously posted by some office joker. It was as kind of cute verse about the boss's secretary and how she had such a nice fanny. It described how all work by male staffers came to a halt when she walked through the work place deliberately swinging that fanny.

While the verse was quite flattering about the secretary's physical appearance, I could understand her discomfort. No one likes to be made fun of and the note could be considered sexual harassment. But it was not my kind of investigation, so I declined to test all the males in the room. That was the kind of thing that should have been handled in-house. There was no reason to spend a lot of money on high-priced outsiders.

My old investigator partner had taken over as head of security for one of the better known labs. I stopped by to visit him while on a routine visit to his area. "Man, I've got a big case going here and I might need a little help," he said.

My ears perked up. This was a man I had worked murders and arson and kidnapping and riots with. I doubted that he needed any help, but I said, "I'm game, what've you got."

"I call it the Twinkie case," he replied. One of our female guards left a couple Twinkies in the guard room refrigerator for her lunch and when she came back they were gone. "I don't know how I'm going to manage," he said with a sad look.

I could go on for a long time in the same vein, but I need to get on with the story. A wise friend once told me, "If you don't give an employee something important to do, the next thing you know, he will start thinking what he is doing is important." While I did not think there was a great need for security at the site, I learned that view was not shared by everyone.

I had been alerted by one of my old FBI contacts that the security contract was about due for renewal and that there were plans to expand the program by several million dollars. I expressed disbelief and with a laugh he explained the thought process behind it.

He told of a case involving one of the Middle East countries having organized a terrorist cell. They had sent three operatives to America, allegedly to blow up a government installation, but something went wrong. He said that when the plane arrived in the United States, one of the so-called terrorists turned himself in and asked for asylum. One fled back where he came from and the third was an undercover government agent reporting on the other two. Even though nothing came out this particular misadventure, the thinking was that a more serious attempt might happen in the future.

I agreed that could happen and asked him what he thought of the possibility that a terrorist might come to Idaho. He laughed and said: "I hate to say it, but I'm not really sure where Idaho is. I don't want to make you feel bad, but I don't think Idaho is on anybody's radar."

A short time later, I learned of another incident that had also been a catalyst in expanding security at the Idaho site. A small group of young men in Washington State were leaders of the local Aryan Nation gang. They robbed an armored car in California, fleeing with quite a stash of money. Three came to Salmon to hide out.

They rented a house and lived in Salmon for several months without drawing attention to themselves. Salmon is a small, isolated town and most of the people there still live by the "Code of the West," which means "You mind your business and I'll mind mine." They avoided trouble and no one in authority would have ever known they had been there except for one mistake. They had taken a liking to their neighbor. As they were preparing to leave town, they stopped by his house and gave him their fishing boat and several hundred dollars worth of groceries they had stocked up on. The neighbor thanked them, but as he thought about it, began to suspect something might be fishy and reported it to the sheriff.

Within a few weeks, the three were traced to a house in Seattle where they made a stand and died in a shootout with the FBI and local police. It turned out that one of the dead gang members had in his possession a blueprint of the plans for a dam on the Skagit River, which flows out of the Cascade Mountains near Seattle.

I had not yet gotten to the place where I could truly appreciate the imagination our government managers could use to expand contracts, but I was about to get a lesson.

I learned that story had been disseminated through the security system and someone had extrapolated from it that he and his companions planned to blow up the dam. You could also extrapolate that if they were interested in blowing up the dam, than maybe they stayed in Salmon not just to hide out but also to do reconnaissance at the INL.

Salmon is more than 100 miles from the site in a remote mountain area and is probably one of the best places in America to hide out. You can't see anything from any of the highways passing through the site. It would have been extremely difficult for them to gain admittance or get anywhere near the buildings. I rejected the idea as being ridiculous. But then maybe I didn't know everything. Later the security was enhanced with helicopters, swat teams and a large increase in security personal, adding several million dollars to the contract.

A couple years later, a budget crunch and failure of any terrorist attacks to materialize not only did away with the helicopters and manpower increases but also reduced the previous staff. The only action the helicopters got was trouble from the U.S. Wildlife Service for chasing herds of antelope that roamed the site.

My approach was not to judge, but to get in on the action and make a little money doing it. Of course, you don't advertise that as your motive, but try to give the impression you're a part of the American team looking after the country's best interests. I was up to the job and my plan was to be honest doing it. I could see that because I had not yet been bureaucratized, I was in a position to do the job right and maybe save the government a little money.

I was to learn later of my own naïveté. I had been told that in the large-contract bidding world, decisions were usually made in advance. I didn't doubt that, but my experience has been that the best-laid plans often get sidetracked. My job was to do a little sidetracking if I could.

I quickly discovered there was no official agency to get me started. Nor was there any official who wanted to share what they all seemed to feel was proprietary information. I had the feeling I was about to enter a cloak-and-dagger world, closed to outsiders. I was also to discover that being an outsider with no background in obtaining large government contracts was probably an asset.

My ignorance kept me from being discouraged. In fact, it stirred the competitive juices. I felt the same drive and excitement as years before when as a young man I had gone alone on my first grizzly bear hunt in Alaska.

As young men do, I thought the grizzly would be wise to steer clear when he saw me coming. It's good to discover that after all these years you can still feel the same. Instead of a big bear, I was thinking of my competitors for the bid.

This was the time when I learned that having a lot of good friends has distinct advantages. In this case, many were connected to the nuclear site in a variety of ways. When I spread the word that I was interested in the contract and needed help, responses started pouring in. Looking back, I like to think that beyond friendship these folks had the same problems with bureaucracy as I did and helping me jump through the paperwork hoops was a way of thumbing their nose at it.

The bid proposal was an inch and a half thick compilation of requirements and duties required of bidders. As I thumbed through, it was obvious that an enormous amount of work and time had gone in to putting it together. Every little detail was covered. I noted that the first requirement was to have a "Project Organization and Operation plan." That meant I would need to start recruiting a staff of experienced and qualified people. Also, we would need to know how to put together an operational plan better than those pitched by the other bidders.

The operational plans used in my own little security jobs had been based on common sense. That worked well for me, but I knew much more would be needed. In big-time contracts, if anything at all goes wrong, the controlling agency wants to be able to place blame on the contractor. I was going to have to get my hands on some existing security plans to know where to begin.

Sometimes things have a way of working out that makes one wonder about the mysteries of the universe. During my days of doing background investigations around the site, I had met an employee that I instantly liked and we became friends.

We would have lunch or coffee and shoot the bull. I mentioned to him that I was going after the contract for site security and he gave me encouragement and advice about working around bureaucracies. My friend told me he had plans to obtain government contracts on his own in another field.

He called one day and asked to get together. I left that meeting with the security plans for two large well-known nuclear plants in other states. These plants might be obvious targets for real terrorists. Suddenly I had actual blueprints that laid out the formats I needed to follow. Manna from heaven! I offered my friend a place in my company and he declined, saying he was pursuing his own goal. This cloak-and-dagger stuff was turning out to be neither cloak nor dagger, but simply good personal relationships.

Now it was time to put a management team together. I would have to offset my small company size with a staff so experienced and knowledgeable that they would eclipse anything those very large national companies could offer. I felt like David entering the field with Goliath, but I had a weapon those big companies didn't have: a plan to share profits.

In my snooping around, I had learned how much money can be made in big government contracts. The government believes in paying well for security. Profits can run as high as 10 percent of the contract's cost per year. I was going after an $18 million job that was going to increase to $24 million in the near future.

The company that held the contract had been notified that the next four-year contract would be opened to other firms. They had immediately offered to work those next four years at cost if they could continue with the contract.

As I asked people why they would agree to work for no profit, I learned there is often a considerable spread between what some companies spend for equipment and supplies and what they charge the government for expenses. In the business world, that spread is sometimes called kickbacks.

I was learning a lot. When you're dealing in millions of dollars, a small spread can really add up. You can make lots of money without profit. I didn't like the idea of doing business that way and my plan was to play everything straight, to only charge the government what I had to pay and save the taxpayers money. I thought that might be a selling point.

Even without working those angles, the profits were, in my world at least, extremely high. I had never been motivated to get lots of money at any cost and I was willing to share equally with those who would be willing to step out with me.

They would be taken into my company as board members and aside from their salary, each could receive a portion of the company profits. I could still visualize ending up with a few million in the bank and that there would be opportunities for other contracts after we had established Idaho Protective Specialist as a big-time player. That brass ring was starting to look tantalizing.

For many years I had been interacting in one way or another with the management team of the existing contractor. They were a national firm and their management staff would be transferring to other company jobs throughout the country. I was well aware of some of their shortcomings, so the Department of Energy's dissatisfaction did not come as a surprise to me.

I had not been very impressed with the people they had running things. I knew and was good friends with candidates who were head and shoulders more qualified and now my job was to recruit them.

Our plan was to keep the existing guard staff and to supply only the management team. Our team would be able to correct the behaviors and missteps that led to the company losing its contract.

I had one of them working with me. Our corporate certificate listed me as president, my wife, Marilyn, as secretary treasurer and one of my longtime friends, Darrol, as vice-president. Darrol and I had started our law enforcement careers together many years before and each of us had gone on with our careers in different directions while remaining close through the years. Darrol had ended up as a very competent and popular warden in the Idaho prison system.

We retired from the government about the same time and were doing private-sector work. He joined with me and quickly obtained the needed secret clearance to do INL work, as well as taking on some of the criminal defense cases coming our way. He was in on this new adventure from the beginning. One by one we came up with our perfect management team.

Using our purloined nuclear plant security material, we drew up what we considered to be the ideal staffing plan. It began with a project manager who was to be in total charge of the job. We were able to recruit a friend I had worked with for years and was managing another security site.

His resume contained four pages of on-the-job experience in security and related fields. His bachelor's degree was in industrial security and his master's in criminal justice administration.

We were later told by the bid-selection committee that he was the most qualified candidate with the best recommendations on any job they had experience with. We were off to a good start.

The choice for the deputy project manager was Darrol. His experience included assuming control of a broken prison system following a tragic riot in the main prison that resulted in considerable destruction.

Darrol had overseen construction of a new prison and instituted a wide range of security-based physical improvements designed to make sure that no riot or hostage situation could ever take place again. He designed and instigated proper training programs and rebuilt morale in the workforce, resulting in a very high retention employee rate.

He also created a public relations program that restored public confidence. Prior to his retirement, the Idaho penitentiary system became an example of excellent management and drew observers from surrounding states trying to emulate his successes. His expertise was unquestionable and unmatched in the security world.

Probably the best coup we were able to pull off was to recruit our mutual friend, Hal, to join us as finance and administration manager. He had been a longtime friend and advisor and had recently retired from the government.

Hal wanted to stay active and liked the idea of "a small group coming out of nowhere to pit themselves against the big boys." What we liked was that his resume would have qualified him as business manager for any major corporation in the world. His undergraduate degree was in accounting and his masters in business administration and he had been the accounting instructor at the University of California Berkley.

He had also been employed by the Atomic Energy Commission as an auditor in their San Francisco operation and had at various times been responsible for the audits of all operating contractors. Hal's expertise included work with the Department of Energy, Department of Defense, NASA, State Department and many prime contractors. We doubted that any of America's large security firms could find a better-qualified business administrator than our little Idaho company.

We had another secret weapon. For years Bill, who lived in Michigan, had been coming to Idaho to go elk hunting with my partner, Jim, and I. Before coming to Idaho, Jim had worked with Bill to organize and operate Michigan's police academy system. We wanted him as our quality assurance manager.

We knew he was nearing retirement and had fallen in love with Idaho's wilderness. Bill's bachelor's degree was in police administration and public safety (graduated with honors) and he had a master's in criminal justice. His resume revealed experience as project director on another management team and listed him as the supervisor of the Michigan Law Enforcement Officers Training Council, which meant he was responsible for formulating and supervising the implementation and evaluation of all police standards throughout the state. He was recognized as an expert in the conduct of a comprehensive job-task analysis, which was an absolute fit for our plans to make the best use of all personnel.

Our man, Roy, was almost the capstone for our position of operations manager. His degree was in law enforcement subjects and was a FBI graduate. He and I worked together for years as policemen, with him attaining the rank of lieutenant, until he had gone on to be an Idaho sheriff. He was an excellent polygraph examiner, an expert in employee prevention of drug use and had an extensive background in employee arbitration functions. That coupled with a reputation for possessing a unique ability to engender loyalty from his staff and subordinates, made Roy the kind of manager you dream of having with you.

And last, but certainly not least, was a former criminal investigator who had worked for years with Jim and I. He had since taken employment in the nuclear security industry in a highly sensitive position, meaning we cannot use his name.

He had an exceptional working knowledge of the Department of Energy's security methods, implementation, evaluations and corrective actions. This was a man whose knowledge would be expected to keep us out of trouble. His degree in criminal justice coupled with his security background made him the ideal choice for our position of deputy operation manager.

Because we knew each other and had, in many cases, worked together, we were able to present our team as a cohesive group of exceptional and qualified men of high standards and moral integrity. Our dream team was together. But we didn't stop there.

Being a state investigator and having been involved in cases across Idaho for years, as well as having provided personal protection for most of the state dignitaries at one time or another, had put me in a unique position to get endorsements. The governor and all four members of Idaho's congressional delegation wrote us glowing letters or recommendation.

This was kind of fun, so we kept going. We solicited letters from sheriffs, chiefs of police and mayors from eastern Idaho, where we were best known. The stack of endorsements got thick enough and so we detailed our plan to contract with eastern Idaho's vocational schools to train security guards and recruit a well-known arbitration company to handle any personnel problems.

We were aware that a concern for the government was the possibility of the guard service unionizing and going on strike, which would leave guard posts unmanned. We did not have trained nuclear security guards we could tap for replacements, so we worked up a plan to use the services of six local county sheriff departments and their auxiliary staffs to aid us in such an event.

Those departments were happy to accommodate us and we drew up an elaborate emergency staffing plan with each sheriff signing off on it and presented it with our bid. With all our plans detailed, along with the management staff and endorsements, our response to the request for proposal was as thick as the original request.

Geri had spent much of her time typing up and putting our proposal together to make us look good. All was left was to submit it and wait and see if we had succeeded.

The wait was only a couple of weeks and the word came that a large and nationally known security firm won the bid. It was not like it hadn't been expected; we knew we were a long shot, but I was a little upset so I appealed their decision, which allowed me a hearing to present my case. We knew there really was no case to present. We had done all we could and unless we could prove we had been the victims of some sort of fraud, we would be dead in the water, so to speak. But I don't believe in giving up easily.

The hearing turned out better than I expected. We were welcomed in a very friendly manner and told with what seemed genuine regret that our proposal had been considered and that they found much to admire in it, so much so that they were willing to say that if they had been looking for a small company, we would have been it. We learned there were seven other companies bidding for it. Their first pick had more than 12,000 trained nuclear guards and years of experience.

We were thanked for our efforts and asked to try again. We will never know if the decision had been made before the bid was put out by officials at a higher level, but I like to think that was probably so. We were all able to put our disappointment aside and laugh together as we looked back at this adventure.

I was reluctant to express my feelings for a while, but I eventually felt relieved. I knew, as did the others, of the task we would have faced had we won the bid. The next four or more years would have been full of bureaucratic wrangling, petty little pseudo emergencies, personality quirks and differences … all things that make my teeth hurt.

I felt a little like a wild animal that had escaped his cage. I kept thinking about those elk who, after being set free, filtered back down out of the mountains to spend their lives as captives waiting to be fed each day. I was free to continue my life as I pleased. It is nice not to have to sacrifice yourself for money. I'm looking forward to the next adventure and I plan to steer clear of brass rings.

Ten

LEAVING THE HERD

I'm not done, but I'm getting older. I've found as we age, we pause and take more time to think about our experiences. What's the meaning behind everything? What is it all about? And where does it all end? Or, does it end?

My life did not start very well, but it got better as the years passed. Now I find every day a joy. Early in my life, I learned not to trust others, particularly when they claimed to have answers about purpose and meaning that were unverifiable using tools available to me. I have lived in what best can be described as the physical world. I like that world. Everything about it seems to fit.

I mastered it early on. I can not only look after myself, providing those things that make a good life, but I can also look after others. But I am curious about the beliefs held by so many who are certain they have answers to their place in the universe.

It has stoked my curiosity that those people can be observed practicing the tenets of such a diversity of recognized religions, and all sure they are the only ones on the right track. There obviously is some component in human makeup that cannot accept the limited confines of existence that animals and insects and lesser creatures accept as a matter of course.

And whether I like it or not, I have, ever since I can remember, had a feeling that there is much more going on than just what the physical world has to offer. I assume that most of mankind has the same feeling, and that's why we are divided up in such a variety of spiritual belief systems – with none having any absolute proof that their way is any better than anybody else's and all failing in one way or another.

A detective's life is about evidence. In my working career, there have been mind-boggling changes in evidence used to prove guilt or innocence.

Eye witnesses were at one time believed to be the strongest evidence you could provide. Now they are recognized as one of the worst. Confessions used to be irrefutable. We have since learned that false confessions are almost as easy for a trained interrogator to obtain as a real confession. Physical evidence metamorphosed through sloppy conclusions and dishonest presentation until our prisons became full of innocent people, many who have been cleared, through DNA, of crimes they had been convicted of. It appears that evidence is fluid and changes as we gain knowledge.

Is it possible that there is more to our existence than obvious physical limitations? I have noted that there are a great many persons of seemingly high intelligence who avow that this life is all there is and they appear content with that premise. I take pleasure in pressuring those people to explain some of the unexplainable little things we all hear about but try to ignore.

For instance, during the World War II, my grandmother woke up in the night, distraught and sobbing. "Jimmie's been hurt," she said. Jimmie was her son and a soldier fighting in the Battle of the Bulge and there had been no contact with him for many months.

My grandmother learned that Jimmie had been badly hurt at the same time she had awakened. It is one of those things I have pondered from time to time. Jimmie recovered only to be killed a few years later in the Korean War.

For a long time I made it a point to ignore things for which I had no explanation. That didn't make them any less real, just easier to handle. I suspect many people handle those things the same way, although many are not going to believe anything that's not easily explainable.

I have done my best to grasp everyone else's religious views, but something deep inside knows there's much more than that. Now I understand that my feeling was right. Let me tell you how I arrived at that conclusion.

My first unexplained experience took place when I was a child. I was 9 or 10-years-old and lived with my mother, grandmother and sister in California. My grandmother, Amanda, was a strong-willed and self-centered woman who managed to hurt everyone she was close to throughout her life. We often butted heads.

My mother, the bread-winner of the family, divorced my father before I was born. She was a sweet woman but totally dominated by her unpleasant mother. Looking back, I realize my grandmother resented me being a part of the household, but as a boy I didn't know why. From what little I was told, the principal reason my mother and father split up was because of my domineering grandmother. There had been bad blood between them and as his son it extended to me.

I slept alone in my small bedroom. I awoke one night and saw a woman I didn't know standing at the foot of my bed and looking at me. My hair was standing out straight and as I rubbed my head my hair flattened back down. I had no fear and she didn't speak.

"Who are you," I asked. If she answered, I didn't hear and she disappeared. I got out of bed thinking she must be somebody my grandmother or mother had invited in, which was not unusual. I went to the living room and kitchen looking for her. She wasn't there so I went back to bed.

The next morning I dressed and went into the kitchen for breakfast before going to school. "Who was that lady who was here last night," I asked. My mother and sister said there was no lady here last night. And my grandmother accused me of cooking up a story to start trouble. I sassed back at her and left the house. This always distressed my mother.

When I came home from school, I heard my grandmother alternating between playing the piano and a harmonica, some old songs from her past. My mother told me to stay away from her as her younger sister had died in Texas the previous day. Playing music was her way of grieving. I recall wondering if there was a connection between this news and the woman by my bed. As I started to bring it up, my mother held up her hand.

"Don't talk about it," she said. "You'll only cause trouble."

I didn't talk about it at home but I remember sharing it with some of my school friends, who seemed interested and for a few days I was kind of a big shot with them. The adults at the school, as well as others I told the story to, went out of their way to explain to me these kind of things don't really happen. I knew it happened to me, but I learned to keep my mouth shut about it. This experience stayed with me. To this day, so many years later, it remains vivid.

Another experience I had about that time involved another kid my age. We took it upon ourselves to explore an estate located in the San Fernando Mountains, a few miles from our homes. The large house was located in a canyon and separated from the world by a six-foot hurricane fence with three strands of barb wire. I suppose they thought it was impregnable, but for two pre-teen boys, scaling it was a lark.

We stayed away from the house, but explored the grounds. I recall a large structure made of steel pipe that was covered with chicken wire.

There were a lot of exotic plants and trees on the property and the structure had several trees growing inside of it under the wire. When we got close, we were able to see that it was occupied by hundreds of birds of different sizes and every color. We speculated that somebody had to have a lot of money to have all those birds, but we didn't understand what an unusual sight we were seeing. I've never seen anything remotely like it since, even in big city zoos.

We followed a trail leading further up the mountain until we found a concrete dam with about an acre-sized lake behind it. We climbed around to the back of the lake and decided to wade into the water to cool off. The sand under our feet was firm until we got out to where the water was just above our knees. Suddenly, the ground gave way and we slid down an underwater slope. Suddenly we were in deep water. My friend couldn't swim and I wasn't much better. He turned and grabbed me, pulling us both down.

I was under the water, thinking that I was drowning and he was going to drown as well. The next thing I knew, I was lying on the hot sand and my friend was near me, hacking and coughing. We laid there for what seemed a long time. I was totally beat and he thanked me for pulling him out.

"I didn't pull you out," I said. "I thought you pulled me out."

"Somebody pulled me out," he said.

"There ain't nobody here but us," I replied. "There's no other tracks in the sand and I didn't do it."

I remember as we hiked back down the trail and scaled the fence that we were subdued and didn't talk much, nor did we ever talk about it again. But I have thought about the incident many times and have no explanation. Somehow we were removed from that water.

A few years went by and I was getting into trouble a lot. I recall spending much of my time trying to figure out a way to leave home. One of my plans was to steal a car, take it to my grammar school, break in, steal all the typewriters and sell them for enough money to go live by myself.

I recruited another kid my age to help me and we got caught in the act. Just as I was turning 12, I ended up in reform school. My grandmother told the judge she and my mother were unable to control me. When I was released, my grandmother took me to her brother's home in Texas where he operated a cattle ranch and was supposed to keep me on the straight and narrow. My grandmother, mother, sister and I all moved to Milano, Texas.

I have a vivid memory of entering my great uncle's house, being introduced and seeing a chiffonier in the foyer with the framed pictures of two older nice-looking women sitting on it. "I know that woman," I said, pointing to one of them.

"Those are your great aunts," my mother said.

My grandmother had one of her fits. "You've never met them," she screamed at me. "You don't know them."

That's another scene I remember well, my mother trying to calm my grandmother down and my poor great uncle with a look on his face as if saying, "What the hell is going on here?" After that, I kept my own counsel about it, but knowing that woman was the one who stood by my bed in California a few years before.

In Texas, life did not improve much for me or my sister. But as we grew, we both became more adept at coping with our circumstances. Within a couple of years, my sister went to live at the Texas school for the deaf and blind as a student caretaker, where she worked and finished high school. She went on to college and has lived an interesting and successful life.

My grandmother went back to California and I never saw her again. Later I came into possession of a journal she kept as a young mother, who took her daughter, who was 11, my mother, and left her husband in Seattle in 1915.

With a horse and buggy, camping gear and $3.15, they traveled to California to start a new life. The trip took a year and she described in detail the difficulties and travails they endured during that trip. While she had not made my life pleasant, I cannot deny that she was a strong and self-reliant woman with considerable talents. Using that journal and what information I learned from my mother, I wrote a story about her titled "Remarkable Woman." Maybe someone will make a movie or TV series from it.

My mother had difficulty making a living in Texas and had to leave Milano to find work. This left me to live by myself at 15. My great uncle and I had grown apart. He was too old to take on the responsibility of raising a wild young kid, but had done the best he could and I remember him with affection. Those were hard years and resulted in me having experiences that a kid should not go through.

Looking back, it seems that I was being looked after by some entity I was unaware of, someone who kept me from either getting killed or in serious trouble. I did get seriously injured in a swimming accident, breaking my neck, something that caused my life to head in a new direction.

While recuperating from my injury, I went to live with a family near Austin, who agreed to take me in as a boarder while I healed. It was one of the better times in my life. I lived with D.J. Hopkins and his wife, Dele, who had four sons and two daughters, teenagers up to early 20s. These were not cultured or refined people. Nor did they have much money. They joked about being hillbillies, but it was the most enjoyable household I've ever been in.

They treated me as one of their own, including the constant practical jokes they pulled on each other and the always-present laughter.

Any time I want to raise my spirits, I think back to those days. Even then I was aware there was something different about these people, something so rare I haven't seen anything like it since. They didn't go to church or talk religion, but they had been touched by something different.

I was wearing a body cast and was limited in activity and D.J. suggested that I go down the road about a eighth of a mile and talk with Richard at the blacksmith shop. I took his advice. After meeting Richard, I visited every day. We became friends. Richard was in his late 80s or early 90s. He wouldn't admit to any age and I came to know that he didn't know exactly how old he was.

Richard was of mixed ancestry. He claimed to be half black and half Indian, but his face was weathered to the point no one could see any race in it. He was unable to read or write, but successfully ran his blacksmith shop, making his living doing what he wanted to.

 Richard did not believe in using electricity. He suspected electricity was something the devil thought up to complicate our lives. I couldn't argue with him. If ever there was ever a man who seemed content with life, it was Richard. Everything he did in the shop was as it had been done 100 years before.

Each morning he threw the front and rear doors open so he would have light to work by, and then fired up his forge. I took the job of turning the manual crank on the blower, providing air to the coals to heat metal hot and soft enough to become pliable and easy to work with. He built his own horseshoes and we had a steady stream of horses provided by local cowmen wanting his special shoes.

I was fascinated by his skills. I learned how to weld, sharpen plows, repair wagon wheels, including shrinking the metal rims, and how to take raw metal to build boxes, buckets and farm implements, all using the forge, anvil, pinchers and a variety of hammers. It was as if I had stepped back in time.

The best part of spending my time in that shop was having the old man share stories of his life and philosophy with me. His mother had been a slave who fled to Texas after the Civil War. She met his father there, but he was shot and killed in a skirmish with the law, forcing Richard to grow up on his own. He became a cowboy and told me about his experiences driving cattle up north on both the Chisolm and Goodnight trails.

Richard faced incredible hardships and dangerous living conditions. As he talked, he would show me scars he'd picked up over the years. Some appeared to be gunshot wounds. Richard said he never looked for trouble, but that it came from every direction; partly because of the work he did and partly because he was black and Indian in a world hostile to both.

I was being told about a life that was of the past and would never be lived again. I had a persistent thought that what he was saying was important to me and I had been guided to this place to hear it. In later years, I came to believe it was not just D.J. who had sent me to Richard but that an unknown entity was looking after me.

I don't recall ever feeling sorry for myself, but after hearing of Richard's life, every bad experience, at the time and in the future, paled in comparison.

Richard possessed a spiritual side, even though he expressed contempt for religions and churches. He shared with me the mysterious things that had happened to him throughout his life and convinced him the things we see and are told of in churches are only a small part of what is around us. At that time I was too young to understand what he was talking about, but I never forgot what he said. And he prompted me, although I was unaware of it, to be aware of the unusual and the unexplainable.

Many times, Richard said this to me: "Kid, get out of the herd, leave the herd." Being an old cowboy, he used cowboy language. "Them cows in the herd are on their way to the slaughterhouse." It took me a few more years to understand what he meant.

My injuries healed and I went on with life. The next step was the Army. I never met anyone there who made any particular impression on me, though I did make many friends and have several adventures. An event that I found inexplicable happened shortly after my training period ended. I was assigned to the Second Armored Division and in the summer of 1950 we boarded a large ship and sailed out of New Orleans, headed for Europe.

This was something new for me. I had been to the beach but never out on any large body of water. We cruised down the Mississippi, which was surreal as our big ship was much higher than the land sliding by below us. Enormous levees held water in a channel and I remember thinking there would be a flood in the future.

When we sailed out into the gulf, most of the troops headed below deck to lounge and play cards. I felt compelled to stay on deck and take in everything there was to see. It didn't take long to get out into the Atlantic and as I watched Florida fade out of our view, I experienced a strange feeling. I was in my glory, my element. I felt like I had come home. I was thrilled to be out on that ocean. I would go below to eat, but most of the time I and a handful of others slept on the deck because the weather was good and the ocean fairly calm.

This feeling remained with me the next six days until we docked in Germany. I, of course, believed my pleasure during the trip had to do with the balmy weather and the fact that I was experiencing something new.

About two years later, it was time for me to return to the U.S. This time it was during the winter and I shipped out on a smaller troopship heading to New York. I was told to be prepared for a rough and miserable trip as we would be going north in a big arc. One of my friends said it "was the same route the Titanic took."

The moment we left the English Channel, we entered rough seas that never let up until five days later when we hit New York Harbor. I had mentally prepared myself for a tough trip and as we plowed into the giant waves I found the same feeling coming over me as I had on the serene first crossing, only more so.

There were in excess of 500 troops on that ship and I would guess 450 were sea sick. They were everywhere, retching and moaning and lying in bunks, in passageways and on bathroom floors. The few of us that were left on our feet gathered in the mess hall, which was in the lower center part of the ship where it didn't roll quite as much. We had the run of the galley because the sick ones didn't care to eat. We prepared sumptuous meals and most played cards. Not me. After eating, I went out on deck.

I spent my time on the upper deck, as it was too stormy to allow anyone on the lower decks. The waves were breaking over the bow. It was cold up there and the salt spray was constant. Again I was in my glory, hanging onto the slippery rails, watching the bow of the ship crash into the big swells, go under, shudder, then come up scattering foam and water. I couldn't get enough. I found myself laughing … until a sick soldier rushed up to the rail next to me to throw up. His stomach contents blew back over both of us, causing me to empty out also. My pain was temporary. I ate again and was back out on my post living it up.

One of the ship's crew members came by from time to time. "You've had a life out on the sea haven't you," he asked me.

"No, not until I joined the Army," I answered.

"I mean one of your former lives," he said.

I didn't know what he was talking about, but the thought stayed with me through the years.

Many years later, my daughter, Beth, who was attending Pacific Lutheran College in Tacoma, got a chance to go to England for a semester in a student exchange program. She wanted some company on the trip and Marilyn and I decided to go with her. We flew to London, saw the sights and got Beth lined up on her assignment. Marilyn and I rented a car and set off to see England, Scotland and Wales. We had no particular itinerary, no reservations; we just planned on roving whenever our list of places to see took us and stay in bed and breakfasts wherever we found them. I cannot imagine a better way to travel. We had a wonderful time and saw much more than we had on the list.

We found that when we stayed in the bed and breakfast places, the owners and other guests would graciously fill us in on the area, suggesting points of interests and places we should see. A couple of times we were told: "Be sure you check out the village of Warrick and the castle there." So, we headed that way even though it was off the beaten path.

As we were nearing the village, things started to become familiar to me – the landscape, hills and trees. I had a very intense feeling that I was coming home. It was the same kind of feeling I had years ago on the ocean. When we passed through the village, it all seemed familiar and as we approached the castle I realized I knew what the view on the opposite side would look like. I became impatient to park and walk through and there it was: the rolling hills with trees scattered about, different from the side we had driven up on and exactly the picture I knew I would see. It was exciting, even as I tried to act nonchalant.

There were other visitors and I didn't want to act loony. I knew that I had been there before, just as I knew I had been at sea before. We spent some pleasant hours there and continued our trip and I, as usual, kept my mouth shut.

After my military career, my next stop was Alaska. I was young, single and anxious for adventure. I ended up living with an Indian family and the extended tribe during my first year there. The experience was different than anything I had been exposed to, but I fit right in. As we were fishermen, we spent much of our time traveling by boat to the various Indian villages throughout southeastern Alaska.

It was a source of amusement to me that the major villages and towns contained missionaries, mostly from Protestant churches, who were trying to introduce the Christian religion to them. I met many of the missionaries and they seemed to be very nice people who were sincere in their beliefs that they were doing the right thing by my Indian friends.

At the same time, I had observed and learned the spiritual beliefs of the Indians. They were different and, in many ways, better, given their lifestyle and background. By exposing myself to their beliefs, I learned no group had a real grasp of what it's all about, nor does one system fit everyone's life. My mentors there also had strong feelings that they were being looked after by unseen forces.

I'm convinced the unseen force looking after me made sure that I met that young nurse who had gone to Alaska to work in the Native American hospital. I had decided that marriage would not fit into my lifestyle and my plan was to stay away from any serious entanglements. However, she was meant for me and I immediately knew, even in my ignorance, that she was the one. She was there and I was drawn to her like a magnet and almost 60 years later as I write about this we are still sharing a good life together. She influenced me for the better from that point on.

My career as a lawman came next, starting as a young policeman. From the beginning, I had the feeling I fit it naturally. That is to say that I fit in with the good ones and quickly learned there were many policemen who were misplaced and shouldn't have been there. I've written about them in another book, "Better an Honest

Scoundrel," and will not repeat myself, but I quickly learned to ignore them, to not be influenced by them, to follow my own path, which sometimes put me at odds with some in the command structure. My goal was not to please everyone, but to make a difference.

I learned quickly that there is more to the life than putting people in jail, although that's what I did with many who I thought deserved it for one reason or another. With the job came opportunity to do some good, such as influencing young people and protecting those who couldn't protect themselves.

Within a year, I became a detective and co-chairman of a police club to help young gang members and troubled teens. I also became a member of the mayor's juvenile committee. We established a live-in group home named Harbor House for kids who, through no fault of their own, had no place to go. I was also active in the mayor's anti-discrimination committee, my interest in that subject likely prompted by living in Texas at a time when blacks were viciously persecuted. Somehow, I knew it to be wrong.

My experiences gave me an ability to communicate with troubled people, as well as those living on what we now call the dark side. That ability later allowed me to concentrate on becoming an interrogator and successful polygraph examiner. I was in that line of work to make a difference and I think that I did.

At the same time, it didn't take me long to realize law enforcement doesn't pay very well and that I would have to find another way to make money. Marilyn worked and we started saving money and investing in parcels of land, houses and commercial buildings. By the time retirement from law enforcement arrived, we were comfortable enough to do a little world traveling, which helps broaden one's perspective, meaning a broadening of mind, in spite of yourself.

When I married Marilyn, she was a Lutheran and I knew it would be wise for me to join that denomination, though my beliefs did not coincide with hers. It worked out well. I was determined that our marriage work and I made every effort to accept the doctrine in spite of my doubt. I found many areas of agreement and common ground and there was much to like, particularly the people we associated with. We had many good times together and I suspected that many of them were like me, not necessarily believing everything but wanting the good life that went with belonging. For me, always in the background was that feeling of "knowing" there was much more, that this dogma was too narrow, that things just didn't work the way the Christian religion promoted.

For my own satisfaction, I knew that virgin births cannot happen, no one survives in the belly of a whale and considerable imagination sometimes goes into selling an idea. I was to be tested in strange ways, and those changed my life.

I had left the city police department after 15 years to accept a position as a criminal investigator with the Idaho Bureau of Investigation. It was one of the best moves I ever made. My horizons broadened and the deputy commissioner of law enforcement and I had become friends. I had some successes and was asked which school I would like to attend. I wanted to go to a polygraph examiners school, specifically the Backster School of Lie Detection in San Diego. I had been told it was the best. I later learned the commissioner told them when they signed me up that I was the best interrogator in the state of Idaho and maybe the country. While it may not have been true, I think that statement focused the school's attention on me in a way I had not expected.

The school's director, Cleve Backster, had a stellar background as a polygraph examiner, had once headed the polygraph division of the CIA and was responsible for the latest innovations in testing procedures. Somewhere I had heard him described as a genius and that intrigued me, as well as rumors that he dabbled in spirituality. I was anxious to meet and challenge him. At that stage of my life, I thought I had spiritual matters pretty well sorted out.

The school was intense with about 20 students attending at any one time and an enormous amount of things to learn quickly. I did not meet Cleve until we had been in session a couple of weeks and only then after he was scheduled to teach an ethics class. My experience had been that ethics was a gray area in law enforcement. While I thought I had the subject pretty well nailed down, I worked with policemen who skirted the fringes of the subject. I expected more of the same.

That class was the first time I had heard anyone in the enforcement game insist that ethics was the most important criteria a police examiner could bring to the table: that the examiner's loyalty must not be to the department he worked for or the criminal justice system but to the individual he was testing or interrogating. You owed that person honesty and that was never to be violated. He was talking my language. I knew that approach worked best and that at the end of the day you could feel good about yourself.

It didn't take long for me to get over my desire to challenge Cleve's extracurricular activities. That class on ethics and some good-natured bantering between classes convinced me he was a very unusual man. He was obviously smart but also self-effacing in that he was full of humor, open and with the kind of self-control I'd noticed in people who march to a different drumbeat. I felt comfortable discussing religion with him, even though I found out we were polar opposites. I was still trying to make sense of Christianity and he had adopted what I could best describe as an eastern religious philosophy. We laughed and joked as we discussed topics such as reincarnation, activity beyond death and the purpose behind everything. I didn't tell him, but I was receiving answers to many of the questions I had been pondering.

One day, Cleve put out an open invitation to the class: "I know some of you have heard I have other interests besides polygraph examining," he said. "The top floor of this building is where I have my laboratory. Tonight you would all be welcome to come up there about 6 and I'll be glad to show you what I do."

We knew he did some sort of research on plants, but didn't have details. Most of us said we'd be there. As we were leaving he called me aside and asked if I knew anything about my fellow classmates that might be embarrassing to them. I knew a detective from the Midwest told us he was a married man with children and that we had seen him meeting a young lady in the hotel bar each night. Cleve asked when he gave me a signal if I would start an interrogation about that girl. I was intrigued and agreed.

At 6, I went to the lab and discovered that only half the class had accepted his invitation. This baffled me as this was a major event. We knew this man had a worldwide reputation. He had written books and gave lectures around the world. His videos disappear as fast as they are released. Why would half our class decline to hear what he had to say? As the years went by, I saw this kind of thing on a regular basis. People who have a belief system of any kind, be it religion, politics, how they do their job or live their lives, when faced with any kind of challenge, immediately put up barriers to resist anything that might force them to reevaluate their thinking.

I have watched many friends flee from exposure to new ideas or information, as if they thought the devil might be after them. They often are not aware of their fear. Exploring new thoughts does not seem to be a virtue with most humans.

Cleve had a large and comfortable laboratory, well lit, clean and orderly. On a long table sat four large healthy-looking flowers in standard pots. Next to each was a polygraph instrument with the wire leads from the instrument component that measures electrical changes or variations attached to leaves in the plant it was adjacent to. Each instrument contained video cameras to record the movements of the pens, which trace the patterns of electrical variations on moving chart paper. The setup was the same as one would use to measure variations in the electrical or nervous systems of human beings as they were being tested for truth or deception.

On the wall above the plants was mounted a split screen. The screen was split into four segments, each one showing the pen and chart paper action from the separate plants. Our curiosity was obvious and I don't think any of us could have been dragged out of that room by wild horses.

After greeting us and thanking us for coming, Cleve told a story: Many years before, he was in a borrowed office in New York City and had made arrangements to conduct a polygraph examination on a police chief from one of the southern cities. The chief was late and had called to say that his plane had been delayed and he would be there as soon as he could. It was an important exam, with a lot riding on the results, so Cleve elected to wait.

Being bored, he looked around for something to occupy his time. Finding nothing else of interest in the office, he turned to his polygraph instrument, thinking to recheck all its functions for accuracy. While fooling with it he noted a plant and decided to hook his electrodes to a leaf, pour water in the pot and see if the instrument can detect the water moving up through the stems into the leaves. Cleve was amazed to see he was getting a wave pattern that was exactly what he would have gotten from a human being.

As he watched, the reaction on the chart seemed to show the plant had life that could be measured and the pattern seemed to indicate the plant had an awareness of its surroundings just like a human. Cleve found this fascinating and decided to light a match and hold it under a leaf to see what would happen. As he thought about doing that, Cleve observed the needle on the chart made a small jump. That prompted him to decide he was actually going to do it. The exact second that entered his mind, Cleve observed a major jump on the chart, exactly as a human might react when being threatened with being burned by a match. "From that moment on my life was never the same again," Cleve told us.

Cleve detailed how he continued experimenting until he was absolutely certain that all plants were aware of their surroundings, that they reacted to not only physical stimuli but also knew what humans in their presence were thinking. Before that night was over, I knew that my life would never be the same again, discovering that there are tangible things going on around us we had never had a clue about, that no one was talking about, that nothing was written about.

I thought back to my days with the Klinket Indians in Alaska and how they seemed to have a reverence for all living things: trees, plants, animals, sea creatures. I remembered how they included those things in their thinking and language and how I had privately scoffed, content with my worldly knowledge.

There is a parlor game I've played in family gatherings that I found to be great fun. A small handheld device with a button is passed from player to player. When the button is pushed the device starts ticking loudly and each player is required to answer a question as they are holding it. What makes the game fun is that the device will stop ticking and buzz loudly at random times. There is no way to tell when it will happen. The object of the game is to not let the buzzer go off while you are holding it, quickly answer your question and pass it on or lose points. The game produces a lot of laughter as the passing gets faster and faster as players try to get rid of it.

Cleve showed us a laboratory device that was very similar. He referred to it as a mechanical concentric circle. It had a small round platform that turned around and around. Like the game piece, it was designed to tip over at random times. The randomness was built into it so the operator had no control or knowledge of when it would tip.

Next to and beneath the device was a pan of boiling water on a hot plate. He had a glass bowl of water which contained a lot of small fresh water shrimp. After explaining that the shrimp had very short lives, mostly spent attempting to reproduce, we saw that they were very active. He placed the bowl on the platform. Before switching it on he said: "When the device tips, it will upset the water and shrimp over into the boiling water, which will, of course, kill the shrimp. None of us can know when it will happen. The shrimp know and will somehow communicate to the room their alarm of their impending death. The plants are going to pick up that message and react violently to it several seconds before it happens."

He switched it on and the platform started turning slowly around. After what seemed like a long couple of minutes, the split screen came alive with all four pens waving frantically. We looked back and forth from the device to the screen and in a few more seconds the bowl flipped over spilling the shrimp into the boiling water where they expired. The pens made a final upward sweep and then returned to a normal pattern. It appeared to me that the final upward swing was a response to the shrimps' primal death scream, the one we didn't hear, but the plants did.

Cleve asked one of our members to take a seat at a table and had the rest of us gather around. He asked the detective to place his hands apart out on the table top and explained that he had a small and harmless spider that he was going to put on the table between the detective's outstretched hands. He instructed the detective to use his hands to keep the spider corralled in one spot. Whatever direction the little spider tried to run, he was to block his escape with his hands until it gave up and remained still.

With a grin the detective rose to the challenge and soon the spider stopped running and hunched down, watching the detective's hands circle around it.

"I'm going to ask you to suddenly pull your hands away and when you do the spider will look around, evaluate his options to escape and make a decision to make a run for it," Cleve said. "When he does, the plants will pick up on it, but we won't. That is we won't unless we're watching these plant reactions!" Our eyes jumped back and forth from the spider to the split screen as Cleve gave the order: "Remove your hands."

A few seconds went by and the spider came up out of his crouch. More seconds passed and suddenly, as before, the pens started waving about in unison. About five seconds later, the spider, in a burst of speed, cleared the tabletop and disappeared under it and out of sight. The pens returned to normal. I still marvel at the dynamics we viewed with that simple test.

We were all standing around, comfortable with each other and our surroundings, exchanging thoughts and I happened to look toward Cleve, who had stepped behind us and noticed that he was giving me the prearranged signal. I was still game. I walked over to my target and in a friendly way started asking him about his city and department that he worked for.

I liked this detective and early on realized that he was very sharp. He obviously realized that I was up to something and, like most savvy investigators, took pleasure in any kind of challenge. Everything got quiet and all attention was on us. I moved from his working conditions to his home life. He, with a puzzled look but friendly manner, played along, telling me about his home and family, saying he was married with kids and that his life was pretty good.

I changed my tone: "With that kind of situation, I'm sure you would never do anything that would be embarrassing or damaging to your home life," I said.

"Of course not," he replied.

I glanced at the split screen, something I would not normally do, but my curiosity was now in charge. The pens were exhibiting what we were learning was a heightened reaction. I couldn't resist. I looked back at him and said: "What about that girl you're meeting in the hotel bar every night?"

I watched him turn red and switched my eyes back to the screen. The pens were going wild.

Everyone had picked up on what had happened. I laughed and smacked his arm and he laughed with me. But I could see that all of us, including our detective friend, had just been exposed to a profound truth. Those four plants had picked up on his wariness and caution and his embarrassment or lie. One of the lady detectives present said, almost in anger: "Why haven't I known about this before?"

"There are people who instinctively know plant life has awareness and understanding and the deeper we explore the more we become aware there is so much more than this going on around us that we refuse to want to learn," Cleve said.

We talked about Indians who know of medicine trees and my thoughts went back to my friends in Alaska, who talked to trees and plants in their language and how I thought that was so dumb. I was glad I had kept those thoughts to myself.

Cleve told us of another test I later saw on film. Using grad students from USC who were interested in his work, Cleve asked one to take a position at a table in front of the room. His assistant took two healthy-looking cabbage plants from a cooler and set them on the table.

Cleve gave the volunteer a stick and asked him to start thinking about things that really made him angry and to take out that anger by beating one of the cabbage plants with the stick. The student really got into the program, obviously working himself up into a rage and literally beat the cabbage to a battered pulp. He was to later say his anger was over an expensive traffic ticket he had received that he definitely did not deserve.

At that time, the uninjured cabbage plant was removed from the table and placed back in the cooler. The following day, the same uninjured plant was brought back to the table and connected in the usual way to a polygraph instrument. The grad students were asked to line up in the hallway outside of the room while the one who had beaten the other cabbage was asked to pick a random spot in the line. They were called one by one to open the door and slowly come into the room. As the instrument was turned on, the pen began a normal waving action and the students were called to enter. They came in at short intervals. The pen made the usual blips as each came in as if indicating acknowledgment of their presence. Suddenly it showed a major reaction and a few seconds later the guilty student appeared at the door.

I could go on about those and other tests, some conducted by others and a few I conducted myself, but I think it is enough to say it was time for me to start looking for answers to the question about what actually is going on around us and why.

I found that when you allow your mind to be unshackled, and you're actually watching and questioning, it's like throwing off a big load you've been carrying on your back and didn't realize was there before. It was exciting to see with new eyes. Unusual experiences kept popping up in my work and my life. One experience that had a profound effect on me came about as follows:

During my early cowboy days in Texas, I had developed a love of horses. When we moved to Idaho and settled in, I began acquiring a small string of gentle saddle horses and used them for hunting in Idaho's wilderness areas and many pleasure pack trips into local mountains and the backcountry of Yellowstone Park with family and friends.

Our scrapbooks are full of pictures of the beautiful sights. I acted as the outfitter guide and took enormous pleasure in those trips ... so much so that I played with the idea of becoming a legitimate outfitter when I retired. To do so, I would need a jump-off place near scenic mountains. I had in mind a small dude ranch. I eventually chose my place in Leadore on the Lemhi River, but before I did I spent time looking for the ideal spot.

At that time I was working as a state criminal investigator, a job that took me into some of the remote smaller counties in Idaho when local sheriffs needed assistance with major crimes. To reach a town I had been called to from my base in Idaho Falls required me to travel on a highway that crossed a small mountain range. The road was quite scenic, winding up a large canyon several miles and then dropping abruptly into the valley.

There was a small abandoned ranch about halfway up. It looked good to me and I stopped to check it out. It featured a green meadow, a nice stream and a couple old buildings. I could see possibilities. But I was in no hurry and had not yet done a search to find an owner to talk about the possibility of buying the place.

One summer day, I had been working with the sheriff in that town on a case and, as often is the case when you like what you do, we worked late into the evening. It was past midnight when I drove over that summit and headed down the canyon toward home. There was almost a full moon. As there was no traffic on the road, I turned my lights off and was surprised to find I didn't need them. I was approaching the old ranch and, as I was tired and a little sleepy, I decided to stop there and stretch my legs and see what the place looked like in the moonlight.

I pulled off the pavement, parked, got out and climbed over a gate wired shut with old and rusty barb wire. The setting was beautiful and serene as I strolled on the drive toward the buildings.

Suddenly and without any apparent cause, a strong feeling came over me that I was in danger. It was not the first time in my life I had that feeling: suddenly realizing a huge grizzly bear was charging my hunting partner and I; or when guns came into play as I entered a building where a felon was hiding. But those times I was aware ahead of time there might be some danger. In this case, there was only silence.

A lot of thoughts were racing around in my mind: a bear, a cougar, an abominable snowman hiding in the brush or in the deep grass. Or worse, a human with twisted thoughts. It would not have been the first time

I've run into a bad guy in the woods with evil on his mind. One of the major life lessons I learned early on was, if faced with something that might be dangerous, your best option is to attack it head on and fast. My big pistol came out and I moved forward. Whatever lay ahead was in deep trouble.

The moonlight was good to me. Everything stood out. I had no flashlight and didn't need one. I moved slowly around the old buildings noting that the grass and weeds were knee high and showed no sign of having been disturbed. The only evidence that anybody had been there were my own tracks behind me. The buildings were empty. My feeling had grown to something approaching dread and I didn't like it.

I was ready to shoot something. I turned my attention to the deep grass and brush, systematically, back and forth, trying to cut some tracks and at the same time swinging around to watch my backside. Nothing was going sneak up on me. As I moved away from the buildings in ever larger concentric circles there was nothing there.

Realizing I couldn't search the whole mountain range, especially in the dark, I returned to the old house. The feeling of dread and danger seemed to increase. I was absolutely sure something bad was present and it galled me to think I was going to have to leave without discovering what it was. The feeling was so strong that when I left, I backed down that lane to the gate, reluctant to turn my back on whatever it was but also knowing I would be back when I could see better.

The next morning, I got an early start and headed back. The drive took a couple hours and I spent the time pondering how I was going to handle whatever it was that

I was going to find and how I was going to explain going back ... if anybody asked. By the time I drove up to the gate, I hadn't figured out any good answers.

The sun was shining, the grass was green and the water in the creek made that kind of peaceful sound water makes as it gurgles around rocks in the stream bed. The stately pines on the mountain side above were dark green and still. The picture was right out of a storybook. I climbed back over the gate and walked up the lane toward the old house waiting for my senses to tell me something bad was about. It didn't happen. The only tracks around were the ones I made the night before.

The bad feeling didn't return that day or any of the times during the coming weeks when my travels took me by the place and I stopped to check again. One of those times was late at night as before.

I think one of the essential qualities a detective must have is insatiable curiosity about things that don't make sense, that don't fit, and a willingness to look for answers or solutions. What happened that night? I wasn't going to leave it alone until I found out. I searched for the owner of the ranch, who turned out to be a woman living in Europe.

Her interests were being handled by a local law firm. I talked to them, as well as some of the local ranchers in the area and learned the history of the place. In the early 1930s, it belonged to a bachelor. A couple of the old-timers described him as not being very sociable. The Great Depression was on and things were tough. He committed suicide at the ranch.

His nephew inherited it and also lived there. World War II broke out and the nephew joined the Army and fought in Europe. He married a European woman and after the war brought her back to America. They lived at the ranch. My informants told me the nephew committed suicide in the same house as his uncle. His widow returned to Europe.

The night I searched the place – and the following day when I found no evidence – convinced me nothing was there that represented any part of the physical world. I was beginning to awaken to the obvious. Those suicides were a part of something I could feel.

My thoughts returned to my old blacksmith friend in Texas, who told me of having to back away from some places where he said the spirit was wrong. Now I knew what he meant.

I have also stumbled upon places that were just the opposite, in which a sudden feeling of serenity and calmness came over me. These, I learned from others, are places where the spirit is right. There is a beautiful small bowl in the high peaks of the Lemhi Mountain Range where I sometimes ride just for the pleasure of soaking in the scenery. This is a high mountain meadow with scattered weathered trees surrounded by peaks.

On each trip, I get the same great feeling. It's so great that I asked my son, after my death, to take my ashes to that meadow and scatter them. If anyone wants to communicate with me, even though I may not be there, they will be rewarded for their trip by the same spirits.

I wasn't through learning about things that don't fit. During a stage in my criminal investigation life, I became a certified police hypnotist. It was easy for me. During my Army career, I served with a professional hypnotist who had been drafted into the service, interrupting his life performing stage shows. We hit it off and he trained me in hypnosis and using what I learned from him, I had fun hypnotizing willing fellow soldiers in our unit.

Many years later, a movement started in the police world of using hypnosis to help witnesses recall events they had seen but had difficulty remembering. I volunteered, went to school and became state certified.

Hypnosis is a fascinating subject and I'm not sure many people understand how it works or what is happening when it does. And for the record, those of us who use it don't really know the full reasons for its existence or its potential for understanding where it can take us in the big picture of purpose and existence.

In the police world, it became a valuable tool. We all like to think that our minds are well organized and that all knowledge we have been exposed to is readily available to us. The truth is that there is so much more than we can ever imagine. A small part of it became available to police when it was realized that almost all of what goes on around us is noted and stored by, for lack of a better word, our subconscious.

As an example, in a bank robbery there are often several witnesses. The event usually elicits emotional reactions and sometimes traumatizes both victims and witnesses, who often can't give a detailed or accurate description of what happened. To the frustration of the responding investigators, they may have conferred with each other and those who are not sure what happened will conform to another witness who seems positive of what he or she had seen or heard, which later may be found to be wrong.

Through hypnosis, those witnesses may be taken back in time to the event and can relive it in a safe and non-threatening environment. Suddenly all those things recorded by the subconscious are brought forward. The amount of accurate information hypnosis can provide is often astounding to investigators.

Police hypnotist was added to my other duties and for the next few years, as I responded to requests for help from local agencies, I became involved in its use to help solve all kinds of crimes. I was constantly being amazed at the knowledge people had recorded in the subconscious that they didn't know they had. Things like having seen a car near a crime scene and not being able to describe it except in the vaguest terms and then, when having been taken back to the scene in a hypnotized state, coming up with makes, models and colors.

It astounded me when they not only came up with a license plate but also could name the state that issued it and the sequence of numbers. Sometimes they would give the sequence of numbers backwards, indicating they had read it backward when consciously they didn't even know they had seen it.

I went from one baffling experience to another, like hypnotizing a mentally challenged person who spoke like a small child. Under hypnosis, this person began speaking as a normal adult with a precise and well-modulated voice. In another case, a husband and wife under hypnosis recalled the details of a drunk driver who ran over and killed a jogger on a highway they had been driving at night several months before. This couple was perplexed and astounded to learn they had seen the accident occur. They had responded to a police call for information by reporting that on that night they thought they had seen a piece of metal lying in the road. The license number and car description they provided under hypnosis was the clue that solved that case.

I had developed my skill to the place that I was contemplating writing a book about this exciting and productive new tool. What a boon to law enforcement. It took a few years and the courts were accepting evidence retrieved by hypnosis and then the hammer dropped. It shouldn't have surprised me. One of the phenomena associated with hypnosis is that subjects who have been hypnotized are very susceptible to suggestion. Information and false memories may be implanted by the hypnotist. The hypnotist in the entertainment world uses this to induce laughs and promote wonder. At one time I had done it myself.

One of my standards was to have a volunteer come forward, put him under and plant the suggestion that when he awakens he will go back to his seat with the others and when he hears me say, "the good old red white and blue," he will jump to his feet and very loudly and forcibly shout out, "Goddamn it to hell." I would close my presentation by thanking everyone for being so cooperative, saying "and don't forget the old red white and blue."

The subject would jump up as if a firecracker had gone off under him, shout it out and stand there looking around with a bewildered expression on his face, as if he couldn't believe he had just done what he had just done. That look caused great hilarity in the crowd.

Many books have been written about this phenomena and much damage has been done with its misuse. About the same time police had started using it, some counselors in the mental health field developed a theory that generally stated that if a woman was having problems in her life, marriage problems, employment difficulties, bad relationships and so on, it was probably because she was sexually molested early in her life and usually by her father. She had suppressed the memories and it was the root cause of her dysfunctional life.

We can't say things didn't happen that way sometimes. However, there were rabid believers in the theory who were unable to accept continual denials from whoever they were counseling and after inducing the patient into a hypnotic state would plant the suggestion that "they must remember all those bad things that happened to them."

The patient would respond by imagining that terrible things did happen. Those imagined memories most often involved satanic rites and other bizarre practices and when the patient awakened those memories became very real to them. They would then confront their imagined tormenter and push for criminal charges to be filed, which created enormous problems. I won't go into this, but I will recommend, if you're interested, the book "Making Monsters" by Richard Ofshe and Ethan Waters.

I was to later work on those kinds of cases, attempting to undo some of the damage done. That involvement exposed me to a great deal of human degradation and unjust accusations, which ultimately had the effect of strengthening my awareness that forces are at work we don't know about or understand.

Police are not immune to misusing a good thing, either. There are investigators who are not competent or honest. All were taught that in using this tool one may never lead a subject into telling you what you want to hear rather than what's true but you don't want to hear. In other words, you are not to plant ideas or information into a hypnotized subject.

An example would be if you are asking a subject about a car at a crime scene. You are not to bring the car up at all. You take the subject back to the time he was at the scene and ask him what he is seeing. If there was a car, he will tell you. Then you ask him to describe the car he is seeing.

I've heard horror stories where the detective would be trying to prove what he already believed and ask: "Do you see a red Ford there?" When the subject cooperated by saying "yes," the detective would ask: "Were there two people in it and were they black and did the car have California plates? The courts soon caught on to what was happening and immediately took that tool away, as they should have.

I had re-entered a world I found fascinating and though it was no longer included as part of my duties, I didn't want to move on without learning more. I began gathering information about other uses of hypnosis and found many volunteers in my circle of friends. Without going into details, I used it to help friends quit smoking, lose weight, develop positive attitudes and gain control of emotions … all positive things and again I marveled at the knowledge and power each person within them.

My curiosity took over. In my reading and conversations with others in the field, I was exposed to something called "past life regression." Using my old self-protection bubble, which was a comfortable place to be, I had rejected the idea. I knew about regressing people. I had done it to take people back to a event or crime scene that needed remembering, back to when they thought they lost something like a ring or watch and even to certain events in their lives, such as the first day of school, which can be hilarious when they start talking like a kid. But to go beyond life as we know it meant rearranging one's entire thought patterns. Is there more we haven't been told about? I felt compelled to explore.

To shorten my story, I have to say there was more. I found it compelling that there seemed to be no shortage of volunteers who also wanted to find out. The volunteers I chose to explore with were ordinary and stable people who seemed to have at least one thing in common: They were not locked into any rigid dogma or creed that discouraged searching.

The first time I guided someone into a past life, I had no idea what to expect. Here was a woman describing to me a former life, what she was feeling and seeing and doing and what she had done. And it was credible, something I really hadn't expected, but knew I had to do it again if for no other reason than to double-check. Could this really be happening?

It was. It happened again and again. I learned that not everyone can be hypnotized, but those who could told stories and described places and relived events even to the point of sharing their death in another life. It was staggering to me. At one point, I stopped to re-evaluate. Was I in over my head? Did I know what I'm doing? Was all this true? And then I sat back and remembered how much of my working life was spent learning how to tell when someone was not telling the truth. The signals for deception were not there. It was one credible story after another. I reached the place I could do nothing else but accept what in the back of my mind I had known all along. I had lived before this life, as we all have.

My story did not stop there. My sister, who lives in Alaska and who I touch base with from time to time, is quite smart. Her IQ qualifies her to belong in the Mensa Society. Mine is short of that, though I'm satisfied with it. She has a higher education than I and is a voracious reader who has an interest in everything, including the spiritual realm. I discussed the path I was on with her. She told me about others who had determined that under hypnosis some can be guided not only to past lives but also future lives and the existence in between each of our lives.

This was heavy stuff, but I saw no reason to stop looking around. I have done a lot of reading, especially in the hypnosis arena, and discovered I've been trailing behind. This has actually been going on and the information from those who have spoken of the past, present and between while in hypnotic trances clarified and reinforced my new perceptions.

The search has become not only exciting but also fun. I reached a place where I could not believe I had allowed myself to have been misled so easily. But then I have come to realize "that's the name of the game." Our purpose is to learn and grow.

What is taught by the so-called great religions is very superficial. Many of the doctrines were formulated during a time of ignorance, when few people were educated and those who were had no access to even a small portion of the knowledge available to mankind today. Doctrines had to be simple and they had to revolve around an extension of the narrow outlooks of uneducated people striving to survive: the wise father in our likeness, somewhere in the sky, giving orders and passing judgments and answering petitions for help and protection just like a king on earth might do.

And a heaven and a hell described in terms easily understood as desirable or horrible. It's no wonder the bigger picture is so elusive, especially if we come into life each time as a "start over," where we are allowed, and I emphasize allowed, to have free choice to either grow or sink by our own efforts. With no direct connection with our past, we are left to discover again what we already knew if we can add the new knowledge that has become available since our last trip.

The search doesn't stop, but instead speeds up. I realize I'm way behind others whose intellect and experiences have taken them beyond where I'm at, those who have experienced what I've come to know as enlightenment. I started reading the works of well-known mystics and scientists who have, in my words, "shaken off the chains, dared to explore and conquered the power of conformity." These people, in the words of my old cowboy mentor, "leave the herd."

And then I had what has been my ultimate unexplainable experience.

One of my great pleasures in life is to have spent time, often alone, at the ranch in Leadore. During those times, when I'm not building and repairing, I have made it a habit each evening to go on a ride or a hike in the nearby mountains. During spring and summer months, when it stays light until 10 or so, it is special. There is time to explore and contemplate in wild landscapes undisturbed by humans.

One evening, I decided to hike up a small and average-looking canyon visible from our place on the nearby mountain. I chose that canyon not because of its beauty – it had none – but because I had never been up it before.

I drove my pickup to its base, parked and started hiking. The mountain was steep and the canyon topped out about a half mile up the slope. I thought it would be a easy climb. It wasn't. There was no trail, the brush was thick, the trees were stunted and the rocks were an ugly and drab color and there were a lot of them. The sun hadn't gone down yet and I was soon scratched up, sweating and a little unhappy about my choice.

About half way up, I arrived at a good game trail that crossed the canyon and went up a slope to a nearby ridge. The going was easy so I followed it. As I topped out on that ridge, everything changed.

I find it difficult to put into words, but I felt like I had been picked up. My whole body suddenly felt great and as I looked around, I realized that I was filled with joy or elation. As I looked around me to find the cause of what was happening I realized the rocks under my feet had a quality about them and a new color that shimmered. I had a hard time taking my eyes off them.

From my vantage point on the side of the mountain, I looked out over the valley below. I'd seen that valley a thousand times before, but never like this. The valley, with its river meandering through it, the mountain peaks, the sky … all came into focus and it was beautiful with a shimmering clarity I had never seen before. I could not get enough of that sight.

As I stood there looking around, I knew no person was with me but I was overwhelmed with the feeling I was not alone. I didn't hear any voices, but an understanding came over me. I was with a friend and the friend was pleased with me and the positive message that my searching had been right. The feeling that filled me was that I had just come home from a long journey to a place of welcoming happiness and love. I stood there soaking in the atmosphere, until the sun went down behind the peaks across the valley.

It was getting dark. I would not have made the decision to leave, but something inside of me said it was time to go. The trip down the ridge should have been difficult. I had no light and the ridge was rocky and uneven and tricky to maneuver, but I was floating and didn't care or notice.

This was in the fall and in the mountains, as the sun goes down, the cold moves in. I didn't notice that either, until I found my pickup and drove back to the lodge, where I built a big fire. I sat there watching the fire snap and crackle and relived the experience. I wanted to share, but was alone and there was no way I could have transferred that feeling to anyone else at that time. Since then, I have come to realize that others have had this experience as well. I have read descriptions that parallel mine.

Dr. Richard Maurice Burke, in his book, "The Future of Humanity," written in 1901, described an experience while riding across London in a horse-drawn carriage. His words are more eloquent than mine, but the experience was identical. The light was within me. Burke wrote, speaking in the third person: "All at once, without warning of any kind, he found himself wrapped around, as it were, by a flame colored cloud. For an instant he thought of fire - some sudden conflagration in the great city. The next instant he knew that the light was within himself. Directly after there came upon him a sense of exaltation, of immense joyousness, accompanied or immediately followed by an intellectual illumination quite impossible to describe. Into his brain streamed one momentary lighting flash of the Brahmic Splendor which ever since lighted his life. Upon his heart fell one drop of the Brahmic Bliss, leaving thenceforward for always an aftertaste of Heaven. Among other things he came to believe, he saw and knew that the cosmos was not dead matter but a living Presence, that the soul of man is immortal, that the universe it so built and ordered that without peradventure all things work together for the good of each and all, that the foundation principle of the world is what we call love and that happiness of everyone is in the long run absolutely certain."

And so what have these series of unexplainable events, the reading and the talking and sharing and especially the observations brought me to? And does it matter? I've come to understand that everything matters. Everything is connected and it all has a purpose. And as I describe what I have come to know, no one should feel they have been wrong in their beliefs. Everyone is where they are. It is a searching journey and the conditions of that journey are that it should not be easy. No matter what answers you may come up with, there will be many forces to hinder and divert and deny. The game, the purpose, is to go all the way if you can. Growth and understanding is what you're after. Leave the herd.

Starting with the universal question: Is there a God? I've come to know that there absolutely is, but not a fuzzy image of one in our likeness. In my searching I heard a description that fits what I have learned. Imagine a person looking at a massive skyscraper in a large city. That person will be seeing a great deal – entrances and windows and commercial rentals at street level and the building facade and colors and height.

Many marvel at the sight. What that person is not seeing is the steel structure that it is built around and which holds everything together, that allows it to exist as a building. God is so much larger and more present than the old bearded man Michelangelo painted on the ceiling of the Sistine Chapel, and we as yet don't know what form God exists in or if it is a form at all and not something we are unable to grasp yet or ever.

What I have learned is that God is in us just like the steel is in the skyscraper. Because we have choice, evil is also in us if we choose to use or follow it.

And as God is large, so is his creation. So large that it not only boggles our minds but can astound us with its complexity. This universe which goes, to us, out and out and on and on into, who knows what but which we refer to as empty space, is just a tiny part of what is. But right now it is ours to explore and learn about. Greater things are coming. Quantum mechanics are beckoning us to those parallel universes. Put yourself in the body of a tiny ant living in a colony in the desert and imagine how much more there is in just this earth that it can't visualize or guess at and you are describing all of us.

And what about life? What about our life, who are we? Is there a plan and a purpose? We are real and the plan is so much larger than most can visualize. Did we really think our narrow little view of a heaven of golden streets and pine trees and psalm singing - or a hell of constant torment in a lake of fire or a garden with 72 virgins waiting for us – is adequate in any big picture? We are real, but we are not our bodies. Our spirit is who we are and it has enormous potential and a special place in the big plan.

What makes us special is that choice we have been given: to either improve ourselves or take ourselves out of the game. And we are given a lot of time and a lot of chances to do it. We will cycle through many lives before we're through, if ever we are through.

And in our goal is there a theme? The answer is yes and what is great is that so many of us have recognized it and practiced it without knowing the particulars. The best word for it is love: a word that is tortured, misused and misunderstood, but which prevails over and over and again and again. That's what it's all about. Our purpose is to embrace it and live it and spread it. Each lifetime is to make a difference to others and then take it into our present environment, to love and protect all of creation. That's a big order but if you're in the game for any other purpose, you are eventually taking yourself into oblivion.

So, as with everyone else, the struggle goes on inside of me. There are people I think need to be destroyed and I know it's in me to do it. At the same time, I find myself liking people everywhere I go, in other countries, other races, other belief systems and religions. I even found myself liking some of the criminals I used to deal with, people who have done some very bad things.

I take solace as I remember back in this life that I reached out to and helped people more often than I hurt them. And as this run has ended up to be so great and satisfying, I eagerly await the next. What could be better than to take another run at it and then another and on and on, in competition only with myself, but desiring to catch up with those souls who show up among us from time to time and are obviously are way ahead?

Epilogue

Well, time has passed since I sat under the overhang that afternoon waiting for the storm to pass over. When the storm passed, it was hard to leave. I relished the hours reminiscing about life as a private eye. But the time was not wasted. As I recollected those experiences, I took pleasure in the memories and decided I would share a few with others. I hope others may take pleasure in those stories and learn as I have.

Lots of changes have taken place since that storm. Whiskey is no longer with me. As he aged, he was having difficulty traversing those steep mountain trails and I thought he deserved a rest. I learned of a family looking for an older, gentle horse their little kids could ride around in the corral. Knowing he would have an easy life in a good home, I gave him to that family. It was difficult to say goodbye.

Now I have another horse: a big and powerful gelding from a wild horse herd that roams the mountains near Challis. He's not as pretty as Whiskey, brown with black mane and tail and white legs and just enough white splashes one could almost call him a paint. I wasn't looking for beauty and I'd like to think I was inspired by a verse by Hannah Kahn:

Ride a wild horse with purple wings
Striped yellow and black
Except his head which must be red
Ride a wild horse against the sky
Hold tight to his wings before you die
Whatever else you leave undone
Ride a wild horse into the sun.

I believe she meant that verse to be a prescription for living life. If someone was to see me on my new horse on a mountain pass with the setting sun right behind us, they may see a semblance of her colors; but I don't think those colors are as important as the animal itself and the experience.

My horse is named Ranger and some of his wildness remains as he does a lot of thinking for himself, which means I have to stay on my toes. I admire that trait in people, so why shouldn't it be admired in horses as well?

My best to you.

Appendix

Opinions published by Steve Watts
in the Idaho Falls Post Register Newspaper

Guest Columns

TIME TO CHANGE DIRECTION
Wednesday, April 22, 2015

It pleased me that the Idaho Falls Police Department chose Bruce Roberts (guest column, April 2) to be the first to publicly challenge my assertions concerning police overreaction.

I would compare my long police career to Roberts on any day. Based upon his descriptions of himself and his career, it seems to me that he may be exactly the kind of officer I am attempting to draw attention to.

Americans are witnessing a switch from what used to be called "community policing" to the militarization of police at all levels. We are slowly turning police into military units with military responses to even the most mundane calls for assistance or disturbances.

A day does not go by in America without news that another person was killed by police; and that person, by any decent or moral standard, should have been helped, not killed.

The national police mantra, "to protect and serve," is out the window. We may have first witnessed it in Waco, Texas, when the feds took over from local law enforcement allegations of sexual misconduct by the leader of a sect who could have been taken into custody as he jogged each morning away from the compound.

The feds moved in with armored vehicles, including an Army tank, crashing into the main building, setting it on fire and killing women and children.

The same response was repeated at Ruby Ridge in Idaho. In both cases, the cover up began immediately. Promotions were made and medals passed out. The public didn't know what a fiasco these events were until the courts started awarded million-dollar settlements to survivors, your tax money.

Community policing is local. Neither citizens nor the police need to be afraid. We should remember that gunmen have always been a part of our history. Right here in Idaho Falls, I can tell you many stories about police officers, including myself, who disarmed or took down would-be shooters. Being forced to kill was very rare.

The best authority on this subject is a government publication dating back to 1968: "The challenge of crime in a free society." It relies heavily on good recruitment of personnel to train recruits in self-reliance and confidence and how to react to mental health emergencies, rather than using weapons.

The publication focuses on teaching law enforcement officers how to move out into the community, establishing rapport and winning trust. Also recommended are citizen review boards. That means wise, knowledgeable community leaders who work from a moral imperative rather than just trying to find legal excuses.

I'm told there is a morale problem in our local police department. The police solution is to ask citizens to build a $10 million station. Community policing is done on the streets, not in a building the public is locked out of because the people inside are afraid of them.

Idaho Falls has some good young police officers who joined the force for the right reasons. They want to make a difference. We owe it to ourselves and them to change direction. We need the right kind of leadership to make that happen.

Watts is a former police officer, state criminal investigator and polygraph examiner who lives in Idaho Falls. In 2002, he published a book, "Better an Honest Scoundrel, Chronicles of a Western Lawman."

OFF THE DEEP END
Wednesday, March 25, 2015

T wo incidents in Idaho Falls tell us our local police
need to stop and think about the tactics they use to
protect the public, writes **Steve Watts**.

On March 12, my wife and I attended a lecture on the
role of chemistry in crime solving as part of the Museum
of Idaho's exhibit on that subject.

It was a good lecture, but poorly attended. That
might have been because people couldn't get to the
museum. The nearby streets, including Yellowstone
Highway and Broadway Avenue, were blocked off. Police
cars were everywhere, blue lights flashing. It was quite a
show.

We later learned a 16-year-old boy was on the roof of
the fruit warehouse by the D St. underpass, shooting
pigeons with a tiny caliber pellet gun. If someone hits
you, it may sting a bit.

This is not a new phenomenon. It probably has been
going on since the town began and pigeons moved in. In
my younger days, when I worked as a policeman in Idaho
Falls, I recall running many kids off roofs doing the same
thing. It was never a big deal.

So, we had a phalanx of police cars that came
screaming up to the building. My guess is guns were out.
That seems to be the style, even in some traffic stops.

They must have gotten a good look at the boy and his weapon. Pellet guns look like pellet guns, even with those small scopes they use on them.

Not one, but two, SWAT teams were present. SWAT stands for "Special Weapons Attack Team" and they are prepared to kill, if necessary. This was a situation that didn't amount to a hill of beans.

This is not the only time I've witnessed city police going off the deep end.

I attend the Unitarian Church on E St. About a year and a half ago, we had a board meeting. That same evening, a young man robbed a nearby store. We knew what he looked like because one of our members had been in the store at the time of the robbery.

Our treasurer is a scientist at the Idaho National Laboratory, doctorate level, super-intelligent, a family man with children. He looks nothing like the robber.

We looked into the church parking lot and saw an armada of police cars with lights flashing. Half a dozen officers had our treasurer pinned up against his car. All were hostile and excited. They searched his car and billfold and verbally attacked him.

At one point in my career, I taught robbery investigations at the Idaho State Police Academy in Boise. Everything I was seeing was ludicrous. These police were so excited and focused on our treasurer that I saw it as a very dangerous moment. So did he.

Our treasurer remained calm and cooperated, which was wise, though he didn't have to. There was no warrant and a difficult stretch to find probable cause. There are many who would not have submitted.

I hesitate to use the words, but I was reminded of pack of rabid dogs after their prey: too many aggressive police in one area, following each others' lead, common sense out the window.

The bad part is this mentality leads to what we are seeing across the country, citizens of all stripes killed without justification.

It's time to step back. We don't have to go in this direction. This trend will only get worse without a course correction.

Acknowledging the Good
Sunday, September 14, 2014

T he Veteran's Administration has received plenty of criticism lately, but that should not take away from the excellent treatment vets receive locally, writes **Steve Watts** .

As a veteran, 21-year survivor of prostate cancer and user of the Veteran's Administration medical system, I am concerned that all the recent publicity about the VA falling behind in treatment to new veterans will undermine all the good work that is being done.

For those who don't know, veterans in eastern Idaho are part of the Salt Lake veterans' hospital system. That system covers all of Utah, southeast Idaho, southern Wyoming and eastern Nevada.

Following the first revelation that Arizona was way behind in scheduling treatments for veterans, the national VA initiated a comprehensive inspection of all regional hospital systems. It did not surprise me that the Salt Lake system passed with high grades. In fact, some Salt Lake staff members were transferred to Arizona for the purpose of getting that system back on track.

I cannot speak for everyone, but many of my friends who are veterans have shared with me their satisfaction with the treatment they receive locally. My best view of the Salt Lake system came when I first started my cancer treatments.

I was required to stay in the Salt Lake hospital for eight weeks. As I was ambulatory, I spent my free time visiting with other patients and becoming acquainted with staff. I was able to observe the inner workings of the hospital and share with others our experiences and concerns.

I didn't expect it but, other than being away from home, this was one of the most fascinating and enlightening experiences I have gone through. During my time in Salt Lake, I witnessed so many acts of kindness and compassion - some by other veterans and some by hospital staff.

One example is a young veteran dying of cancer who volunteered to stand by the hospital entrance. Whenever anyone came in confined to a wheelchair, and there were many, he offered to wheel them to wherever they needed to go. He told me it was a good way to spend his last days. He was only 37.

There were a few instances when some of our older, crotchety veterans would show up at the hospital wanting a special favor or treatment. And while I thought they ought to have a swift kick in their pants for being rude and obnoxious, I observed staff members bending over backwards to be cooperative and understanding. I could go on and on.

My association with VA staff members in the Pocatello and Idaho Falls satellite clinics has been every bit as good as what I observed in Salt Lake. My view is that good people doing good things should be acknowledged, just as bad people offering bad services are always recognized.

On Learning from Life
Sunday, November 3, 2013

For the average American, knowledge comes from two sources: formal education and the life we live thereafter. Hopefully, the longer we live the more we learn. I'm edging up in age and can attest that life teaches us things formal education cannot.

Much depends on what we decide to do with our life, how we make a living, where we choose to live and who our associates are. I'm talking about myself here, so I'll cover what I have learned.

I began as a cowboy in Texas, enlisted in the Army and worked as a commercial fisherman in Alaska. My wife and I chose Idaho. She had a job as a nurse and I fulfilled a desire to get into law enforcement, mostly as a detective and criminal investigator.

That career lasted 28 years and was exciting, productive and satisfying, though it didn't pay very well. But it was what I wanted to do and I supplemented our income in the private enterprise world of real estate. I took early retirement to operate a private security investigation company for the next 15 years, than retired a second time, though I still dabble as a private detective.

This life has required that I associate with all social levels of Americans, from the top to the bottom, the rich to the poor. Years ago, in a sociology class I attended, the professor described the two political parties, stating the

Republicans' position was one of social Darwinism, the strong survive and the weak perish, and the Democrats' position was one of social Christianity, those who are strong and able help those who are weak.

Those words resonated with me and my observations since have been that he was mostly right. Like others, I have come to see all Americans as family. Families look after each other, the sick, the less able, and those who disappoint us. We give our family members a leg up, educate them, and help in every way we can. What kind of a family would not do it that way?

I count many rich people as friends. They are go-getters, talented and ambitious. They don't really need big tax breaks, supplemental payments or weak laws and regulations that allow them to cheat.

Conversely, I know many poor people who need and deserve extra help. Some from broken families. Some in jail. Some under-educated. Some handicapped. Some mentally ill. And some with diminished capacity and unable to compete.

Let us, as a country, act like the family we are and see that every member prospers. In the end, we won't be able to justify having done anything else.

That's what I have learned from living this life.

What about you?

DYING WITH DIGNITY
Sunday, January 27, 2013

Americans need to have serious conversations about the conditions and expenses associated with end-of-life care, writes **Stephen Watts** .

It was gratifying to read last week's letter from Celeste Eld reminding us that Hospice of Eastern Idaho, which turns no one away, is a nonprofit organization, meaning all monies collected from insurance policies, private donations and, most importantly, Medicare are used, after expenses, to provide end-of-life care for indigents unable to contribute to the expense of their own death. Those costs would be picked up by taxes if it wasn't for that non-profit organization.

Death -- it's such a hot button word in our culture. For many, the thought of preparing for it is too distant or scary to contemplate. To be born and to live and then to die being the eternal plan for every living thing is unacceptable for many who seemingly want to leave the dying part off.

This attitude, combined with modern medical science, has made dying an incredibly expensive production. I recently was told that up to 90 percent of health care costs are spent on end-of-life expenses, and this is particularly important when we concern ourselves with the continued funding of Medicare. Everyone has a similar story of their own mythical Uncle Jack on his death bed when his children, who he has not seen in 20 years, show up and make demands on doctors to keep poor Uncle Jack alive because they love him too much to let him go.

And so, three months later, Uncle Jack, who is comatose and extremely uncomfortable, and having been kept alive by machines, finally gets put out of his misery by dying. Now there's a million dollar bill that needs to be paid. Medicare pays up to 80 percent, and neither Jack nor his kids can pay the remainder.

We can't blame the doctors and hospitals. Their purpose is healing people, and our legal system does not protect them from making life and death decisions on their own. Nor can we blame the myriad new private, for-profit hospices that have sprung up -- started by entrepreneurs who have learned that since Medicare has picked up end-of-life costs, money can be made as long as they pick and choose patients.

It is our own fault we are in this fix. But we are not totally helpless. It is a simple matter to get copies of living wills and write addendums to spell out the conditions you wish to depart under and get them on the record by filing them with the Secretary of State. Lastly, when you choose a hospice, opt for one doing the most good for the most people.

Let's keep Medicare alive. Let's all join the conversation about dying and the reality that sometimes living is worse than death -- and no more silly talk about death panels.

LOOTING OUR HERITAGE
Thursday, April 4, 2013

I daho's public land should be preserved for everybody and not sold off to the highest bidder, writes **Stephen Watts** .

The Legislature passed a resolution demanding that the federal government cede title to all federal land within Idaho to the state.

Some of my friends laugh and shrug it off as just another loony right-wing fringe group venting their hatred for the U.S. government. If one was to believe everything promulgated by this group you could get the impression they think Idaho is a separate country and no one outside its borders should have a say in anything that goes on here.

The idea that the U.S. government is an enemy baffles me. Idaho was created by Americans, blood was shed by multitudes of our countrymen and all of us own Idaho as we do every other state in our magnificent country. That the federal government sends more money into our state than we pay into it makes it evident we in Idaho are part of the United States family.

The idea that Idaho is better able to manage our federal lands is being sold as an opportunity for the state to wring more money from cutting timber and selling off choice blocks of land to private interests.

All this is true. More money could come into state coffers in the short term. What worries me is the long-range price we will pay. We have seen in other states when private interests are put first that the public finds itself locked out of scenic lands once available to everyone. The hunting and fishing opportunities have to be purchased at high prices from the new landowners. There is no evidence that state agencies can manage our forests, mountains, rivers and prairies as well as the U.S. Forest Service and Bureau of Land Management. What a state can do is plunder and degrade and that is what I don't want to see.

Let the super rich and special interests look after themselves. Idaho's future is best served by capitalizing on its availability for ordinary citizens to enjoy hiking and camping in pristine forests, fishing in unpolluted streams and rivers, climbing in roadless mountain terrains, riding on traffic-free trails and hunting in wilderness settings as opposed to shooting game confined to escape-proof pens.

Idaho has the most scenic and beautiful places in the contingent states. As the population of America grows, Americans as well as foreigners will be drawn, with their money, to share this beauty with those of us lucky enough to live here. They do not need to stumble over industrial-size mines and logged-off mountains and pillaged properties.

We are all in this together. We look after each other. The only people having their freedoms taken away are those who want the freedom to loot our heritage.

Do Your Homework
Friday, October 26, 2012

Those who accuse Jefferson County Sheriff Blair Olsen of wrongdoing in office are completely out to lunch, writes **Stephen Watts** .

Having worked with Jefferson County Sheriff Blair Olsen for many years and knowing him well, I am not surprised that he is paying no attention

to those who attack him by insinuation and half truths.

Blair is the quintessential embodiment of what a lawman should be. He looks the part. Tall and dignified, carries himself well, but the real person behind the appearance is what is impressive. He is honest and straightforward almost to a fault, intelligent, fair with everyone, personable and would be a credit to any county that was lucky enough to have him.

That he was chosen from a long list of potential candidates by Gov. Otter to represent eastern Idaho at the Peace Officers Standard and Training Council and then to be elected as the chairman of that body seems to indicate that these qualities are recognized throughout our state. Jefferson County can take pride.

In this particular election season, I can picture him as a lion moving through the jungle with a pack of jackals at his heels. Like the lion, he doesn't pay a lot of attention to anyone yipping at his heels. His political opponent, a former deputy who at one time worked for him and was assigned by Blair to an investigator's

position and who was unable to function well in that position, was called in to be given a patrol assignment and he quit in anger. That kind of reassignment is standard in all police bodies, allowing leadership to find the best role for individual officers.

For him and his supporters to approach the press and county commissioners to complain that Sheriff Olsen might have pocketed travel money used on county business or in representing

the county when this in fact did not happen is reprehensible. Anyone doing their homework will find that all reimbursements owed the county went into the county's account at the Zion's Bank, the same bank that Blair has his personal account. Press reports indicating that reimbursement checks being deposited in a Zion Bank might possibly be Blair's account when they were not is sloppy reporting.

Maybe we can fault Blair, who knows he has done nothing wrong, and maybe the county commissioners, who after looking into the matter, also concluded he did nothing wrong, for not seeing the accusations worthy of reply. I think even bad accusations in the public square need to be answered. My answer to Blair Olsen's accusers is, "Put up or shut up."

RESTORING SANITY TO GOP RANKS
Sunday, September 16, 2012

The quickest way for moderate members of the GOP to right their party ship is to stop supporting those who hijacked the party, writes **Stephen Watts** .

A group of us older guys meet regularly for morning coffee. One told us of a time when he was a boy. His father farmed in the north valley area and he recalls coming to Idaho Falls in their old 1937 Chevrolet truck. Where the Northgate Mall is today was just a sagebrush field and when they arrived a circus had come into town and was being unloaded from the train at that field.

He described seeing an elephant pulling a cage on wagon wheels with a lion inside and a tent larger than any building he had ever seen. He said when he went home that night he was sure that he had seen "all that there was in the world to see and that he would never again see anything as grand as what he had seen that day." And so we are all reminded about the changes we have seen in our lifetimes. They came often and were hard to keep up with.

My thoughts turned to politics. In my youth, I lived in Texas, which was considered a very Democratic state. I became a Democrat, and when I left that state I saw no reason to change. But, Texas changed. With the enactment of the Civil Rights Act under President

Johnson, it, like the rest of the south, turned into a solidly Republican state almost overnight.

They tell me there are signs it might be swinging back the other way again; which brought me to the recent column written by Kathy Stanger lamenting that Democrats were having such a field day castigating Republicans. I know Ms. Stanger mostly by reputation and regard here as an intelligent and delightful person who has been an excellent spokesperson for the Republican Party as long as I can remember. Our group sees her as a class act.

It's probably not necessary to remind Kathy about change. She will know change as we all do. But sometimes it slips up on us. It appears from the outside that the Republican Party of rational conservative people that she has loved and served so well may have slipped away while she and her like-minded friends were not looking. Would it be too much to suggest that maybe the loony right has hijacked the party and taken it in a direction even most of my Republican friends are disgusted with?

I've seen this happen in the Democratic Party from time also. When that happens, I vote Republican to send a message. I would suggest to Ms. Stanger that she would be welcome to cross lines and vote Democratic for a while. If you do, it will hurry the return of reason and sanity in Republican ranks.

No Fear of Oversight
Friday, August 12, 2011

In regard to concerns about police killing community members and then shutting off any inquiry until they have completed their own investigation, my 29-year police career has caused me to be familiar with this issue. I can say without doubt the police believe sincerely they are doing the right thing.

Within police ranks, there is an unspoken belief that the public does not understand their jobs, and the problems and dangers they face. And they are legitimately aware of elements within society who range from being unsympathetic to openly hostile towards them.

There is a real belief that the public may not be fair in the judgment of their actions, or that it would have adequate knowledge to see their reasoning clearly.

However, the issue of trust cuts both ways. An "us vs. them" attitude poses danger both to police and the community. In my rookie years, it was fairly common to connect with situations where guns were being brandished and many times pointed at policemen. Learning from the veterans, it became obvious to me that not everyone with a gun wanted to shoot me. Divorce, loss of a job, alcohol and mental problems sometimes cause people to temporarily go off the deep end. I learned to talk some of them into giving up the gun and how to disarm those who declined. Most old-time police can recite dozens of cases they handled that way. There were rare exceptions when we brought our own guns into play, but our purpose was not to kill except as a last resort. We have noted changes and trends during recent years that most of us feel are not good.

The SWAT Team is designed for the purpose of keeping the community safer and that may be the problem -- an overemphasis on police safety as opposed to community safety. Most of America witnessed this at its worst during the Columbine disaster in Colorado. Children were killed as police waited outside, protecting themselves.

Killing is a serious business that needs the whole of society's involvement -- the legal system and the checks and balances of community input. The trend to give frightened policemen carte blanche authority to kill when killing may not be necessary or desirable can only lead to a tragedy waiting to happen -- when somebody gets killed that our community doesn't think deserved death, such as returning war veterans who may have PTSD and go off the deep end temporarily.

The citizen review board is a good idea. It makes partners of the community and the police. The police, if they are doing the right thing, should have no fear of oversight. It is lack of oversight that should cause fear.

A JOB WELL DONE
Tuesday, December 7, 2010

E astern Idahoans should be pleased that the Post Register went to such lengths to inform the public about a shooting in Lemhi County last year, writes **Stephen** T. **Watts** .

I thought I would allow someone else to applaud the Post Register for pursuing the story of the four state policemen being shot at near the ghost town of Gilmore last year.

It is too easy to put off doing the right thing in our busy lives. But, even belatedly, I will be the one to step forward.

Four state policemen rode snow machines into the Lemhi Mountains out of Gilmore. They stopped at a building and one of them tried to open the locked door when someone started shooting at them. They fled the scene, abandoned their machines and hiked out through deep snow with one of them at risk because of a breathing problem.

This story is so incomplete it is almost laughable, but when the Post Register reporter made inquiries, she was told by police that they were unable to discuss the case as it was under investigation. Shooting at policemen is serious business, and the Post Register took the position that the public has a right to know what's going on. They ventured financial resources and considerable effort and sued the state for the complete story.

When I first heard the story, I was at a get-together with some of my old retired police friends. They are tough, cynical guys who know how the system works. To a man, they declared there was a lot of lying going on and considerable derision over policemen who being shot at did not shoot back.

Saying "you can't talk about it" because "it's under investigation" is the oldest dodge in the police world. You save yourself from embarrassment and it appears to the public you are secretly working on some big deal while implying you need the support to not foul up your case. The problem comes if the nosy press insists on knowing if there is a criminal out there who will gun down any hapless snowmobiler who stops for a rest at the site; who might also want to know why surrounding law enforcement personnel and backup support officers and resources were not called to respond and assist in catching such a dangerous shooter before he was allowed to escape during the several-day blank period between the incident and the reporting.

We need to be very pleased that the Post Register, the paper we all complain about at one time or the other, asked those questions and sought answers.

The issue is not about embarrassment or possibly interfering with a dope case. The issue is about a free people in a democratic country having trust in those they choose to enforce the laws they enact. Thank you, Post Register, keep up the good work.

About the Author

B orn in San Francisco in 1932, Steve Watts spent a large part of his youth in Texas on a ranch and later, in Alaska as a fisherman. Idaho Falls was his home since 1957. He had been a police officer, a detective, criminal investigator and polygraph specialist. Throughout his long and distinguished career, Steve's compassion for the victims of crime and his pursuit of justice affected and changed the lives of many people from every walk of life. He was a painter, builder, inventor, author and story teller. He was also a columnist for the newspaper Post Register. His first book, "Better an Honest Scoundrel: Chronicles of a Western Lawman," was published in 2003. "Lemhi Overhang," his second book, tells fictionalized stories based on his experiences. He passed away on May 9, 2015.

www.ingramcontent.com/pod-product-compliance
Lightning Source LLC
Chambersburg PA
CBHW030922260626

47169CB00002B/357